PROXIMAL TO MURDER

A
Steve Raymond, D.D.S.
Mystery

Also by Eric B. Olsen

Fiction

The Seattle Changes
Death in the Dentist's Chair
Dark Imaginings
Death's Head
If I Should Wake Before I Die

Non-Fiction

The Intellectual American
The Films of Jon Garcia: 2009-2013
The Death of Education

PROXIMAL TO MURDER

A Steve Raymond, D.D.S. Mystery

Eric B. Olsen

authorHOUSE®

AuthorHouse™
1663 Liberty Drive
Bloomington, IN 47403
www.authorhouse.com
Phone: 1 (800) 839-8640

Published by AuthorHouse 01/05/2018

ISBN: 978-1-5462-2159-3 (sc)
ISBN: 978-1-5462-2158-6 (e)

Print information available on the last page.

For my father,
Dr. Raymond P. Olsen, D.D.S.

Introduction

Proximal to Murder was written in a white-hot fever of inspiration in 1992. I had completed my first novel, the medical thriller *Death's Head*, almost a year earlier and throughout that year it went through several edits and eventually made its way out to publishers and agents. Though it was a first novel, I was nevertheless disappointed that it wasn't picked up by anyone. So the question at the time was, what to do next?

I wanted to make my mark in the world of genre fiction, and in order to do that was sure that if I could come up with a unique idea that was well written I could gain a foothold in the publishing industry. And that's all I really wanted. I was more than willing to put in the effort necessary to build an audience for my work over time. I felt I was in the right place and at the right time to be able to do that. My work at the University Bookstore had given me access to regional book reps from all the major publishing houses and I had cultivated solid relationships with several of them. I knew that if I could get a novel published by a New York house, no matter how small, I could build a significant readership in the Northwest and eventually branch out from there.

In December of 1991 I hit upon an idea. My father had been a dentist, and while I was growing up I had become familiar with the inner workings of his office and his practice. I had even worked for him briefly in his lab trimming dies and doing denture repairs. In addition, I had also worked for a short time at a dental laboratory in Seattle before I found my job at the bookstore. Then I began to wonder if there had ever been any mystery novels written with a dentist as a protagonist. After looking around I found only one, a series by Rick Boyer about an oral surgeon and amateur sleuth named Charlie "Doc" Adams. But those novels dealt primarily with his hobby of boating and the plots revolved around more action-adventure oriented stories like modern-day piracy, the illegal ivory trade, and treasure salvaging in the ocean than dentistry.

What I wanted to do was get into the office, with patients and assistants and a receptionist. I wanted my dentist to do fillings and root canals and lab work. I wanted him to be an amateur in the truest sense of the word. It was with that in mind that I stumbled upon another writer while doing my research: Parnell Hall. Though his protagonist, Stanley Hastings, is technically a private investigator, his inexperience and self-deprecating humor were exactly what I was looking to replicate in my own work and so he was a major inspiration for Steve Raymond.

The choice for my amateur detective was easy. Steve Raymond had been the protagonist of my first novel. His father had been a physician, and after his death Steve had taken a step back from medicine at the end of the book. It was an easy shift, then, to have him go to on to dental school in order to avoid matters of life and death in his practice. That was one of the ironies that I loved the most about his character. The creation of police lieutenant Dan Lasky was slightly more interesting. He had also appeared in *Death's Head*, as a detective, but his genesis began much earlier. Before either of us had written a novel, my friend Patrick and I hit upon the idea of co-writing one, thinking it might be easier. Our idea was to simply begin writing, with no outline, and write one chapter at a time. When one of us had finished a chapter we would hand the whole thing off to the other and continue right where they left off. It was a horror novel called *Blood Hunt* and it only made it to the second chapter. But one of the characters created by Patrick was a police detective named Dan Lasky, and when I asked him if I could use the character after the novel stalled, he gave me his blessing.

I began writing the book in December of 1991, and finished it a scant ten months later at the end of October the following year. The title came from a comment I overheard one day at the dental lab where I had worked. Two of the guys were gossiping around the time clock about something interesting that had happened in the lab the day before—probably an argument between two of the other employees—and when one of them asked the other what had happened, the response he received was, "Unfortunately, I wasn't proximal to that situation." This was several years before I started writing, but I had always remembered that line and thought it a perfect way to title my first dental mystery.

After a couple of complete edits, *Proximal to Murder* was ready to send out to agents and publishers. And though it received more positive comments than my first novel, no one wanted to take a chance on it either. So I plunged ahead and continued to write and completed a horror novel—something I had always wanted to write—before deciding to write a sequel to my dental mystery. The thinking was, if I could show that I had it in me to become a series writer, I might be a little more attractive to prospective publishers. But that didn't really work, either. The only regret I had during the whole process was that my father hadn't been alive to help me work on the novels. I could never escape the suspicion that somehow, had he collaborated on them with me, they would have contained that indefinable element that would have made them more appealing to publishers. It also would have been a tremendous amount of fun.

It wasn't until a few years after I had stopped writing

fiction altogether and went back to school that I thought about giving the New York publishing world another try. At the time, a recent technological advance in on-demand printing began a resurgence in self-publishing that hasn't abated to this day. I was toying with the idea of publishing my mystery series myself, but before I did I wanted to give the legitimate publishing world one more chance. So I sent proposals for the two books out to several agents and, to my complete surprise, one of them wanted to represent me. She was the sole owner of a small agency in the Southwest, and it turned out she really enjoyed the novels and my protagonist, genuinely understanding what I was attempting to do in my mysteries. But after several months of effort she was unable to place the series either, and so I decided to go ahead and publish the first novel myself in 2000.

One of the things I had to do before going ahead was to take a look at things that needed revising in the material. The biggest change came in the form of the music that my protagonist listened to. When I originally wrote the novel I had wanted him to be a musician who loved jazz. But I really had no idea what good jazz was at the time. I tried buying CDs on my own, looking through the racks at Tower Records and guessing what might be good. But nothing was. I eventually settled on a few smooth jazz groups that weren't completely horrible. My friend Patrick—who was very knowledgeable about jazz—could only shake his head in dismay but was reluctant to make suggestions. Fortunately, in the interim, my stepfather Bill introduced me to Horace Silver and Art Blakey and Blue Note records, setting me off on a new course of discovery by exposing me to the best jazz in the world— exactly the kind that Steve Raymond would listen to. The only other major change had to do with First Avenue in downtown Seattle. When I wrote the book the buildings on the northwest end of the street were pretty dilapidated, but in the intervening years the whole place had undergone a serious renovation so I had to make that adjustment as well and decided that I would just write it into the story.

Reissuing the novel now, however, also poses a different problem: whether or not to completely re-write the story to include cell phones and the Internet—things not available to my amateur sleuth when the book was originally written. The argument for even considering this comes out of my own experience as a reader. I had read the novel *27* by William Diehl while I was working on *Death's Head*. It was set in pre-war Germany and because of the similarity with my own work I had enjoyed it quite a bit and I was eager to read his next novel when it came out. That book was *Primal Fear*, his best-known work, but I was only a short way into it when I realized it was set almost a decade earlier. I don't know why, but I was really disappointed that he hadn't simply updated the setting—regardless of when it was written—in order to have it occur in the present day.

In thinking about it, though, the situation with *Proximal to Murder* was quite a bit different. The book is nearly thirty years old now and, as I had done with *Death's Head*, I decided that the writing and the time period were of a piece, and I couldn't see that completely changing everything was going to have a net positive effect. More importantly, however, updating the novel would have necessitated eliminating Ray Brown and Gene Harris from the story, and I could not allow that to happen. In fact, Gene Harris had already left Ray Brown's trio when I updated the story the first time, and I was compelled to leave him in even then. As a result, I kept the novel set in the late 1990s and simply make the corrections to the book that I had missed on the first edition.

What this revised version of the book does allow me to do, however, is to include a Steve Raymond short story that I wrote in 2005 called "Lying Through Your Teeth." At the time I hadn't done any serious writing since the mid nineties and when I decided to see if I still had it in me to write more fiction I thought I would begin with my old friends Steve Raymond and Dan Lasky. It was an easy way to get back into writing, and if I could come up with an interesting story it wouldn't be too much of a time commitment. After I finished writing it I submitted the story to *Alfred Hitchcock's Mystery Magazine* on a whim and again, to my surprise and delight, it was purchased for their March 2005 issue. Chronologically, the story takes place after the second novel in the series, but since this first book was so much shorter than the second I decided to include it in this volume.

Finally, this reissued version of *Proximal to Murder* also allows me to take advantage of advances in cover and interior design that have taken place in the industry since that first, simplistic version of the book came out in 2000. By adding the new story and this introduction, hopefully it will give readers something worth taking a look at, as well as allowing the novel to take its rightful place within the overall arc of my series of unpublished fictional works, six manuscripts that began with *If I Should Wake Before I Die* in the late eighties and early nineties, and ended with the last novel I ever wrote, *The Seattle Changes*, in 2005.

I've had a lot of positive responses to *Proximal to Murder* over the years. I even submitted the book to the *Writer's Digest* self-published book contest in 2001 and received an honorable mention. What I'm most proud of, however, are the kind words from readers in the dental field. I even received an email from a real dentist named—that's right—Stephen Paul Raymond. If you enjoyed the novel the first time, hopefully it will be just as good the second time around, and if you're coming to it for the first time, thanks for reading.

Eric B. Olsen
August 11, 2017

"What would you guess he did for a living?"

"I — dope, maybe. He had the gold chains and all that thug stuff. I don't know. He could've been a dentist."

— Bernard Schopen
The Big Silence

"Hell of a way to make a living, Doc."

"Well, you should have married a dentist."

—Kim Basinger &
Alec Baldwin
The Getaway, 1994.

1

I bit down hard, my lower central incisors digging deep into the callused groove on the inside of my lip. The added pressure against the reed sent my saxophone into orbit, and the piercing scream of my horn suddenly made me think of the high-speed drills back at my office.

Despite this unwanted reminder that I should have been in bed hours ago, I held the note through several bars, letting a slight vibrato creep in just as the chorus was about to turn. Then I relaxed my embouchure and descended into the verse in a swirl of chromatics, like water down an old-fashioned spit sink. After the singer hit the microphone I laid out, content with listening to the fairly tight comping of the impromptu rhythm section as they ran through the changes of James Cotton's version of the classic blues, "Rocket 88."

It was Monday night at the Owl Café in the Ballard District of Seattle, and every Monday night for the last ten years I'd been coming down here to play. Some guys like football—I like music. Between an opening and closing set performed by a host band, the stage was open to any amateur who wanted to grab a little of the musical spotlight for him- or herself.

You gave your name at the door as you came in, your instrument permitting entry without paying the cover charge, and the manager would put together as many ad hoc groups as he could. If there happened to be a shortage of a certain instrument, a member of the host band could usually be persuaded to join in. The last time I missed a "Blues Nite" at the Owl was eight years ago, the night my daughter was born.

The chorus was coming around again and I pushed my alto sax out in front of me, drawing the white strings of my cheap neck strap taut like dental floss, and guided the mouthpiece home. I played a backing line behind the singer and then laid out again while he went into a guitar solo. Once you became a regular here—and if you were any good—the manager usually tried to put you together with some of the better musicians. This bunch was okay.

For someone like me, who had to work during the days and didn't have the time to invest in his own band, it was a good gig. I was always dead tired at work on Tuesdays, sometimes having dragged myself in at two in the morning, but it was worth it. I still loved the feeling of being up on the bandstand. I had played professionally for a while out of high school, and when that didn't pan out I swapped my saxophone for schoolbooks and put in four years at college.

My father had been a doctor, so I naturally applied and even made it into med school, but my first year was interrupted by my father's death. I never went back. Since I already had the science background, I decided to give dental school a shot. Now I hang out my shingle five days a week doing fillings and root canals—the easy ones anyway—from seven to two in the Magnolia District. The sign on the door reads *Stephen P. Raymond, D.D.S.*

To my knowledge, no one at the Owl knows I'm a dentist, and I haven't really thought it necessary to tell them. I mean, who wants to listen to *Gee, Doc, I've got this tooth that's been giving me trouble . . .* all night long? Around here I'm just Steve who plays the saxophone, and that's good enough for me.

Onstage, from the end of the long narrow room, I looked out over the sea of tables on the left and the bar that ran the length of the room on the right. Stacy, the bartender, caught my eye and I nodded, then she held up an empty schooner and I nodded again. It was the last song of the set, and she knew I was going to need a cold Heineken when I was through.

Looking back at the half-filled room, I thought about how I'd met my wife in this very bar when we were both still in college. She used to come and watch me here every Monday and I missed seeing her blue eyes out in the audience looking back at me. Busy daydreaming, I hadn't been paying attention to the music, and when the next chorus came around I wasn't ready.

I was just swinging my horn up to my mouth, knowing I was going to be half a bar too late, when the rhythm guitarist brushed passed me and broke off the end of my reed. I'd tried to move out of his way as soon as I saw what was going to happen, but he still managed to turn that thin sliver of cane into a jagged mess. When I heard the crunch I winced as though it had been a part of my own body, and not because I couldn't afford to buy a new reed—I had half a dozen in my jacket pocket. It's just that a saxophone reed is such an inconsistent commodity, when you find one that really plays well you want to hang on to it as long as possible. This one had been perfect.

I loosened the ligature on my mouthpiece and extracted the reed like a bad tooth, while fishing in my pocket for another. That's when I noticed that the guitarist who'd broken my reed kept on going—right off the stage. He took a header onto the dance floor, his axe unplugging with a loud electrical pop and his skull hitting the floor with a dull thud. A gasp went up from the dancers, and the musicians stopped playing, except for the drummer, who blindly banged out the last few bars of the song.

The final cymbal crash was still resonating in my ears when I jumped down off the bandstand. If there was some unconscious reason that I had wanted to keep my being a dentist a secret, it was too late now. Though I was a doctor in name only I'd taken many of the same classes M.D.'s take in med school, and the frozen stares of the people in the club made it a sure bet I was the only doctor in the house.

I yelled for Stacy to call an ambulance and she gave me the thumbs-up. The new fire station was only a couple of blocks away so I knew it wouldn't be long. When I felt his neck and didn't get a pulse, I managed to enlist some of the braver dancers to help me turn him over. He was lying face down and I unfastened the guitar strap first and took his head in my hands, then all of us gently rolled him onto his back.

He looked about my age, early thirties, but a bit on the scruffy side. He had a beard and long hair that hadn't been near a bottle of Head & Shoulders in a while. His clothes weren't much better—well-worn jeans, heavily creased with dirt, a gray, stained sweatshirt, and a thin pair of canvas sneakers with no socks.

As soon as I put my hand around his throat again I knew, but I began CPR anyway. When the ambulance arrived three minutes later, my diagnosis was confirmed: he was dead.

2

Things were pretty hectic at the Owl for the next half-hour or so. The cops showed up just as the ambulance was leaving, they took a statement from me and a few other people, and then, almost as soon as it had happened, it seemed, it was over. A new group of musicians had taken the stage, the music started up again, and I headed out to my pickup with my saxophone in tow.

I was halfway home before I realized I hadn't had my Heineken. "Damn it," I yelled, just to hear the sound of my own voice, and hit the steering wheel with the heel of my hand for emphasis. But I was more disappointed than angry. Still a little shaky from the whole experience, I really could have used a beer. Life and death situations have a habit of scaring the hell out of me, especially when they end in death. That's probably the reason I opted out of medical school.

I was driving northbound on Holman Road, and a couple of blocks before home I swung into Art's, a local grocery chain that stays open all night. Tiny droplets of rain began to streak the windshield as I pulled into the lot, and I tried to remember the last time I'd had to use my wipers. Though it rarely snowed in Seattle, we had our fair share of nasty weather, especially during the winter months. But this winter had been a mild one and, all things considered, it was pretty warm for February.

I locked up after stepping out of my truck and just stood for a moment in the rain, breathing deeply and letting my smoke-filled clothes air out. Finally, I walked up to the automatic doors and into the store. It was only a little past 12:30, and since you can buy liquor in Washington State until 2:00 a.m. I still had plenty of time.

Despite the bright and cheery atmosphere inside the giant supermarket, the place seemed deserted. I didn't see anyone until I rounded the corner of the beer aisle and noticed a clerk up at the far end mopping the floor. I hoped I wouldn't have to come back and get him just to ring me up.

After a quick glance through the cooler, I spotted the familiar green Heineken label, pulled a couple of six-packs out of the way and reached back deep for a cold one. Then I cradled it in my arm and walked up to the register. Luckily, a gal wearing a red apron was nearby stocking shelves. Once she'd spotted me, she hustled right over.

Running the carton of bottles over the scanner, she gave me a funny look, and then said, "Could I see some I.D.?"

I had been smiling up to that point—in spite of the grand finale by the rhythm guitarist, I'd had a damn good night on my horn—but now I had to laugh as I took out my wallet and fished for my driver's license. I have been blessed, some might say, or cursed—I, myself, haven't decided yet—with the kind of face one could refer to as boyish. The fact that I prefer to keep it clean-shaven only serves to accentuate the look. But that wasn't the only reason she'd asked me.

In addition to my youthful face, I have rather long hair. And when I say long, I mean *long*. Even tied back, my ponytail reaches well down between my shoulder blades. Add to that the silver hoop earring in my left ear and the effect is . . . Well, let's just say that even at thirty-one I get carded fairly often.

"Oh, my God," she said, and started laughing herself when she finally figured out my age. "You're older than I am."

That last part had obviously slipped out and a blush began

to creep up her neck as she handed back my license and took my money. "That's okay," I said, giving my standard reply. "It's good to know I'm aging gracefully."

She smiled again as she handed me my change, showing a rather high lip line that revealed a mismatched assortment of crowns and stained composite fillings. For a pretty girl her teeth weren't helping any. She probably worked part-time, though, and wasn't eligible for dental insurance. I wanted to give her my card and tell her I could really help her smile, but I resisted. It usually comes off sounding like a bad pick-up line or, if someone is self-conscious, it embarrasses them. Her earlier blush suggested the latter, so instead I thanked her and left.

Back outside it was raining for real and I jogged out to my truck, pelted by thick drops. I had to resist the urge to pop open one of the bottles once I was in the cab, but it wasn't too difficult, especially since I didn't have a bottle opener with me. So I fired up the engine and drove home as fast as the speed limit would allow.

My apartment building is a white, three-story box up in the Greenwood District on the north side of town, and I pulled in under the covered parking beneath the building and walked up the stairs to my two-bedroom unit on the third floor. The front door opens onto the kitchen, and as soon as I let myself in I put the beer into the fridge, saving out one bottle for immediate consumption. I popped the top and took a long pull, then walked out into the living room, turned on the TV and VCR, and fed a tape into the machine.

The sliding glass door in the front room opens onto a small balcony, and I just stood there for a moment in the semidarkness looking out through the rain-streaked glass at the city. On a sunny day you can sometimes see all the way across Puget Sound to the Olympic Mountains, but most days I have to be content with a fogged and cloudy view of nothing. At the moment I was gazing at the lights of Seattle, when I heard my daughter Cathie call out to me.

"Hi, Daddy."

"Hi, sweetheart," I said without turning, and took another sip of my beer.

It was my son, Timmy, who spoke next. "Daddy, Daddy, don't forget about me."

"Well, who do we have here?" I muttered, before I finally had to grab the remote control and mute the sound. Video dad, that's me. The occasion on the tape I was watching was Cathie's eighth birthday party, recorded last summer. Even though I'd seen both of my kids earlier that day, the sound of their voices brought on a fresh pang of loneliness.

I crossed the room and turned on the stereo, put on *Parker with Strings*, and sat down on the couch as Bird launched into "April in Paris." Leaning back, I closed my eyes and thought of Janet. It was nearly a year to the day that my wife and I had separated, and I had never stopped missing her.

I missed my kids too but, as it turned out, I saw them a lot more often. My office hours were such that I could pick them up after school and stay with them until Janet came home from work in the evening. It was good for me, it was good for Janet, and it was good for the kids. But even that didn't stop me from being lonely; I still had to go back home at night.

I watched Cathie for a while longer as she entertained her friends, and although I'd seen the tape enough times to have memorized the dialogue, I still laughed when Timmy's cake fell off his paper plate. I yawned once, killed off my beer and was thinking about another when Charlie Parker eased into "Summertime." I was feeling maudlin enough already, so I went out to the kitchen instead, rinsed out my beer bottle and put it in the plastic recycling bin the city so thoughtfully provides. Then I turned off all the electronic hardware and finally went to bed.

3

The next morning I was up at six. I sandwiched a shower and shave between cups of industrial-strength coffee and dressed for work. My preference is rayon suits in dark shades. I put on a slate-gray jacket and slacks, with a matching paisley tie, over a white shirt, then slipped on some black dress shoes and I was ready. After pouring another cup of coffee for the road, I was on my way by 6:45.

My office is located in the Magnolia District of Seattle, a few miles south of my apartment. I don't have to use the freeway, so it only takes about ten minutes to get to work in the morning, even during rush hour. The office is small, with just three operatories, but I own the whole thing. Technically. I'm actually mortgaged up to my wisdom teeth, but at least I don't have any partners; it's a one-man show. Well, that's not altogether true, either. I have four other people working for me, so it's more like a one-man and four-woman show.

If I had one complaint about my practice, it would have to be the location. The building I'm in houses about eight other dentists and is part of the monolithic conglomerate of health facilities collectively known as the Elliott Bay Medical Center. My affiliation with the hospital enables me to offer a nice health care package to my employees and family, but as a result of the dental overcrowding, I seem to end up with a lot of empty space in my appointment book.

I'm not really complaining, though. After paying the bank, wages, and malpractice insurance, I still have enough to live on. Janet has a good job and she's able to take care of the kids. The house they live in, across Lake Washington in a pricey little suburb called Medina, is paid for; I inherited it as part of my father's estate.

As I pulled into the medical cul-de-sac where I practice, Nona, my receptionist, was already unlocking the door. She's the only other person, besides Janet, who has a key. I trust her implicitly. None of the other dentists in my building begin office hours until eight, and in the scramble for patients I've found that many people can't—or won't—take time off work to have their teeth fixed. So at least I'm busy from seven till eight.

"Good morning, Dr. Raymond," Nona said as I came in the front door.

"Hi, Nona." One of my little idiosyncrasies is that I have all my employees call me Dr. Raymond in the office, even when there are no patients around. It's not so much a question of self-importance as it is professionalism, not to mention the fact that it's fairly common practice in most doctors' offices. I want my patients to feel that they're in the hands of a professional, and if they hear the assistants and receptionist referring to me as Steve, well . . . let's just say that I have enough strikes against me in that department with my looks. I don't care what they call me in private, but within the confines of the office I'm Dr. Raymond.

"So," said Nona, "how'd it go last night?"

The people at the Owl might not know about my private life, but with Nona I have no secrets. "Ah, it wasn't too bad, except for the guy dying onstage."

"Well, what do you expect when you play those jam sessions all the time? I don't know why you don't start your own band."

I suddenly realized I hadn't made myself very clear. "No,

I mean he really died—fell right off the stage onto the dance floor."

"Oh, my God. What happened?"

I shrugged. "Not much after that. The ambulance came a few minutes later, but there was nothing they could do. He was already gone when they put him on the stretcher."

Nona simply stared at me.

"What?" I said.

"That's it?"

"That's what?"

"A man dies onstage in front of a crowd of people and that's as detailed as you can get?"

I smiled. "Gee, if I'd known it was that important to you, I'd have brought along my video camera. It really wasn't that exciting, and besides, I wasn't even involved." I hated lying, but death wasn't one of my favorite topics for morning conversation, or anytime for that matter.

She was still staring.

"Honest."

Shaking her head, Nona hung up her coat and walked back to the lounge to make some coffee. Good thing, I thought, and promptly yawned. I was going to need it.

My practice, wedged as it is among my fellow dental health professionals, is a fairly straightforward affair. You enter the waiting room through an outside door, and directly ahead is the open reception desk. To the left are chairs and a play area for children, and another door that leads to the rest of the office. After that, it's just one long hallway with operatories on either side.

Behind the reception desk is an empty room that's used for storage, and an alcove that houses the panoramic x-ray machine. My office is the first door on the left down the hallway, and that was where I went now to mentally prepare myself for the day. Across the hall is operatory number one, with numbers two and three the next rooms up on both sides. In the back is an employee lounge to the right, and on the left, a small but well-equipped laboratory where I like to go to get away from it all. Some people like to meditate—I trim dies and make denture repairs.

A few minutes later, Nona came into my office with a cup of coffee, something she's done every morning since her first day on the job. I must have tried a hundred times to convince her that it was unnecessary, but I eventually gave up and learned to accept her generosity. This was the time when we usually went over the day's schedule. Secretly, I think she brought me my coffee because she liked to talk in my office rather than at the reception desk.

In spite of her maternal demeanor, Nona was a very attractive brunette, married, but with no kids. She kept her hair short, her face set off with stylish glasses, and wore elegant but comfortable clothing. In the four years since I had opened my practice I had grown to depend on her more than anyone else in my life, with the possible exception of Janet.

Along the right-hand wall as she entered my office were shelves lined with all of my dental textbooks and medical reference books, and on the wall behind my desk were framed diplomas from Bellevue Community College and the University of Washington. My diploma from the University of Washington School of Dentistry is out in the hall in plain view of the paying customers—just in case they get that far and still have any lingering doubts.

My desk is more of a table, with no drawers beneath, my blotter typically surrounded by dental journals, files, and pictures of Janet and the kids. Nona, thank God, keeps the bills out front and has become quite adept at forging my signature on my business checks. Next to my desk, on a separate stand, sits a PC and a large viewer for slides and x-rays. I keep everything else I need on the shelves above me to the right.

"So, what are we looking at today?" I asked.

Nona was sitting in the chair across from my desk, and I leaned back to sip my coffee. "You've got a final crown seat at seven, but nothing after until two checkups at eight. A chipped tooth at nine. Mrs. Bonney's having trouble with her bridge— she's at ten. And then a Mr. Spencer's coming in at ten-thirty to get started on his dentures—I left that one open till noon. And after that . . . nothing."

Nona took a sip of her coffee and I marveled again at her remarkable memory. She did the work of three people, taking care of my appointments, filing insurance claims and even doing my taxes. I made more money on paper, but Nona didn't have my overhead and she ended up with almost as much take-home pay as I did. And even with that, I still managed to feel guilty at times for not being able to pay her more.

"All right," I said. "I have some lab work I can do, so I think I'll stick around this afternoon, just in case."

Nona's eye's widened.

"You know what I mean," I said, and she grinned. It was just something I said. I mean, it might be fine for a beauty salon, but you don't get too much walk-in trade at a dentist's office. Still, there are emergencies, and I have gained a couple of loyal customers that way. Not to mention that I *did* have lab work that needed to be done.

At that moment my two assistants, Laurie and Susan, walked past the office talking animatedly, and Nona stood up to leave. My fourth employee is a dental hygienist named Julie, who only comes in on Fridays.

"Let me know when my seven's here," I said.

"Okay," Nona answered, and closed my door on her way out.

Later that morning at about seven-thirty, after three unsuccessful attempts to seat Mrs. Sandstrom's crown, I was ready to throw the damn thing across the operatory. It's supposed to be a snug, but not tight, fit. The crown should set down fairly easily because of the microscopic layer of room allowed for the glue that's used to cement it to the prepped tooth, but this one stubbornly refused to go all the way down.

I finally lowered the overhead light and gave the inside of the crown a close inspection. I really should have known better. I usually use the Nakanishi Dental Lab over in Bellevue—Dave Nakanishi makes all my crowns personally and does a terrific job. But I was in a hurry last week and was going to be late picking up the kids, so I called a lab in town to come in for the impression. Big mistake. I went back to the die—the plaster cast of Mrs. Sandstrom's prepped tooth that the crown had been made to fit—and brought it over to compare with the real thing. That's when I saw it.

There was a tiny dimple in the die which wasn't on her tooth, undoubtedly from a bubble in the plaster, which meant that the crown had a bump on the inside that was preventing it from seating. At this point the best thing to do would have been to take another impression and have Dave make the crown right. But Mrs. Sandstrom had been very patient during the whole ordeal, and the thought of having to do the crown all over again made me angry.

Throughout the appointment Laurie was doing a brilliant job of keeping Mrs. Sandstrom occupied, maintaining a line of patter that didn't require any response on the part of the patient, but with which she could seemingly go on forever. Laurie was an athletically-built blond, my age, and was the best dental assistant I had ever worked with. In addition to her technical expertise, which was considerable, she was dedicated to the job, and I really valued her ability with patients. Mrs. Sandstrom was in good hands as I ducked out to fix the crown.

The defect was extremely small, but that was all it had taken to keep it from seating. I went to the lab and, using a bur in the belt-driven hand piece, removed the bump in no time.

They were still talking when I came back in, but when I moved in over Mrs. Sandstrom, Laurie was right there, giving me her full attention. This time the crown seated perfectly.

The margin line was dovetailed well and I had Mrs. Sandstrom bite down on a strip of soft metal to make sure the crown wasn't riding too high or too low. It was within acceptable limits and I proceeded to cement it into place. Afterward I walked her out and we chatted—one of the benefits of a light patient-load—and then Mrs. Sandstrom left. Another satisfied customer. I, on the other hand, went back to my office with fifteen minutes to spare before my next appointment, yawning, dead tired, and thankful that everything had worked out.

4

After lunch I was busy doing lab work when Nona stuck her head in the doorway. I had decided that with certain patients I would take the time to make my own crowns. Not only would it save me money but, no offense to Dave, they would also be done right. I was in the middle of waxing up a model when she said, "There's someone here to see you."

"Who is it?"

"Pamela Nations."

"Do I know her?"

Nona shrugged. "She says she wants to talk to you."

"Well, give me a couple minutes before you send her in."

"Too late. She's already in your office." And with that, Nona was gone.

I set down the model and turned off the Bunsen burner, then removed my lab coat and headed down the hall. The door to my office was closed when I arrived. I opened it and walked in, but before I even had a chance to shut it behind me I was assaulted by a cloud of perfume. Though I tried my best not to react visibly, it wouldn't have mattered. The woman seated in front of my desk barely looked at me.

She had long, blond hair that was set in loose curls. She wasn't overweight, but hadn't missed too many meals, either. And she was wearing sunglasses. I walked over to her and offered my hand. "Ms. Nations?"

She didn't take it. "Mrs."

"Excuse me," I said, and took refuge behind my desk. "Can I get you anything? Coffee—"

"That would be fine."

I immediately jumped up and headed for the door, but when I opened it Nona was already on her way in with a steaming mug in her hand. She walked right by me to "Mrs." Nations and handed it to her.

"There you go, Pam."

"Thanks, Nona."

Nona swept back out the door and left me standing there with what must have been a stupid expression on my face. After I had walked back to my desk and sat down, I took a good hard look at Mrs. Nations. She was wearing a dark-blue suit with a white, ruffled blouse, and a gold chain with something sparkly hanging on the end. Nice legs. She took a sip of her coffee and this time there was no missing the rock of a ring she was wearing on her left hand.

"So, Mrs. Nations, what did you need to see me about?"

She sighed. "I feel like such a fool coming here."

"Oh, please don't," I said. "I'd really like to help you if I can."

"The thing is . . . It's just that . . . Well," she sighed again. "I thought you were a *real* doctor."

Ouch! That was hitting below the belt. Dentists seem to have a built-in inferiority complex as it is without having their noses rubbed in it. Even though we go through just as much schooling as medical doctors—four years, and two extra for specialists—some dentists subconsciously feel that they don't deserve the title *Doctor*. Thank God I'm not one of them. Still . . .

"I'm sorry, I don't think I understand."

"Oh," she said. "I saw your name on the police report. You *are* the one who found him?"

"Found him?"

"My husband. He died last night."

I felt my face turn red. Never in a million years would I have connected the grimy guitarist who had fallen off the stage at the Owl with *this* woman, who looked, for lack of a better word, rich. The only thing I could do was try and talk my way out of my embarrassment.

"Yes," I said, nodding. "That was me. I'm very sorry about your husband."

There was an awkward pause while she smoothed out her skirt.

"Did you find out what happened?" I ventured.

"Only what the police told me, which wasn't very much. I didn't realize when they called me last night that they were going to make me identify his body."

I nodded again. "Is that what you wanted to see me about?"

She took another sip of coffee, but with her eyes hidden behind the dark glasses I couldn't tell if she'd heard me or not.

"When I saw your name on the report, and that you were a doctor, I thought you might be able to find out why he had died."

I squirmed a little in my seat. "I see. Well, I really think that the hospital might be in a better position to tell you than I would."

"I know, but Rick didn't have any insurance."

Then she stopped. Reluctantly, I thought I was going to have to tell her again that I didn't understand, when she continued. "And I was hoping that his death might be somehow . . . work related."

Now my hackles were up. This didn't sound like something I wanted to play any part in. "You know, Mrs. Nations, what I think you really need is a lawyer."

"I suppose, but I'm not from around here. I just thought if you were a real doctor you could talk to somebody, the coroner or something, and find out if he could have been poisoned, contaminated on the job."

Now, in spite of my not being a *real* doctor, I did have friends from my medical school days, one of whom just happened to be a pathologist at Bay Med Hospital, and I *could* have done what she requested. But Pamela Nations was leaving a bad taste in my mouth and I thought I'd just as soon have her out of my office and get back to my lab work.

"I'm not positive, but I think you can request an autopsy from the medical examiner."

She perked up at this. "Really? You'd be able to do that for me?"

My head was shaking before she had finished. "No. I *really* think you need to find yourself a lawyer."

The corners of her mouth turned down. "You wouldn't happen to know of any offhand, would you?"

This time I sighed. "Not really. If you left me your phone number, though, I could contact you if I think of anyone."

"That wouldn't work. I'm staying at a hotel right now. I'll only be in town for a few days."

Just long enough to start a wrongful death suit against your husband's former employer, I thought. It was definitely time to end this discussion, but as soon as I opened my mouth she began to speak.

"I hadn't seen Rick in years," she went on. "I live down in California, and I was quite surprised when the Seattle police contacted me."

"I can imagine," I said, trying not to sound condescending, but secretly hoping I did.

"Of course, I flew up immediately."

"Of course."

"I live in Glendale now, but when Rick and I were first married we lived in San Francisco. That's where I met him. He was playing music full-time then, and for a while it was one band after another. He was happy, though.

"Well, at that time I was working for First Interstate Bank, and about a year later I was transferred to one of their Los Angeles branches—they moved all of the loan-servicing departments from the individual branches to one location, and since I was the head supervisor in the downtown San Francisco office they naturally offered me a job at headquarters."

I cleared my throat, desperately trying to end this thing. "Yes, that's—"

"But Rick was just catching on with this new group. They were based in Oakland and, oh, I don't know, I guess he thought they were going to make it big, but I thought they were all losers. You could just tell."

She looked at me as if for affirmation, and I jumped at the chance to get rid of her. "I know exactly—"

"That's when the fighting started. For real this time. I mean, we'd had fights before, but then everybody does. They don't mean anything, really—they're just fights. But this time it was different—there were way too many things we disagreed on. For instance, I wanted to have kids but he didn't want to be tied down. He knew my new job was going to pay me a lot more—we could have afforded it—but he didn't see it that way. He thought I was trying to break up the group. You can't believe what kind of strain that puts on a relationship. The long and short of it was that he told me he wasn't going to L.A. I told him I was, and I did.

"We wrote to each other for a while—we were still married, after all—but once the band broke up, just like I knew it would, he said he still wanted to stay in San Francisco. I couldn't believe it. That's when I knew there had to be somebody else. I mean, *I* was dating, but it wasn't like it was anything serious. And then one day he just disappeared. My letters were returned, and when I tried calling, his phone was disconnected. He just vanished.

"Well, I filed for divorce immediately, but you know how it is—I never got around to taking care of the finalities. I suppose if I had met someone worth marrying, that would have been different, but . . . I don't know."

Miraculously, she stopped and leaned over to set her coffee cup on my desk. Without a moment to lose I blurted out, "Hey, you know what?" I *do* know a lawyer who might be able to help you, after all."

Here eyebrows arched over the dark glasses and I scribbled a name and number on one of my prescription pads, tore the sheet off and handed it to her.

"Thank you," she said succinctly, and I seized the moment to stand and head for the door. I opened it and walked her to the reception desk where she thanked Nona again for the coffee and ignored me as she left.

Afterward, I took a deep breath and ran my hands over my head as Nona looked on. I was exhausted. Nona didn't say anything but I could tell she wanted to.

"Don't ask," I said, and surprised myself by yawning.

Nona was smiling now. "I take it you're going home early, then?"

I looked at my watch, more for effect than anything else, and affirmed what I had wanted to do the moment I walked into my office and laid eyes on Mrs. Nations.

"Yes."

5

As soon as I walked in the door of my apartment I headed for the bedroom and crashed for a couple of hours. I had set the alarm first, and when it woke me up I dragged myself out of bed and down to my truck, and then drove over the 520 floating bridge to Medina to pick up the kids from school.

My Toyota SR-5 short-bed was only two years old, and had come equipped with a factory tape deck that was more than sufficient for my musical needs. I had a handful of cassettes in the glove box and I put on one containing cuts I had recorded from compact disc. Tenor saxophonist Ralph Moore, playing Bud Powell's "Un Poco Loco" blared out from the speakers in my doors as I raced across Lake Washington, minutes ahead of rush-hour traffic.

Janet dropped Cathie at school on her way to work, while the housekeeper who came in weekday mornings took Timmy there on her way home. Janet could afford to hire a housekeeper but I never asked her for money, and she never offered.

Among the crowd of children in the fenced playground, I spotted two in particular as I pulled into the lot of Medina Elementary. The older was a girl with long, dark hair and a tiny round face reminiscent of my own. She had on a bright-purple raincoat—which she had begged her mother to buy for her—even though it wasn't raining. The boy was two years younger, with the lighter hair and more angular face of his mother, and was wearing a small brown ski jacket. Both of them came bounding up to the truck as soon as I stopped.

Cathie was in the second grade, and Timmy was in the afternoon session of kindergarten. We exchanged greetings and kisses and then I strapped them in for the six-block drive home. I had walked about the same distance when I was in grade school, but things have changed considerably, even in the relatively short time since I was a kid. It's a sad commentary on our society that I felt there was no way they could safely walk home alone.

As we drove, I became immediately and pleasantly immersed in the inner workings of Mrs. Dassel's second-grade class, and I added thoughtful nods and "Hmm's" where appropriate. My son, on the other hand, could only stare in rapt fascination at the gold star Mrs. Kogan had placed on the picture he had drawn that afternoon. The trip home was much too short.

It had been my idea for Janet and the kids to stay at the house, but it was mostly for the kid's sake. They had grown up in that house. I felt that they had more of a claim on it that I did, and I wasn't about to take it away from them. Cathie and Timmy had their friends, and school, and in spite of what had happened between me and Janet, I wanted it to stay that way. A few minutes later I turned into the driveway and was greeted by the familiar and welcoming sight of my own childhood home.

The house had been my parent's originally, and the property had been passed on to me when they died. It's a fairly modern affair, with a cedar-shingled exterior and a single, sloping roof that extends down over a carport in back. Out front is a large deck and a virtual wall of windows and skylights. Inside there are three bedrooms and four bathrooms spread over three stories. I parked the truck next to my Porsche, another legacy from my father, and the three of us clambered out together.

My dad's car is a late model 928, and though I take it out

a couple of times a month, I don't like to drive it all the time. For one thing, the maintenance on it is a killer: a couple of tires can put me out nearly a month's rent on my apartment. And I also don't like leaving it parked downtown as an invitation to car thieves. But the real reason, I suppose, is that I'm just not a sports-car person.

Once we were in the house, my previous fatigue came back with a vengeance, and as the kids ran off to their bedrooms I veered right, into the TV room, and collapsed on the couch. The next thing I knew, Cathie was shaking my shoulder.

"Daddy, wake up."

"Huh? What?"

"Mommy's here."

"Oh," I said, sitting up. "Thanks, hon'."

I rubbed my face and saw that the kids were on the floor in front of me, coloring. The TV was on, but the sound muted, and when Janet came in the door I stood and walked over to her.

She had shoulder-length brown hair, combed straight back from her forehead, and was wearing a dark-burgundy suit, a white blouse, a single strand of pearls, and had her wedding ring firmly ensconced on her left hand.

Janet had a light-complexioned, oval face that needed little makeup, and the most luminescent blue eyes I had ever seen. When she saw me she smiled, and kissed me when I reached her.

"Thanks a lot," she said, her face suddenly deadpan.

"For what?"

"Pamela Nations."

"Oh, Christ." In my blissful slumber I had forgotten that I had foisted Pamela "Mrs." Nations onto Janet. "I'm sorry," I said. "I didn't know what else to do with her. She was in my office and she was driving me crazy, and I thought maybe someone in your firm could—"

"No, I mean it. I think Pam just might have a case."

25

I was confused. Had she really just said "Pam?" Was I missing something? Was she talking about the same self-absorbed woman who had accused me of being something less that a medical professional only a few short hours before?

"Since when have you started trying civil cases?"

"I haven't. It's just . . . I don't know. I like her. Besides, who says it's going to go to trial?"

I could only shake my head.

The year I'd begun dental school was the same year Janet had decided to pursue a law degree. Thinking back, it was hard to imagine how we'd managed it. Cathie had been born the year before, and it was tough. Very tough. But we both liked what we were doing and we persevered. Janet had become an associate in a Bellevue firm, and was earning quite a reputation in the Seattle area for her criminal defense work. That's why I was more than a little surprised she was taking on the Nations case herself.

"Daddy and I are going upstairs for little while," she yelled to the kids. Timmy was the only one who mumbled back an okay. Both their heads remained buried in their coloring books.

Janet took off her jacket and began unbuttoning her blouse as I followed her up the stairs.

"She tells me you were there last night at the Owl when her husband died."

"Yeah. It was really strange."

"I'll say."

"No, I mean aside from the obvious."

"How's that?"

We were at the top of the stairs now and I followed her into the master bedroom.

"Well, for one thing," I said, "there was no warning."

"Yeah?" She kicked off her shoes while I climbed up on the bed and stretched out, leaning back on the pillows against the headboard.

"When someone dies unexpectedly like that, it's usually preceded by something, convulsions, or seizures, or they grab their chest if they're having a heart attack, or warn you if they can't breathe. You almost always know it's an emergency before they pass out."

"And that didn't happen?" Janet had carefully removed her skirt and slip, placing them on the chair next to her desk. Then she began on her nylons.

"Not that I could see. I hadn't paid much attention to him onstage, so I'm not sure what happened right before, but when this guy landed facedown on the dance floor he was already dead. It was like he'd died on his feet. There was no pulse that I could feel. He wasn't breathing. He was just . . . dead."

Finally, Janet unhooked her bra and tossed it on top of her nylons; then she cupped her naked breasts and vigorously massaged them for a moment. "God, I hate wearing those things," she said, and promptly stripped off her underwear before heading into the adjoining bathroom. "I'll just be a minute," she yelled, and I heard the shower turn on. "There's Heineken in the fridge if you want one."

"Thanks."

The last thing I needed was a beer, unless it was to stick down the front of my pants in lieu of a cold shower. Some people are belligerent drunks, or happy drunks—I'm a tired drunk. After too many beers all I want to do is curl up into a ball somewhere and go to sleep. I was so tired already that it wouldn't have taken more than a couple of sips to put me out for the night. But then again, I thought, that might not have been such a bad idea after all.

With the image of Janet's incredible body still dancing across my retinas, my heart was racing a mile a minute. The problem was I couldn't tell whether it was from lust or fear. I don't like being scared of people, and Janet scared me. But before I had a chance to decide, the shower turned off, and a few minutes later Janet came in the room wearing only a towel—a very short towel.

She climbed onto the bed beside me and gave me another kiss. This time I kissed her back, and it was anything but unpleasant. I indulged myself in this highly enjoyable act until I noticed that her towel had come undone. My hand was moving across the smooth skin of her stomach and slowly making its way upward. If I didn't stop now there might be no turning back. I pulled away from her gently and sat up. She closed her towel, but couldn't hide the disappointment on her face.

"So, what kind of case does she have?" I said, trying to get my mind on something else.

She blinked her eyes hard a couple of times and then took a breath. "Well, when she picked up her husband's personal effects from the hospital, she went through his wallet and found out that he had been working for Lacroix Chemicals here in Seattle."

"I thought they were based in Tacoma."

"The headquarters, sure, but they have a small plant on Harbor Island."

I nodded. Harbor Island is a man-made island at the southern end of Elliott Bay, between the two forks of the Duwamish Waterway. Its easy access to shipping makes it an ideal location for the many heavy industries that are located there. "You really think his death was work related?"

"It's a definite possibility," she said, hopping off the bed and discarding her towel in one motion. "Especially with something like industrial chemicals. But I won't know for sure until I get the autopsy report later this week. Then I'll know if I have a case." She slipped on her robe and turned back to me. "Do you want to stay for dinner?"

God, I hated this. A couple of times a month Janet would try to seduce me into staying the night. It had been three weeks since the last time. It wasn't that I didn't want to—on the contrary, I wanted to very much. But the fact was I couldn't. I don't know why we hadn't filed for divorce right away. Maybe it was like Pamela Nations had said: we never found anyone else we wanted to marry. I didn't have a girlfriend, and I wasn't really looking for one. I knew Janet didn't have anyone else either. And, of course, there were the kids. So, a couple of times a month, it came down to this.

"I'm sorry, hon'. I just can't."

She looked at me as if I'd slapped her in the face. "How many times do I have to apologize, Steve? Tell me how many times and I'll do it."

"Janet, please—"

"What else do I need to do?"

I could see the tears welling in her eyes and I pushed myself off the bed in the hopes that I could avert them. I went to her and held her tight in my arms. "Hey, come on. I don't want to leave like this."

"Then don't," she said into my shoulder. I could feel the hot tears through my shirt. "I love you, Steve."

"I love you, too."

She pulled back from me at that. Her cheeks were wet and she snuffled a couple of times. "Then what are we doing? Why are we still living like this?"

"Janet—"

"I swear to God it won't happen again. I promise. I don't know what else you want me to do."

"Janet, I'm not asking for anything but time. Please. I wish there *was* something you could do, something that would make everything better, but there isn't. I just have to work this out on my own."

She took a deep breath and wiped her eyes with the sleeve of her robe. "I know," she said. "But I miss you so much. Sometimes I can't stand it."

I couldn't think of an answer for that, so I gave her another kiss.

"Are you sure you can't stay? *Just* for dinner?"

I didn't hesitate, only because I didn't want to make things any more painful than they already were. "Not tonight, okay?"

She nodded and I kept my arm around her as we walked downstairs to the door. Cathie and Timmy both gave me hugs and kisses and I told them I'd see them tomorrow.

"Let me know what turns up on the autopsy report," I said on my way out.

"Why?"

"I don't know. I was there when the guy died. I'm just kind of curious."

Janet smiled and said, "All right." Then she kissed me goodbye and I drove back home across Lake Washington to my empty apartment.

6

The next morning was gray and rainy, typical for Seattle. But after a light dinner and an early bedtime the night before, I woke up feeling rested and restored in spite of the wet weather. In fact, I felt so good that I skipped my coffee at home and made it to work before Nona.

Wednesday was another average, slow day, and though I did have a couple of appointments in the afternoon, the vacancies in the morning more than made up for them. My first patient that morning was a young woman I had come to know well over the four years I'd been practicing. Her name was Andrea Paul. She saw me every six months, religiously, and her visits had become almost routine. But it hadn't always been that way.

Andrea Paul was not a fortunate young woman. Through either bad genes, bad luck, or a combination of both, she had been born with weak enamel. In practical terms, it meant that in spite of diligent brushing and flossing, she was still prone to getting cavities. Even worse, they tended to be right along the gum line between her teeth, where the enamel was thinnest anyway.

The first time I saw her was when her mother brought her in right after I had opened my office. Andrea was an angry and confused eight-grader then, and she made it perfectly clear that she was not happy to be here. To put it simply, she hated dentists, all dentists, and that included me. After talking with Andrea's mother, I began to understand why.

This was a girl who had grown up without once uttering the phrase, "Look, Ma, no cavities." Even suggesting a trip to the dentist was tantamount in her eyes to suggesting a visit to the torture chambers of the Inquisition.

At the time of that first appointment, she hadn't been to the dentist in over a year. She was a freckle-faced girl with glasses and straight hair who wore a perpetual frown—at least she did when she was in my office. She'd had four cavities that day, which wasn't bad considering the amount of time since her last checkup. But in addition to those, I decided to replace two discolored composite fillings in her front teeth, one each on the mesial edges of her upper lateral incisors. I made a good match on the materials and it immediately improved her smile, so much so that she was willing to come back five months later.

She only had one cavity that time, but I replaced a few other discolored fillings near the gum line in her lower teeth. I followed this up with a treatment usually reserved for small children and applied a pit-and-fissure sealant to the few remaining occlusal surfaces that hadn't been filled. Next, I had her show me how she brushed and flossed, and then I corrected her technique and pointed out some trouble spots that she should pay special attention to.

It had taken a little extra time on my part but, back then, time was a commodity I had plenty of. As it turned out, it was well worth it, and on her next visit I was able to give Andrea a clean bill of health. She was fifteen by then, with a smile on her face that not only looked good, but that she began to show more often.

After those first two visits, Andrea usually left my office without having any work done at all, and believe me, I was as happy about it as she was. She was now a senior at Ballard High

School, a star volleyball player with a steady boyfriend and a vastly improved outlook on the dental profession.

I said hi as I walked into the operatory, and talked to her a little about what was going on in school. Her freckles were mostly gone now, contact lenses had replaced her glasses, and her formerly stringy hair was lush, permed and stylishly cut. But the changes weren't just physical; her personality had blossomed. She was vibrant and outgoing and I liked to think that somehow I'd had a hand in her transformation. That's why I was a little reluctant to give her my diagnosis.

I'd had my eye on a couple of potential cavities on her upper bicuspids. I'd told her about them as soon as they'd become evident, so that she wouldn't miss them when she was flossing and brushing. On her last visit, it had been a judgment call and I'd let them slide, but now they needed attention.

"Bad news," I said, and she looked at me with resignation.

"How many?"

"Two."

Andrea breathed a sigh. "Are they the two you've been warning me about?"

"Yeah."

"I worked my buns off brushing those suckers," she said, her eyes focused forward.

Susan, a twenty-five year-old brunette who had been with me less than a year, smiled at me from across the chair and began to ready a syringe.

Andrea looked back and forth between the two of us and shrugged. "Sorry."

"Flossing, too?" I asked.

"Are you kidding? Sometimes I think I'm personally responsible for keeping Johnson & Johnson in business."

"Well, everything else looks great, if that's any consolation. You should be in and out of here when you come back after graduation."

"I can't wait," she said with a relaxed smile, then slipped the headphones over her ears and leaned back. I have a Sony Walkman in every operatory for those patients who like to tune out during the procedure. It's a nice distraction and the patient can still hear me give instructions.

"Open," I said, and we were underway.

After I had finished with Andrea and lunch, I picked up a file from Nona and entered operatory number one for an appointment I'd been looking forward to all day. The patient's name was Daniel Lasky. He was a Lieutenant in the Seattle Police Department's Magnolia Precinct, right down the street from Bay Med.

If Andrea Paul was unlucky, Daniel Lasky was exactly the opposite. Though he made nominal attempts to keep his teeth clean, invariably he wound up with a tremendous amount of plaque and calculus buildup. He came in twice a year to see Julie for a prophy, but sometimes it seemed like even that wasn't enough.

Lieutenant Lasky wasn't big on flossing, and even though I tried my best to scare him straight with the horrors of periodontal disease, he wasn't convinced. And it wasn't hard to figure out why. His reasoning was based on something much more visible than the mysterious inner workings of gum tissue: two cavities.

During his forty-two years of life, Dan Lasky's teeth had succumbed to dental caries only twice. Both of the fillings in his mouth had been put in about fifteen years ago and each replaced once since then. The guy had enamel like galvanized steel and, for all practical purposes, was a veritable dental *Übermensch*.

"Hi, Dan," I said as I walked into the operatory.

A sandy-haired man in a rumpled brown suit and tie returned my greeting. "Thanks for squeezing me in on such short notice, Steve."

"You bet," I said, and smiled to myself. Lasky had called only yesterday saying that one of his fillings had broken. It had not been a problem finding space for him in my busy schedule.

After washing up and donning a fresh pair of gloves I took my seat next to Lasky and lowered the chair so his head was resting in my lap. I asked Susan for an explorer, adjusted the overhead lamp, and then said, "Open up."

The first thing I noticed was that an entire cusp of his first molar—where one of his duo of fillings was located—had completely broken off about halfway above the gum line. "Do you realize that a whole chunk of your tooth is missing?" I said, and removed the explorer so he could talk.

"Hey, no kidding? I felt a sharp edge with my tongue but I just thought a piece of my filling had broken out."

Somehow it didn't surprise me that he hadn't actually looked.

"So, what happens now?" he asked.

"I'm going to replace the filling. It was getting pretty worn anyway. Let's have another look."

This time I checked the rest of his teeth, removing what calculus I could with the explorer before finally asking for a scaler. Not a cavity in sight; it was unbelievable. My next appointment wasn't for an hour, so I did a little impromptu cleaning before replacing his filling. Since part of the structure was missing I would need to put a thin metal collar around his tooth to hold the amalgam in place while I sculpted a replacement cusp. Once I'd given him the anesthetic, Dan and I talked for a few minutes to let it take effect; then I asked Susan for a matrix band and a holder, and started in.

Nine years earlier, Janet and I had gone into the Magnolia Precinct to report a missing person. That missing person had been my father, and the incident had ended in his death. *Detective* Lasky, then, had been very helpful, but once I became mired in the tragedy that followed, I had virtually forgotten about him. Imagine my surprise when six years later he showed up in my waiting room to schedule an appointment.

Since Dan didn't have a regular dentist at the time—and obviously didn't feel as if he needed one—he'd decided to look through the listings in the phone book. He recognized my name and thought he would stop by and tell me how sorry he was about my dad.

Well, I checked him out and was happy to inform him that his "toothache" was, in reality, pain originating in his sinuses due to a cold he'd recently recovered from. He decided right then to make me his regular dentist, and as if that weren't enough, a few months later he brought in his wife and kids and added them to my sparse patient list.

Though Dan and I had never been what you'd call close friends, two or three times a year after that first appointment we would entertain each other's families, usually at backyard barbecues during the summer. His kids and mine enjoyed playing together, and Janet and Dan's wife Rena got along famously right from the start. Things tapered off quite a bit after Janet and I separated, but since Dan worked in the area I still saw him every once in a while.

When I had finished and Dan was trying in vain to rub out the numbness in his lip I decided to pop the question. "Listen, Dan, I was wondering if you'd be able to do me a favor."

"Sure. What do you need?"

"It's kind of unofficially official."

He looked at me with a little more interest now. "Yeah?" he asked guardedly.

I explained to him all about the incident at the Owl on Monday night and he grunted appreciatively. When I relayed my encounter with Mrs. Nations he nodded his head sympathetically. Then I came to the reason I needed the favor: Janet.

"She told you she's taking the case?" he asked.

"Yeah. She seems to think there's something there."

"And you don't?"

"It's not that—it's just that the guy was dressed pretty shabbily and musicians are notorious for drug abuse."

"What did the autopsy say?"

"There hasn't been one yet, as far as I know. And Jesus, you know how long toxicology reports take." Dan nodded. "It could be another month before Janet knows what he actually died from. I just thought you might be able to run his name through your computers and if he *was* in there for something drug related, at least Janet would know that going in."

"And be able to bail out of the case?"

"Something like that."

"How are you two getting along, anyway?" I paused and Dan shrugged. "I'm sorry, I—"

"No, it's okay. We're doing all right, I guess. Things are still up in the air, though."

Dan rubbed his lip again and then pushed himself up off the chair. I picked up his file to return to Nona, and walked him out to the reception desk. Once we were there he stopped and turned to me. "So, what did you say this guy's name was?"

"Nations," I said, and smiled. "Rick Nations."

7

Thursday morning Janet called me at work. "What the hell is a nonspecific cerebral hemorrhage?"

"Excuse me?"

"I just got the autopsy report back, and it says here that Rick Nations died from a nonspecific cerebral hemorrhage. What's that?"

"Well, hello to you, too."

She laughed. "Didn't Nona tell you it was me?"

"Yes, but—"

"I'm sorry. I'm a little excited because I still don't know if I have a case yet. So, what do you think?"

Although I wanted to be mad, I had to laugh as well. Janet was as determined as they came when she smelled blood. Then I said, "It just means that they couldn't find the cause of the bleeding in his brain."

"Why not?"

"Most likely he was bleeding in several areas—it wasn't specific to a particular vessel."

"That's fine, but what does it mean?"

"I have a pretty good idea, but you're not going to like it."

"What?"

"I think you might be looking at an adverse reaction to drugs."

39

Janet was silent for a moment and then said, ". . . or chemicals."

"Not necessarily."

"But can you rule it out?"

"It's not that simple—"

"Yes or no?"

"Don't cross-examine me, Janet."

"All right, I'm sorry. It's just that we've already started the preliminary investigation and I want to make sure we're not wasting our time."

"Investigating what?"

"Lacroix Chemicals."

"You're going ahead with it, then?"

"Unless you can tell me that there's no possible way it could have been chemical exposure."

She had me on that one. "I guess I can't."

"Okay. There was something else I wanted to ask you. It says here that the drug screen is going to take two weeks. Will that tell me if he was poisoned by the chemicals?"

"If it *is* a poison, no, they would have to be testing specifically for that chemical. I thought you knew all this."

"Are you kidding? Most of my clients either stabbed or shot someone. I don't usually need to wait around for a toxicology report. Okay, so they test for drugs, how much longer do I have to wait after that?"

"I'm just guessing, but I'd say another two weeks."

"Are you serious?"

"Yeah. It's not that easy. There's no general test on blood that's going to show you every chemical that's in it. You have to test for specific substances."

"In other words, you have to know what you're looking for in order to find it?"

"That's about the size of it."

She sighed. "Okay, so all together it's going to be about four weeks?"

"Unless it was drugs—then it's only two."

"I guess we won't know until then, will we?"

"I guess not."

"Would you be able to go over the report tonight if I brought it home with me?"

"Sure."

"Great. I'll see you tonight, then."

We said goodbye and hung up. The more I thought about Rick Nations that day, the more a cerebral hemorrhage made sense. With something like a heart attack, a person is usually able to flop around for a minute or two before the lack of oxygenated blood causes him to pass out. But if the pressure inside a person's skull from internal bleeding damages the body's control centers, it's like throwing a switch that shuts everything down. Reactions such as Rick Nations' were not unheard of, and to my mind fit perfectly with everything that happened on Monday night.

I didn't learn much more than Janet had already told me when I went over the report with her that night. She was understandably eager to find out which of the chemicals Nations was working with might be responsible for his death. I was just as sure it had been drugs. There were any number of amphetamines that could have caused the hemorrhaging, and if Nations had been drinking, too, it would have made the reaction time that much quicker.

I tried valiantly to warn her about jumping to conclusions, but Janet wouldn't listen. *Pam* had insisted that Rick never use drugs. It was a losing battle, so I decided to let it go. Either way, the toxicology report wouldn't be completed for another two or three weeks and there was no way to be sure until then. Janet told me that while she was waiting, she would be proceeding with the investigation. I wished her luck and hoped that I would be hearing something from Dan Lasky soon.

*   *   *

The rest of the week had passed before I knew it. Friday was a light day for me at the office, with Julie using two of the operatories most of the day for her hygienic work, so after school I took the kids to a matinee showing of *Peter Pan*, which was making its septennial rounds in the theaters. Janet was already home when we arrived back at the house, and since she already had dinner prepared and, more importantly, since I was starving, I decided to stay. Predictably, I had caved in when the kids had wanted popcorn during the movie, and so they spent the entire meal pushing food around on their plates before asking to be excused. Janet and I had a nice talk afterward over coffee, but I still went home that night.

In addition to the seven-to-eight hour in the mornings, I've found that Saturday is a prime day to see patients. Nona always offers it, and it's usually the first day in my weekly schedule to fill up. My grandfather had been a barber and, like the Barbers' Union, I take Sunday and Monday off. It's a nice schedule, and since I don't have to pick up the kids on Saturday, I can usually book the whole day solid.

Sundays I have all to myself. That Sunday afternoon I had the TV on, watching the Sonics duke it out with Utah. But I also had the sound muted and the stereo playing. I was listening to Harold Land's *The Fox*. Not only did the album feature one of my favorite pianists, Elmo Hope, but it also contained one of the few performances by a nearly forgotten trumpet great, Dupree Bolton. It's a fantastic album and I had the stereo turned up rather loud.

A little after two the sky had cleared for the first time in four days, and I could actually see the Olympics out my windows. I had the sliding glass door open and was standing out on the balcony, the cold crisp air smelling faintly of the spring that was to come. One of my hands was on the railing and the other was wrapped around a bottle of Heineken.

Harold had just finished ripping through the changes of Elmo Hope's "One Second, Please" on his tenor sax when the phone rang. It was a good thing the song was almost over or I might not have heard it. I went back inside, eased back the volume on the stereo and picked up the phone.

"Hello?"

"Hi, I'm looking for Steve." The voice was soft and raspy with a faint East Coast accent.

"This is Steve," I said.

"Hi, I'm Bobby Stutz." The name sounded familiar but I couldn't place it. "We're playing down at the Ballard Firehouse tonight and I'm trying to get a sax. You play sax, don't you?"

Now I remembered. Several months ago Bobby Stutz and the Bearcats had been the host band at the Owl. Bobby had asked me after my set how he could get in touch with me because the saxophone in his band was thinking of quitting. I'd told him I would be glad to sit in, but that I wasn't looking for a full-time commitment. He had taken my number anyway.

"Sure." I said.

"Do you think you'd be able to play tonight? I don't know how much we're gettin' paid, but you'll get something."

"Yeah, I could do that. What kind of stuff are you doing now?"

"Sixties soul, same as always—Wilson Pickett, Sam and Dave, James Brown, Marvin Gaye . . ."

"That's no problem."

"All right, man, all right. We start playing at nine, so you should be there by eight-thirty. Do you know where the Firehouse is?"

"It's just down on Market, isn't it?"

"Right."

"Do I need to bring a microphone or anything?"

"Nah, we got it all taken care of. Just bring your horn."

"Okay."

"All right. Hey, thanks, man—I really appreciate this. I'll see you tonight."

After I hung up the phone I turned the stereo back up and sat down on the couch. I always enjoyed sitting in with an established band. Whereas amateurs spend most of their time fumbling around, making sure they're all playing the same thing, a group that has been together for a while provides a solid background that's a pleasure to play over. And since I had Monday off, the late night wouldn't interfere with work.

As far as the music went, I'd cut my teeth on Atlantic soul years before, back when the Blues Brothers first hit it big. I remembered having a heated "discussion" with my father after graduating high school about my decision to go to Vegas with a white soul band—years before the Commitments came along. I went despite his objections and I had a lot of fun that summer, but I don't think I was cut out for a career in music. So I turned up at home three months later and made my father very happy by enrolling in college that fall. I still enjoyed playing the sax, though, and I smiled at the thought of the evening ahead.

My smile disappeared, however, when the score of the game flashed on the TV, and I had to blink my eyes to make sure I wasn't seeing things. The last time I had looked, the Sonics had been up by twelve points going into the fourth period, but in the time I had gone out on the balcony and then talked to Bobby on the phone, they had fallen behind by six. I shook my head, killed off the Heineken, and padded out to the kitchen for another.

After the game I picked up the novel Susan had loaned me the week before, *Fatherland* by Robert Harris. It's widely known around the office that I love historical fiction, especially when it involves either of the World Wars. Though it wasn't exactly historical, Susan had thought I would like it. She was right. I only had a hundred pages left, and spent the rest of the afternoon reading.

Engrossed in my novel, even through dinner, I managed to finish it by seven-thirty that evening. I hopped in the shower afterward, then dressed in my standard playing attire: black Levis, black jacket, black tie, and red cotton shirt. I felt the nervous knot in my stomach that I always had before playing, but I felt pretty good as I grabbed my sax and headed downstairs to the truck.

8

I'd only been to the Ballard Firehouse once before, to see Duffy Bishop and the Rhythm Dogs, but there was no way I could have missed it. It was only three blocks away from the Owl and I had to drive by it every Monday. The building was an actual converted fire station, with three big glass-paneled roll-up doors in front where the engines used to race out at the sound of alarms.

I walked in shortly after eight, hoisted up my horn to show the bouncer, and walked in without paying the cover charge. The stage was on the right as I rounded the corner into the bar and I tossed my sax case up near one of the microphones in front. There were a couple of people setting up equipment but I didn't recognize them as the band members I'd seen with Bobby before.

Behind the stage was a large banner that read *Clean and Sober Dance*. I wasn't quite sure what that meant until I walked up to the bar and tried to order a beer. I was curtly refused, but the bartender informed me that I could buy a can of soda for a mere two-fifty. I settled on the one-dollar cup of coffee—refills only fifty cents. It was a good thing I was getting paid tonight.

The large room was nearly half full and I wandered over to a table near the stage. Hanging from the rafters amid a cloud of cigarette smoke were the flags of nearly every nation, assaulting the place with color. I sipped my coffee and watched as people continued to trickle in.

About twenty after eight the drummer arrived and began hauling his cases up onstage and setting up. He had long blond hair and an awful lot of equipment, I thought, for the kind of music that we would be playing. Shortly after, a large black man in dreadlocks rolled in a small bass amp and guitar case and lifted them onto the stage.

At eight-thirty the rest of the group arrived: guitar player, late thirties, a snazzy dresser in a beautiful leather jacket; keyboard player in jeans, white T-shirt, and black high-top sneakers; and female vocalist, mid-twenties, wearing a black swatch of a miniskirt and a leather vest with a plunging neckline designed to induce vertigo.

Finally, through the front door, strode the unmistakable figure of Bobby Stutz. He was a light-skinned black man, six foot six, easy, in a white suit, bright-red silk shirt, bolo tie, white Stetson, and snakeskin cowboy boots. I had laughed to myself the first time I saw Bobby in his getup and I did the same again. He flitted around the soundboard and the other members of the band with what was either a lot of excess nervous energy, or a little cocaine—most likely the latter.

I pondered finishing the cold dregs of my coffee, then decided to leave them and walked up to Bobby.

"Hey, how ya doin', man?" he yelled to me before I had even reached him. "Thanks for comin' tonight. I really appreciate it."

"No problem."

He grabbed my outstretched hand in one of his big paws and hauled me over to him so that my eyes were level with his chin. Then he clapped me on the back and yelled, "All right, man! You guys ready to jam tonight?"

Yeah, it was definitely the cocaine. "This is Steve," he said to the musicians onstage. "He's playin' sax." A couple of them actually nodded to me.

After I extricated myself from Bobby, I made my way up onto the stage and began to set up. The guitarist immediately walked over and introduced himself.

"Ted Aykroyd."

"Steve Raymond," I said, and we shook hands.

Ted was a good six inches shorter than my six feet, with a slight build and thinning hair. "So, how did Bobby rope you into this?" he asked me.

That didn't sound very promising, but from what I'd just witnessed it made sense. I lost my train of thought momentarily while I was looking at Ted. There was something familiar about him that wasn't in conjunction with Bobby. In fact, I couldn't remember any of these musicians as having played with Bobby that night at the Owl. "He gave me a call this afternoon." I finally said.

Ted smiled at me. "He didn't promise you any money, I hope."

I rolled my eyes and smiled back. "Should I be worried?"

"No, I'll make sure you get paid."

"So, how long have you been playing with Bobby?"

Ted shook his head. "This is only the second time."

"What about the rest of these guys?"

"Never seen 'em before. I know the bass player plays with a reggae band in town."

"Are any of these guys part of his regular band?"

Ted laughed at that. "Bobby doesn't have a regular band." Oh well, there went my fantasy of playing with a tightly-knit unit. "He tends to forget to pay people and, for some reason Bobby can never figure out, they tend to get pissed off about it and quit."

I shook my head. "Thanks for clueing me in."

"You bet. But don't leave here tonight without any money.

He knows better than to stiff me, and I'll make sure you get something, too. Okay?"

"Okay. Thanks, Ted."

He nodded and went back to tuning his guitar.

As I was readying my horn I searched frantically in my case for a couple of minutes looking for my favorite reed before I remembered that it had been destroyed last Monday night by Rick Nations' death throes. Eventually I found one of acceptable quality and put my alto together, set it on its stand, and went back to the bar for another cup of coffee. The place was nearly full now and I had to search for a seat near the back of the room.

Nine o'clock came and went with no sign of Bobby. At quarter after, the keyboard player came up to me and asked me if I'd seen him recently, and I had to say I hadn't. A few minutes later Ted walked over. "We'd better get up there and play something."

He managed to get everybody together and after he'd given the changes to the bass player and the arrangement to the drummer, we launched into a blues tune I'd never heard before, something about a personified bottle of whiskey. Ted, as it turned out, was a phenomenal guitarist—and then he began to sing. He had a strong, controlled voice with plenty of gravel that put just the right edge to the lyrics. His guitar playing was so solid and dominating that everyone in the band seemed to fall into place behind him.

The rest of the musicians were definitely a cut above the ones who turned up at the Owl and, in my humble opinion, the sound was breathtaking. I was very happy to be a part of it and before too long I was playing above myself. I had forgotten that these people would be professionals, unlike the amateurs I usually played with, and that even if they hadn't played together before, this was their job. The quality of the music showed that.

After the whisky song, we ran through a very nice rendition of "Further on up the Road," and then Ted segued into the opening riff of one of my favorites, "Sweet Home, Chicago." But if I'd thought the five of us were good, that was nothing compared to what happened when Bobby suddenly appeared onstage with his female vocalist in tow. They sang background to Ted's lead vocal and it blew me away.

When the song was finished Bobby yelled out, "Knock on Wood." Ted in turn yelled out the key, counted off the tempo, and we were into the old Eddie Floyd tune before I'd had a chance to catch my breath. I fumbled with the first few notes before finally locking into the opening line. I crowded the microphone, dead on the riff, and Bobby looked over at me and grinned.

Now, even though it was obvious that the crowd had been enjoying the music, nobody had been dancing up to this point. But when Bobby started singing, the tables emptied. It didn't take long to realize why. Even doing somebody else's song, the sound was unmistakable. If you closed your eyes and didn't know he was dead, you'd have sworn to God that Otis Redding was on the stage at the mike. Where Ted's voice had been bright and commanding, Bobby's was dark and soulful, and if he'd been born thirty years earlier, I had no doubt that cover bands today would be playing *his* songs.

Evidently I wasn't the only one who felt that way: the dance floor was packed and the place was jumping. For the next forty-five minutes people came and went, but the dance floor stayed full and by the time the set was over I was drenched in sweat and feeling better about my playing than I had in a long time.

Ted came up to me as I was climbing down off the stage. "Hey, Steve, this isn't really my scene. You want to go down the street and get a beer?"

"You read my mind," I said, wiping my face with a handkerchief. "Lead the way."

Ted ran back and grabbed his leather jacket and put it on as we headed out the door together. Once we were outside he pulled out a pack of cigarettes and fired one up as we walked. "So," he said, after taking a long appreciative drag, "you play around town much?"

"Just down at the Owl on Monday nights."

He nodded. "That gets old after a while." It wasn't a question. "Look, I'm going to be putting together a group here pretty soon and I'd like you to play sax for me."

I was stunned. We'd only played one set together and Ted had spent most of that time trying to direct the other members of the group. I didn't think he'd even noticed me. "Wow. That sounds good, but I'm not sure how much time I'd be able to give it. I work during the days."

"No sweat. Look, give me your number and when things get going I'll give you a call. You can come over and rehearse a couple of times before you decide. I'd really like to have you, though. I like your sound."

"Okay."

Ted stopped in a doorway that I hadn't noticed and he opened the door and we pushed our way through a crowd of people over to a dirty table next to the jukebox. We were in a small, nondescript tavern. There were a couple of pool tables, neon signs above the bar and, like the Firehouse, more people than I'd have expected for a Sunday night. The waitress came over a couple of minutes later. They didn't have any imported beers, so Ted and I both ordered Rainier.

By the time she brought us our bottles, Robert Cray's "Smoking Gun" was playing above the din. Ted and I were content to sit and drink for a while, and then he leaned over to me and said, "Have you ever listened to this solo? This is probably one of the best guitar solos ever recorded. You can hear at first, when he comes home and catches his woman with the other guy, how he's confused and sad."

The halting passages Cray was playing certainly suggested that. "Then he gradually starts to get angry," Ted continued, and Cray's playing began to speed up, one burst of notes followed quickly by another. "And by the end he's in a white-hot rage." Finally there were almost no rests, and strings were snapping against the frets with every run of his fingers, and stretched to the point they sounded as if they were crying. I had to agree; it was an incredible solo.

Then the vocals began again and Ted leaned back in his chair. "That man is the best guitar player living."

Suddenly I knew where I'd seen Ted before. I don't spend a lot of time checking out the music scene in Seattle. My tastes run more to jazz and when I do go out it's usually to Dimitriou's Jazz Alley, or the New Orleans Club. But one night, years ago, when I was still in college and Robert Cray was living in Tacoma, I'd caught his show at the Backstage, and now I was pretty sure who the rhythm guitarist was that had been playing with him that night.

"You were with Robert Cray."

Ted smiled. "Yeah, for a while."

"I saw you at the Backstage."

"I'm not surprised."

"You were great."

"Don't remind me."

"What happened?"

Ted was already shaking his head as he leaned forward and stubbed out his cigarette in the ashtray. "I was with Cray from the start. We did a lot of shows and played a lot of road gigs before we had enough money to record. Well, we wound up cutting three albums on an independent label, and in the meantime I'd gotten married and had a kid.

"We were just beginning to get a name, but it was still slow going, you understand, and eventually it got to the point where

I decided I wasn't going to be able to stay on the road and keep things together at home. So I quit."

He lit up another cigarette. "When *Strong Persuader*, the first album on a national label, went gold, I started having major regrets. I think she could sense it." He shook his head and blew out a stream of smoke. "Then the next album went gold, too, and I really got depressed. By the time the last album hit the charts I was suicidal, and that's when she bailed."

"Divorce?"

He nodded. "How about you—married?"

I hesitated and then said, "Yeah."

He smiled knowingly. "I hear that. I'd still like to give you a call, though. I just might luck out and you'll change your mind."

We finished our beers and then ordered another round. Before long Ted looked at his watch and nodded toward the door. I drained my bottle of Rainier and we headed outside, back down the street to the Firehouse.

9

The stage at the Ballard Firehouse stands a full three feet above the audience, with banks of powerful blinding lights hitting the performers from front and behind, their beams roiling with cigarette smoke. Directly abutting the stage is a large dance floor, surrounded by tables on the carpet that swings around in back and down the left side of the room against the roll-up doors to the entrance. In the very back of the room, baffled off with glass partitions, is the bar itself, running nearly the full length of the back wall.

Onstage to my left playing bass was Jerome, and to my immediate right was Bobby Stutz, singing Sam Cooke's "Twistin'." Behind me was the drummer, Chris; next to him on keyboards, Walt; and to my far right was Ted. But in between Ted and Bobby, banging a tambourine on her hip and doing a tremendous job of singing background by herself, was Lydia.

Even though I have to stay pretty close to the microphone while I'm playing, I'm not exactly static. I like to get into the music, especially when I'm playing well. At some point during the second set, Lydia must have seen me gyrating around the mike with my horn.

Being a good sax player means not only knowing when to play, but when not to play. Generally, I lay out completely during the verses, and that leaves me with some free time on the bandstand. The same is generally true for background vocals, and during "Midnight Hour" I suddenly found Lydia singing next to me.

I must have surprised her the next time the chorus came around, because her eyes widened when I leaned into her microphone and began to harmonize with her. That lasted only a second, though. She immediately flashed me a big smile, displaying an attractive gap between her upper centrals, and we spent the rest of the set doing the bump and singing together whenever I wasn't playing my horn. We had our own little show going on next to Bobby, mugging to each other and dancing together.

When the set was over Lydia turned to me and kissed me full on the lips.

"Nice job," she said. "That was really great."

"Thanks," I said, more for the kiss than the compliment. Then she bounded down the steps and was lost in the crowd. When I had finally recovered I set down my sax on its stand and worked my way back to the bar for another cup of coffee.

By now the place was so full there was nowhere to sit, although after a few minutes I noticed that Bobby, Ted and Lydia had managed to find a table. She caught my eye at one point and winked at me, and I found myself fantasizing about what it would be like to be with Lydia.

She looked a few years younger than I was, twenty-seven, twenty-eight maybe, with a head of thick black hair that was a little longer than mine, and dark Mediterranean skin. I suppose if I had let myself, it would have been easy to get the wrong impression from her intimate behavior. But we were just professionals putting on a show for the audience. I had assumed she was with Bobby, and I really hadn't seen any evidence to the contrary, despite our extremely pleasant stage flirtations.

The second time we made eye contact she waved me over, so I squeezed through the crowd one more time, pulled up an empty chair from another table, and sat down between her and

Ted. Bobby was turned around talking with some people at another table.

"Is this guy good, or what?" Lydia said, putting her arm around my shoulders.

Ted was smoking thoughtfully, and nodded as he exhaled twin plumes of smoke from his nostrils.

"So," Lydia said, "you going to give me your number?"

That took me by surprise. "Sure, I guess."

She grabbed her purse from the floor and began rooting in it until she came up with a pen. "Got a piece of paper?"

I looked around, Ted looked around, and Lydia looked around, but nobody had any paper. Finally, not wanting to miss an opportunity—of what type, though, I had absolutely no idea—I pulled out a one-dollar bill and wrote my name and number on the face. But when I handed it to her, Lydia frowned.

"What?" I asked.

She folded it deliberately and put it in her purse. "I suppose this means I can't spend it."

Ted laughed and crushed out his cigarette. I just shrugged. "Hey, a buck's a buck," I said, and her smile returned.

"All right, my man!" It was Bobby. He'd finally turned around and spotted me. "Nice playing," he said, before jumping up and losing himself in the crowd. Ted followed shortly after, and at last I was alone with Lydia.

I took a sip of coffee, stalling for time, and worked up the courage to ask her when I was going to get her number.

"It's in the book," she told me. Grant. Lydia Grant. I host an open mike out at a tavern in Green Lake every Thursday night—the Lion's Lair—and I thought it might be fun if you came out and played sax once in a while. You think you might be up for that?"

Now it was my turn to frown. "Uh, yeah. Sure."

"I'll call you," she said, and lifted her purse, evidently referring to the single with my name and unlisted home number on it. Then she stood up and left, too. I felt embarrassed after getting my hopes up like that, but at least now I had some idea of the situation. It wasn't long before people were eyeing me and I became aware that I was taking up a whole table by myself, so I stood up and walked over to give my mug to the bartender.

Coming back up onstage for the third and final set, I couldn't help feeling a twinge of pleasure in my stomach when I saw that Lydia had moved her mike stand in between Bobby's and mine. We smiled at each other as I hooked my sax on my neck strap, and I found myself wishing that things could have turned out differently. Oh, well. I could think of worse ways to spend a Sunday night.

Lydia and I continued to enjoy each other's company onstage for the next hour and a half. Several of the songs didn't have any real backup parts, and on those she harmonized with Bobby, including the last song of the night, a truly awe-inspiring rendition of "Bring It on Home to Me." By the time the playing was over I was drained, tired, and very sweaty, but also quite pleased with my performance. I hadn't played better in years.

It only took me a couple of minutes to break down my horn and pack it away in its case, but I heeded Ted's advice and settled down at one of the empty tables to wait. The Firehouse gradually emptied out after last call, and the other musicians began breaking down their gear. Shortly after, I noticed that all of the band members were taking turns walking around behind the stage. When Ted finally emerged after his turn he nodded to me and I went back for what I presumed to be my meeting with Bobby.

I walked into the dark hallway and almost didn't see the shadowy figure standing back in the emergency exit alcove.

"Hey, man," came Bobby's raspy greeting. "You did a really nice job tonight."

"Thanks," I said, and he handed me two twenties.

"Sorry I couldn't give you more, but we only made about three hundred bucks."

"That's all right. I had a good time." I pocketed the money and was about to leave when Bobby spoke up again.

"Listen, I'm booked in here next Sunday night, too. You think you'd be able to play again?"

Would I? Not only did playing with Bobby's band beat the hell out of jam sessions at the Owl, but I'd be getting paid to do it. And what with Lydia and all, it wasn't very tough to say yes.

"Sure."

"All right, my man. I'll catch you next Sunday?"

"You got it. Take it easy, Bobby."

When I returned to the table I felt my stomach twinge again as I discovered Lydia sitting on my sax case. "Think you could give me a ride home?" she asked. This was even easier to say yes to, and after I'd agreed she stood up and handed me my horn. "Thanks a lot," she said. "I came here with Bobby tonight, but he's so stoned, I don't even want to be in the same car with him."

Ah, I thought, so that's why she was keeping an eye on him. I opened the door for her and we headed down the block to where I had parked. In spite of the late hour, and the fatigue I was feeling, there was a definite bounce to my step as we walked together to my truck.

10

Lydia's house was almost exactly halfway between Ballard and the Green Lake District. We didn't talk much on the way there, except for Lydia's giving me directions, and eventually she guided me to a small, white house in the middle of a block crowded with cars. When I pulled into her driveway I left the motor running and she turned to me before getting out.

"You hungry?"

"Starving," I said, and I was telling the truth.

"Why don't you come inside and I'll make you an enchilada?"

"Enchilada?" I asked, amused by her specificity.

"What can I say? I may not be a great cook, but I make a mean enchilada."

"Sounds good to me," I said, and promptly turned off the engine.

We both stepped out of the truck and I followed Lydia up the walk to her front door. Though it was difficult to see in the dark, the yard looked ill tended and the house a little shabby. The walkway was cracked and sprouting weeds and the exterior was in dire need of a coat of paint. And if that wasn't enough, the front stoop had been done in Astroturf. Once the door was open Lydia walked past me to turn on a lamp and I found myself standing in a room full of music equipment.

On one side of the front room were stacks of dusty speaker

cabinets, a couple of guitar amps, a twelve-channel mixing board, an electric piano, and three guitars on stands. Facing these were two microphones on stands, two floor monitors, a small drum set, various effects pedals, and cords snaking out all over the carpet.

"Wow, you have enough stuff here to outfit a whole band."

"It's all mine," she said with a smile.

"Do you play all of these?"

"Guitar mostly, but some piano and drums. I'm putting together a demo tape right now."

"I'm impressed."

"I don't play sax, though."

"That's what you have me for."

She smiled again, and this time when our eyes met I saw something genuinely grateful that went way beyond mere stage flirtation. "Come on," she said. "Kitchen's this way."

I followed her back to what had been built as a dining room just off the kitchen, but now served as a de facto living room. There was a couch and a couple of overstuffed chairs wedged in the corner and a coffee table out in front of them. I flopped down on the couch while Lydia opened the refrigerator and began tossing ingredients on the counter.

"You want a beer?" she asked.

"Sure," I said, and she brought one over to me. I hadn't realized it, but I must have smirked when I saw the can of Buckhorn.

"Hey, you'd be surprised what you can get to like when you're dirt poor. You still want it?"

"Of course. I'm sorry. I didn't mean anything by that."

She nodded and handed me the can. "I'm going to go change. Will you be okay out here by yourself for a few minutes?"

"I think so," I said and took a healthy pull of the beer as she disappeared into a small hallway off the living room. A few minutes later I heard the sound of the shower. It was nice and warm inside, so I took off my coat and loosened my tie and then sat back and sort of studied the place.

Looking around Lydia's house, I could only think of one way to describe it: white trash. To put it mildly, the kitchen was a mess. Dirty dishes filled the sink, and empty cereal boxes, wrappers and murky-looking glasses covered the counters. The rest of the place wasn't much better.

The paint on the walls was a splotchy yellow, and there were numerous cracks in the plaster. The carpet was brown and threadbare, split and showing white fibers in places, and the furniture looked to be third- or fourth-hand. But the most distinctive feature of the house had to be the guitar picks, broken strings, lined pages of notebook paper with lyrics scrawled on them, patch cords, cassette tapes and record albums strewn everywhere like musical flotsam.

It was a wreck, sure, but for some reason I loved it, probably because it told me so much about Lydia. I could see her everywhere and it made me feel good. It was the first time in a long while that I'd ever wanted to know that much about anybody.

The shower stopped and Lydia emerged a minute later from the hallway where I figured the bedroom must be, wearing a thin pink cotton bathrobe and brown slippers, her hair still wet from the shower. Her olive skin looked freshly scrubbed and the small lines on her face told me that she was probably closer to my age than I had first imagined. To my mind, her drab attire was far more sensuous than her stage costume, and I took great pleasure in studying her body as intently as I had studied her home. She walked past me into the kitchen and began to assemble the meal.

"So, were you born and raised in Seattle, Steve?"

"No, but sometimes it feels like it. I was born in Maryland.

My folks moved out here before I started high school. How about you?"

"I'm from California originally," she said as she began to grate the cheese. "Santa Cruz."

"How long have you been here?"

"Since I was sixteen."

"Did you move up with your folks?"

"That's a laugh. I suppose you could say I ran away from home, but I don't think anybody really missed me."

I took another sip of beer and tried to change the subject. "So, where'd you learn to cook?"

"Back home, I guess, taking care of my little brother. My mom sure as hell didn't have time to make us dinner."

"Did she work?"

Lydia grunted. "Nah, she was too busy fucking anything with a cock."

Well, there wasn't much I could say to that, and Lydia mercifully changed the subject on her own. "So, how'd you ever wind up playing with Bobby?"

When I told her about the Owl and how much I'd enjoyed playing with Bobby's band, she just nodded.

"Yeah, I don't know why I bother, though," she said. "Working your ass off for twenty bucks a night is bullshit, don't you think?"

I took another swig of Buckhorn and thought of the forty dollars in my pocket. "Yeah," I said. I was a little taken aback. That must have been the reason that Bobby met everyone individually. But why? In all my experience, after the leader took his cut, everyone was usually paid an equal share.

"Jesus, I could have taken my guitar and played out on a street corner in Pioneer Square or at the Seattle Center and made that much." Lydia was busy dipping the tortillas in sauce and rolling up the cheese inside them.

At last I saw an opening. "Were you serious about having me play at the open mike?" I asked her.

She stopped what she was doing and looked at me. She grinned. "That would be great. If I can get some better musicians in there I might actually start making some money for a change."

When she had placed the enchiladas in an aluminum pie tin and sprinkled the extra cheese and sauce over the top, she put the whole thing in the oven and turned the knob above the burners. Then she came over and sat down next to me on the couch. She lifted the beer from my hand, took a sip, and then handed it back.

"You'd better go easy on that stuff—I only have one more left."

This time it was my turn to smile, and before I knew it, I had set down the can and we were kissing. Her tongue felt cold from the beer as I'm sure mine did to her, but we gradually warmed each other up. I had one of my arms around her shoulders and the other across her hip. Both of her arms were wrapped around my waist and we pretty much stayed that way until the timer above the stove went off.

The aroma of the cooking food made my stomach rumble as Lydia stood up and went to the kitchen. She pulled the pie tin from the oven and dished up two plates, then opened the other beer and brought all of it over to the couch. The food was fantastic. It didn't take long to polish off the meal, and for desert we went back into a clinch.

Without interruptions, things progressed a little further. Before long my shirt was unbuttoned and Lydia was running her hands along my bare back. As for me, one of my hands was roaming freely beneath the ever-widening neckline of her bathrobe. It was only after more extensive exploration on my part that she came up for air. She gently pushed me back and took hold of my hands.

"I better not, Steve. I might wind up doing something I shouldn't."

"Isn't that the general idea?"

"That's not what I mean." She stood up and closed her robe, then gathered our plates from off of the coffee table and walked out to the kitchen to add them to the ones in the sink.

"Well, what is it then?"

"Are you serious? I feel like I'm robbing the cradle."

"What are you talking about?"

She gave me a wizened look and said, "You don't *know* how old I am."

"You're about the same age as me, aren't you?"

"How old is that?"

"Thirty-one."

She didn't bat an eye. "I'm forty-two."

"You're kidding."

"Trust me, honey. I feel every year of it."

"That's hard to believe. When I first saw you I thought you were in your twenties."

Her eyes narrowed as though she wasn't sure whether to believe me or not. Then she shook her head and ran some water in the sink. When she was finished she walked back over to sit down and I welcomed her with another long kiss. "Eleven years isn't really that much," I said, "is it?"

She laughed. "I guess not. But all this time I thought you were twenty-five."

I moved to kiss her again and she shook me off. "That's not the only reason, though, Steve. I have to tell you, things are . . . pretty complicated right now."

I didn't like the sound of that and decided to keep quiet until I had more information.

"This is house is mine, sort of. I own it, but I don't own it all my myself. I have a roommate."

My chin sank down to my chest as she told me. This was not what I wanted to hear. "It's not Bobby, is it?"

"God, no," she said. Then she took my hand in hers and held it tight. "I really like you, Steve. If I didn't, you wouldn't be here. But I'm still trying to work some things out right now."

I leaned back to mull this over. If it had just been a boyfriend, I would never have given it a second thought. But she lived with the guy, and to top it off they owned this damn house together. It didn't seem like there was much hope for us, at least until they decided . . . whatever it was they had to decide. "Maybe it would be better if I just left."

Now she took my other hand, too. "No, please, you're not listening to me. I'm trying to tell you—"

At that moment a door opened in another part of the house. Lydia immediately stiffened and looked toward the hall. Jesus Christ, I thought, he'd been in the house this whole time and now he was going to walk in on us. I couldn't believe it. I pulled my hands away from her and awaited the inevitable as Lydia's roommate emerged from the hall.

Needless to say, I was stunned when a tall woman with short blond hair shambled past us into the kitchen as though she hadn't seen a thing. I, on the other hand, saw plenty. She was wearing a blue robe, completely open in front, with nothing beneath, the tie trailing behind her across the carpet. She was light-skinned with small breasts, and was obviously a natural blond. She pulled open the refrigerator, took a swig of orange juice straight from a plastic jug, then headed back across the room, her eyes mere slits, and disappeared down the hall.

Complicated was right. The last I'd heard, there weren't too many "roommates" buying houses together, and the reality of the situation was sinking home fast. A boyfriend was one thing—at least I stood a chance there—but competing with women was a little out of my league.

"I know what you're thinking," she said, "but let me explain."

I had a pretty good idea what was coming but I let her talk anyway.

"I'd been living with guys all my life, ever since I moved up here. Some of them were probably okay, but I was looking for someone with deep pockets, someone to finance my singing career."

"Jesus."

"I know. I sound like a shit—I probably was—but that's what I thought I wanted. Then, three years ago, I met Diane at the Central Tavern down in Pioneer Square. I wasn't even performing. I think we were the only two women in the place, and she just came up to my table and started talking to me."

"Didn't you know she was a lesbian?"

"I wasn't thinking in those terms. I suppose I did, but it was such a relief to be talking with someone who wasn't trying to put the make on me."

"It sounds to me like she was."

"I know. I guess you had to be there. But it was a lot more easygoing than that, not like a lot of guys who are barely coherent because all they can think about is how soon they're going to be able to fuck you. We didn't even do anything that night. I told her about my music and she seemed genuinely interested. We exchanged phone numbers, and after talking with her on the phone every night for a week, I got up the courage to go over to her house."

"And . . ."

"At the time, I really thought it was what I wanted."

"What do you mean?"

"I mean that Diane was different from any man I'd ever been with, and not just in the obvious ways. And I let myself think that the good parts outweighed the bad. I did some things I shouldn't have. I wanted so badly for a relationship to work out right for once that I guess I looked the other way when it didn't. I love Diane. I love her a lot. But I found out one thing for sure after being with her. I'm not a lesbian."

I slowly linked my hands behind my head as I leaned back on the couch. "Wow. Does Diane know about that?"

"Yeah, she knows, and I feel awful about it. She's been seeing a couple of women, but I don't think she's very happy."

"And you two own this house together?"

Lydia nodded.

"Jesus, what are you going to do?"

"I don't have any idea. Neither one of us makes enough money to buy the other out. I can't really sublet. I don't know what I'm going to do."

"So why invite me inside?"

"I don't know. You're fun. You're a good musician." The corners of her mouth turned up slightly. "And I like your hair. I had a good time tonight and I guess I didn't want it to end."

I was trying to figure out what to say next when she finally said, "You probably should get going. I've got work in the morning, and I'm sure you have better things to do with your time."

Now I was the one who took Lydia's hands in mine. "Listen, are you doing anything tomorrow night?"

She hesitated, and then said, "No."

"Could I take you out for dinner?"

She gave me another smile and slowly nodded. "Yeah, that would be nice. I think I'd like that a lot."

We both stood up then and she walked me to the door. After another clinch I didn't want to leave, but Lydia finally managed to push me out. When I reached my truck I turned back and looked at the house for a long minute before jumping inside and heading home. I was glad I didn't have to work the next morning, because the way my heart was racing I didn't think I was going to get much sleep at all.

11

Monday morning, after a surprisingly easy time falling asleep the night before, I was standing in the kitchen making coffee and thinking about something that hadn't even crossed my mind last night: Janet.

Now, I suppose I should have felt bad about what was going on between me and Lydia but, to be honest, I didn't. And besides, there was nothing going on between me and Lydia. Not yet, anyway. So what exactly was I supposed to tell Janet at this point, or was she entitled to know anything at all? Our relationship, even though she was doing everything she could to get me back, felt tenuous at best. If she found out I was seeing somebody else, I was fairly certain that would be the end of it.

The way things had evolved over the past year, I wasn't sure whether I was still hanging on because of the kids or because I loved her. And for the most part I hadn't tried to analyze it too deeply—there never seemed to be any point. But that had been before Lydia came along. Suddenly I had to make a decision, and by the looks of things it wasn't going to be an easy one.

In the end I elected to go with my first instinct and not tell Janet anything. That might change after my date tonight, but at least I could put it out of my mind for another twenty-four hours.

When it had finished brewing, I poured myself a cup of coffee and walked out into the living room. I had a new paperback on the coffee table, *The Rainmaker* by John Grisham, but I knew I was too nervous about my date to read, so I set my mug down and fired up the stereo, putting on Hank Jones' *The Trio*. It was mostly ballads, and I hoped the slow and easy music would relax me.

Then I sat down on the couch and began to look through the small pile of newspapers for Friday's entertainment section. My plan was to take Lydia to Jazz Alley, but I wanted to see who was playing first. I was pleasantly surprised to find that the Ray Brown Trio was going to be there all week. After that, I hung around the apartment until noon watching TV, and then called in to make reservations.

As I showered, I realized there was something else I hadn't thought of. Lydia didn't know I was a dentist. Under normal circumstances, that wouldn't have been a big deal. I'd have dusted off the Porsche, winded and dined her, and things would have made their logical progression from there. But her remark the night before about someone with deep pockets had me wary. She seemed to like me as much as I did her, and that was without knowing what I did. Still, it might be better just to use the truck. Deception rears its ugly head yet again.

After drying off, I ran a brush though my wet hair, tied it back in a ponytail, and headed for the bedroom. I dressed casually, in jeans and a sweatshirt, and was lacing up my tennis shoes when the phone rang. I picked up the receiver and sat down on the edge of the bed.

"Hello?"

"Hey, Steve, I'm glad I caught you."

I recognized Dan Lasky's voice at once. "Hi, Dan. What's up?"

"I had a chance to run that name you gave me through the

system this morning and I found a couple of things that might interest you."

I was all ears. "Yeah?"

"First of all, I pulled up Rick Nations' file and it turns out he did have a drug arrest on record."

"I thought so. What for?"

"Theft, and possession with intent to sell. Eighteen months ago he was fired as a hospital orderly at Maynard Hospital up on Queen Anne for stealing drugs."

"No kidding?"

"Vice found amphetamines, barbiturates and morphine in his apartment after they got a tip from one of the nurses on staff. It seems he'd been humping her for a couple of weeks when suddenly her key to the drug cabinet turned up missing. She was pretty sure it was him but she was too embarrassed to tell anyone about it. Evidently she was hoping she'd just lost it, but it never turned up. It took her a few days before she was able to screw up enough courage to tell the head nurse. Things happened pretty fast after that. She spilled Nations' name right away and the bust went down a few days later."

"Jesus. Was he convicted?"

"Nope. After they'd had a while to think about it, the hospital decided not to press charges. Didn't want the bad publicity. We charged him on the possession anyway, but since it was a first offense he was able to plea-bargain down to criminal misdemeanor. He did spend a couple of weeks in jail because he couldn't make bail, but that was it."

"That's incredible. If he was still doing drugs he could have overdosed right there onstage."

"It's a possibility. But if they did a tox screen at the morgue I'm surprised Janet wouldn't already know about it."

"He didn't go to the morgue. He was DOA at Bay Med— they were closer. So they're just doing a standard postmortem."

"Hmm. That's still going to be a while then."

"It looks that way, unless you guys decide to investigate."

"I don't think so—nothing there. He's been dead over a week. Anything he had in his apartment would have been cleaned out by now, and besides, you can't charge a dead man with possession."

True enough, I thought. "I guess you're right. You mentioned you had something else?"

"Yeah, and this is where it gets interesting. Besides looking up his file, I decided to do a general search on the computer—anything to do with King County—just to see what I could find, and you'll never guess where his name popped up."

"Where?"

"County Clerk's Office. It seems that a week before this guy kicked, he filed for a divorce from one Pamela Nations in Glendale, California."

"You're saying *he* filed the divorce?"

"Yeah. I thought that was funny, too, because I remembered you told me that *she* filed in California."

"Right. Although she did say that it was a few years ago, and if they hadn't finalized it back then, the time limit must have expired. But if he filed this recently it seems pretty strange that she didn't mention it."

"Well, all I know is that if I were you, I'd tell Janet to make sure she checks this gal out before she goes any further."

"I'll do that. Absolutely."

"Okay. I've got to run now, Steve. I'll talk to you later."

"I really appreciate this, Dan. Thanks a lot."

"Hey, no problem. It took me all of ten minutes at the terminal. You take it easy, okay? And say hi to Janet and the kids for me."

"You got it. See you later, Dan."

Once we'd said our goodbyes I hung up and leaned back against the wall and put my feet up on the bed.

I had never liked Pamela Nations in the first place, and

the more I found out about her the more my opinion was confirmed. She hadn't been honest with me, which was fine as far as I was concerned, but evidently she hadn't been honest with Janet, either. And that was something I wasn't going to take lightly. Whether she liked it or not, Janet was going to get an earful tonight.

I stood up and walked out to the kitchen, tying to keep my anger at Pamela Nations in check, and turned off the coffeepot. I grabbed my keys off the counter and then headed out the door and down the stairs to my truck. The sky was overcast, but there were patches of blue and an occasional glimpse of the sun. God, it felt good outside. Spring couldn't come soon enough for me.

12

I drove east to Aurora and headed downtown, killing the afternoon at Pike Place Market. I had lunch in the basement of the Elliott Bay Book Company and then stopped in at a couple of music stores down on First Avenue before heading across I-90 to pick up Cathie and Timmy.

It seemed as though the day was flying by, until I arrived home with the kids—then the minutes began to drag on endlessly. First I helped Cathie finish a math assignment she was having trouble with, and afterward she went outside to play with a couple of her friends. In the meantime, Timmy had decided to take an impromptu nap on the family room carpet, but I still had another hour and a half before Janet was due home.

I spent most of that time pacing, my stomach churning because I still hadn't called Lydia and I didn't want to do it from the house. I was also worried about what I was going to say to Janet about Pamela Nations, and every time a car drove by I tensed up thinking it was Janet, but it never was.

The three of us were watching television at five-thirty when she finally arrived. I was the only one who got up to meet her, but that was good. In the last ninety minutes I had carefully rehearsed everything I was going to say and it would be easier without the kids around.

"Hi," I said. "You have a good day?"

"Not too bad. How was your day off?"

"Boring. Listen, could I talk to you for a few minutes before I get going?"

"Sure. Come on up to the bedroom."

My rehearsals hadn't included any nude scenes, so I had to do a little last-second improvising. "Could we just go into the living room? I'm playing at the Owl tonight and I wanted to get home as soon as possible. It'll only take a second."

Her face took on a serious cast as I spoke, but she relented. "All right."

I followed her past the kitchen and around the corner beyond the stairway to the living room. Janet took a chair across from me on the couch, a large glass coffee table between us. I took a deep breath and waded in.

"Now, first of all, I don't want you to get mad about this. Don't think that I'm stepping on your toes or interfering in your business, because I'm not. Whatever I did, I did because I wanted to help. It's just that she came to me first, and I feel kind of responsible for the whole thing."

"Who came to you?"

"Pamela Nations."

That elicited the infamous raised eyebrow and I knew I was in for trouble, but I stuck to my script. "I talked to Dan Lasky a few days ago, and he just got back with me today. He told me a few things I thought you should know."

Her face hadn't grown any cheerier. She cocked her eyebrow again and said, "Yes?"

"I asked Dan to run Rick Nations' name through the computers, and he found out that this guy was arrested a year and a half ago for possession."

I was ready for the roof to come down on my head, but Janet just looked at me. Then she smiled. That was the last thing I had expected, and it had me a little confused. Was I missing something?

"Okay," she said. "What's your point?"

"The point is that it may not have been the chemical company's fault. Nations could have been totally stoned out of his mind the night he died. If he was really heavily into it, he may have even inadvertently overdosed." I was on a roll, so I stayed with it. "Now, I don't know what the hell else this Pamela Nations told you, but if she lied about this, there's a good chance she might be hiding other things from you. It might be a good idea if you had her checked out.

"I knew she was trouble as soon as I saw her sitting in my office, and I'm sorry for sending her to you. I just wanted you to know what was going on so you wouldn't waste any more time on this case than you already have. For all you know she's lied to you about everything, and from what Dan told me that might very well be the case."

My speech over, I waited for the fury I knew was behind those intense blue eyes. But, to my amazement, Janet began laughing. I had prepared for many things—anger, resentment, annoyance at best—but the one reaction I hadn't counted on was laughter.

"What the hell's so funny?"

"Oh, Steve. I wish all the prosecuting attorneys I had to face argued like you." She shrugged off the navy-blue blazer she was wearing, pulled her blouse free from the matching skirt, and toed off her shoes. Then she unclasped her pearls and set them on the table.

I was still in the dark, so I came out with it. "What are you talking about?"

She leaned forward and gave me a look that I knew she normally reserved for witnesses on the stand and said, "I appreciate the information you got from Dan—I didn't know about that—but what proof do you have that Rick Nations was actually taking drugs?"

"It's obvious," I responded indignantly. "I just told you that he . . ." Suddenly I found myself sitting with my argument in a heap of rubble at my feet. I closed my eyes and nodded, and a few seconds later I was laughing, too.

"I know you want it to be this drug thing with Nations. And you know, it might very well be. But all we can say for certain right now," she continued, "is that he had drugs in his possession. I don't care if he was some drug kingpin from Miami with his sights on virgin territory in the Northwest—that alone doesn't prove he was using.

"Christ, Steve, you of all people should know what the music business is like, what the money's like. If you want to know the truth, it doesn't surprise me a bit that he was dealing to make ends meet. I wouldn't blame him, would you?"

"All right—"

"And as far as Pam goes, the only thing she ever said to me was that Rick never *used* drugs. Without the toxicology report, is there any evidence to refute that?"

I shook my head.

"So, until the report comes back, she's the only witness I have. More than anyone, I think she'd be in a position to know, don't you?"

"I suppose—"

"Unless you saw him shooting up backstage, for now I'm going to have to take her word for it. Any objections?"

"Okay, okay. I'm sorry. I guess I did already have my mind made up about him. Her, too. I didn't really think it through. But that doesn't mean I'm going to be any less suspicious about this whole thing."

"There's no reason you shouldn't be."

"Just do me a favor and be careful, okay?"

She nodded and, though she'd had every opportunity, to her credit she wasn't condescending. "As long as we're on the subject, you want to know what *I* found out today?"

"Sure."

"I had one of my investigators apply for Nations' job. We faked his resume and he got it. Anyway, Nations worked in the shipping end of the plant, you know, loading tanker trucks with chemicals—"

"Wait a minute. Is that even legal?"

"Are you kidding? Who hasn't lied on their resume?"

She had a point there, and I nodded. Then I began to wonder about my own employees, when she continued.

"We found out that Lacroix has been shipping a batch of industrial dyes all month long. During the breaks in orientation, my man learned that the main ingredient in these dyes is aniline."

The name rang a bell, but it had been a long time since I'd taken organic chemistry in college. "Do you know what the symptoms are for poisoning?"

Her enthusiasm was infectious, and I found myself smiling along with her as she told me of her discoveries. "Uh huh. I talked to the doctor we consult on medical cases and he said that the symptoms for aniline poisoning could very easily account for what happened to Rick Nations."

"Sure, but so could a hundred other chemicals."

"That may be, but he was only handling this particular one."

I thought about that for a second and something didn't mesh. "How in the world did he get that job, anyway. I found out he'd been fired from his job as a hospital orderly. This thing at Lacroix sounds like it would be a big union job, something you have to work your way into."

Janet was already nodding. "He was at the bottom of the totem pole. He wasn't doing the actual loading—this is even better—he was cleaning and doing maintenance on the plant delivery system, the machinery, entry-level position. He would have had even more exposure to the dies than the loaders."

"Come on, it doesn't make sense that a big chemical company like that wouldn't be more careful. You even said your guy had to go through an orientation. I really think it has to be an overdose."

"We've already established that we'll have to wait for the toxicology report. You're the one who insists on speculating."

I was the one speculating? Clearly, this was not an argument I was going to win. I shrugged again.

"Until then we're trying to find out what clothing Rick wore while he was working, and see if there was some kind of defect in the equipment, some kind of leak. The doctor said he could have absorbed the poison through his skin or by inhaling and either one would have had the same effect."

"Don't people who work with chemicals like that have to sign a release or something?"

"Yeah, but that's just a formality. There are ways to get around release forms."

I could only shake my head. If there was anybody I'd want on my side of the table during a legal battle, it was Janet.

"So," she said, standing up. "Is the Owl doing a dinner set now?"

I almost asked her what she was talking about when I realized she'd changed the subject. "No, no, it's nothing like that. I need a couple hours to practice before I go over there." I felt lousy about lying and I pushed myself up immediately to hide the guilty look on my face.

Janet came around the coffee table, linking her arm in mine, and began walking me out. "You may not have what it takes to be a lawyer," she said with a smolder in her eyes, "but you have other talents that more than make up for it."

This was the last thing I needed right before my big date, but that jogged my memory about what I hadn't told her yet. I stopped as we reached the stairs.

"Listen, there was something else about Rick that Dan told me."

"What?"

"Did you know he filed for divorce here in King County a week before he died?"

That started the gears spinning in her head. She pulled her arm from mine and was lost in thought for a moment. "Are you sure?"

"He checked the computer. Did she mention anything about it to you?"

"No, but he may not have had time to mail the papers to her, especially if he didn't know her address. If that's the case, there's a good chance Pam didn't know about it. She still might not know about it."

Once again, a ready defense. Of course, there was the fact that Pamela Nations must have cleaned out his apartment and found the papers by now, but I didn't have time to argue. "Okay. I just thought you should know."

"Don't worry so much. I can take care of myself."

"I don't think there's ever been any doubt about that," I said, and then Janet surprised me. She wrapped her arms around my neck and kissed me.

It was the kind of kiss that reminded me why I had married her. It brought back memories of our college days, and sexual discoveries of each other, as well as the virtuoso performances of married sex that we'd shared. Unfortunately, it also reminded me of why I'd left, and I pulled away a little too abruptly.

A flicker of pain and confusion passed across Janet's face but she hid it well and then ushered me down the hall toward the door. "Come on, you have to get out of here so you can *practice*." The emphasis on the last word was not very comforting, but there wasn't much I could do about it. When we reached the family room Janet told the kids to say goodbye to me.

"Goodbye, Daddy!" they yelled in unison, eyes still glued to the TV.

Janet wasn't going to let that suffice. "Get over here,"

she said, with a subtle undertone of menace that miraculously propelled them from the couch into my arms for the obligatory hugs and kisses. Finally, Janet walked me to the door.

"Have good night tonight," she said. "Break a leg."

"Thanks."

She pulled me close again and gave me another kiss. "I love you so much, Steve."

"I love you, too," I barely managed to answer and, feeling like a complete heel, I climbed into my truck and drove back to Seattle to prepare for my date with Lydia.

13

Traffic is usually light westbound over the Interstate-90 floating bridge, even during rush hour. Monday evening was no exception, but it was still six-thirty before I walked in the front door of my apartment. I went straight to the phone in the kitchen, dug out the white pages, and looked up Lydia's number. It was there just as she'd said, and she picked up the phone on the second ring.

But it wasn't Lydia. A throaty voice that must have been Diane's said, "Yeah?"

"Uh, hi. Is Lydia there?"

There was a long pause and I thought for a minute that I'd called at a bad time. But then Lydia was on the line and I realized that Diane had just dropped the phone and delivered the message.

"I was beginning to wonder if you were going to call," she said after my hello.

"Sorry about that. I had a busy day—I just got home. Listen, I made reservations for seven-thirty. Can you be ready in half an hour?"

"That depends."

"Depends? On what?"

"On where you're taking me."

"Well, it was going to be a surprise, but if you twist my arm . . ."

"Come on, tell me."

"We're going to Jazz Alley. Is half an hour enough time to get ready?"

"Hey, I'm ready right now. You still remember how to get here?"

"Absolutely."

"Okay, I'll see you."

When I hung up the phone, I held my hand on the receiver for a moment, as if letting go might break the connection I had to Lydia. My heart was flopping around in my chest like a fish out of water. Lydia had sparked something in me that had been dormant for a long time—she was really getting to me.

I was just about to release the phone when my eyes were drawn to something else: the naked third finger of my left hand. I jerked my arm away and felt myself flush with embarrassment at what and incredible asshole I'd become. All day long I'd been thinking about how this thing was going to effect Janet, and how Lydia's attitudes might effect me. But not once had I thought of Lydia's feelings. Shit. I still hadn't told her that I was married.

Oh, sure, I was separated, but that was just a technicality. Christ, if our relationship was going to progress any further than some heavy necking after a gig, she had better know what was going on, and damn fast. I thought about calling her back right then, but this was something I needed to do in person. I couldn't risk having her hang up on me.

I hopped into the shower again, even though it had only been a few hours since the last one, and was dressed in a flash. I put on a pair of black cotton slacks, a white shirt, and a black jacket and tie. A pair of black leather shoes, Italian jobs I'd picked up at a men's store in Pioneer Square, added the final touch and I was off.

It was about five minutes after seven when I pulled into Lydia's driveway, and she surprised me by running out of the house before I'd even had a chance to turn the motor off. She was wearing a black cotton dress with a dropped waist and a black sweater. Her dark hair was long and loose, and she looked stunning. At that moment I wanted nothing more than to get Lydia in the cab and start driving, leave my old life behind and never look back. Instead, I turned off the ignition as soon as she reached the passenger door. I wanted her to have an out when I told her I was married, and not feel as if she had to suffer through the entire evening—or make me suffer, for that matter—if she was having second thoughts.

"Sorry," she said as she climbed in. "Diane's in a weird mood tonight, and I thought it would be better if I just came outside."

Her smell was intoxicating as it worked its way over to me, and I took a deep breath before I could say anything. She was three feet away, but it seemed as though I was only inches away from her skin. No perfume, just a clean, freshly washed fragrance.

"That's all right, but before we go, there's something I need to talk to you about, okay?"

"Uh oh, is this going to be serious?"

"Yeah, I'm afraid it is. Before things go any further there's something about me you should—"

"Wait, don't tell me," she said, her hands held up in mock fear. "You bought a house with another man and you're living together."

Though I tried hard not to, I laughed. "You're not making this any easier, you know. I'm trying to be serious."

"Me, too," she said, but she was still smiling. "Just don't propose to me, okay? You know I'm still holding out for a guy who rakes in the big bucks."

This time I managed to stay silent, barely suppressing a grin, and she finally acquiesced. "All right," she said. "No more jokes. Just get it over with. I don't like this serious shit."

I nodded and took a deep breath. "Here goes. I'm not living in a house right now, though I do own one. I have an apartment up on 103rd, and I live there by myself."

"But . . ." I could see in her face that she was bracing herself for what was coming next, so I didn't drag it out.

"The thing is . . . I'm separated right now, but I'm not divorced yet."

Instead of being alarmed, she resumed her flippant manner, different this time by its decidedly disappointed edge. "Hey, no problem. I've been out with married men before." She was sitting stiffly now, looking straight ahead out the windshield, and it was pretty obvious what kind of experience that had been.

"This isn't like that, Lydia."

"Oh, really. Then what's it like?"

"Jesus, I didn't come here tonight just so I could get in your pants. This isn't about my having a fling, or an affair, or whatever you want to call it. Look, I don't live with my wife anymore, okay? I'm not cheating on anybody. I'm here because I want to be with you and that's all there is to it."

She turned and looked into my eyes for a couple of seconds, and then began to rattle off a bunch of questions. "How long have you been separated?"

"About a year."

"Any kids?"

That one caught me off guard and I hesitated for a moment. "Two. A girl, eight, and a boy, five."

"Where do they live?"

"Bellevue," I said for convenience' sake, since it's much more familiar as an enclave of yuppie movers and shakers to most people than Medina.

"You're kidding. What does she do?"

"She's a lawyer."

Lydia was about to ask something else when she stopped

herself. I could almost read the change of thought on her face. "Which reminds me," she said. "I don't even know what *you* do. You're not going to tell me you're a professional musician, are you?"

"No," I said, trying to keep my reservations out of my voice. "I'm a dentist."

"No shit?" All at once she was radiant with excitement. "I just had a dentist appointment this morning. If you'd told me last night, you could have had yourself a new patient."

Lydia didn't ask any more questions but she was still looking at me, obviously lost in thought about everything I had told her. Then I glanced at my watch. "Hey, it's getting late. You still want to go?"

She frowned at me. "Why wouldn't I? You think because you didn't tell me your life story last night I'm going to tell you to fuck off now? Jesus, what kind of person do you think I am?"

I sighed. "The kind of person who deserves to make up her mind for herself, and not feel obligated just because she said she'd go out with me last night."

Lydia nodded thoughtfully for a moment, then she scooted down the seat next to me and gave me a kiss. "I like being that kind of person. Let's go."

I backed out of the driveway and then headed south through Ballard, Fremont, and Queen Anne toward downtown. Along the way I finally got around to asking Lydia where she worked. "Unless the Lion's Lair pays more than I think," I said, "you must do something else to pay the mortgage."

"You may not know it, sir, but you are in the presence of the world's most skilled toilet cleaner."

She had me at a disadvantage because I couldn't take my eyes off the road in the heavy downtown traffic. "Are you serious?"

"Oh, yeah. Most people don't realize there's a fine art to cleaning a toilet. It's not just the bowl itself that needs attention—you have to get under the rim, under the seat, and most importantly, *behind* the bowl. Nobody ever cleans behind the bowl anymore."

It wasn't until the next stoplight that I was able to turn and face her. She just shrugged and said, embarrassed, "I work as a maid in a hotel."

"So, what's wrong with that?"

She rolled her eyes. "Cleaning toilets, for starters."

14

I lucked out and found a spot close by the club to park. Lydia and I walked down Lenora, each with an arm around the other, and up to the entrance in the alley between 5th and 6th Avenue. There was a line and we had to wait a few minutes before being seated, but eventually we were led down the stairs to a table in the middle of the room. I ordered a Red Hook, and Lydia had the same.

The room was one I had been in many times, elegant but functional. The bar and the stage were on one end of the room, booths and tables stretching to the other end, and above us, overlooking everything, was a small, two-tiered balcony with even more tables. I had been seated up there one night and hadn't liked it very much. The view was great, but I felt too far away from the musicians. Since then I always requested a table on the floor.

The wall along 6th Avenue began at the stage and ran the length of the building. It was done in glass and landscaped out front with tall hedges to baffle the noise from the street. Our table was close to the stage, which was already set up with microphones, a small drum kit, an acoustic bass, and a black grand piano.

Once we'd been served our beers, Lydia said, "Tell me about Ray Brown."

"Well, he's the bass player—phenomenal, but so is the

rest of the group. I've probably seen him half a dozen times, and I have a few of his albums. God, he's been around forever. I think he's played with just about every great jazz musician there is, or ever was."

"Even Charlie Parker?"

My jaw didn't actually drop open, but it might as well have, as she invoked the name of the person I considered the greatest saxophonist to ever play the instrument. The look on my face said it all, and I didn't bother tying to conceal it. Lydia was cool, though, and calmly took a sip of her beer. "What, you think a dumb guitar-playing hick like me doesn't know anything about jazz?"

"I didn't say a word." But the expression on my face certainly had. "Yeah, they played together. He recorded with Bird, too, on the *Parker With Strings* album—he and Buddy Rich and, if you can believe this, Mitch Miller."

"You mean the sing-along guy with the goatee?"

"The very same. He played the oboe."

I was able to relax once I saw how much Lydia was enjoying herself, the gap between her teeth prominent every time she smiled. We had been drinking and talking about music for several minutes when she said, "You like jazz a lot, don't you?"

I nodded. "Sure. Next to you, it's my greatest passion."

"I'm glad to see you have your priorities straight. But if you don't mind my asking, what the hell are you doing playing with Bobby? I'd have thought you'd rather be playing in ritzy joints like this."

I laughed grimly and took a long pull of beer. "It's not that easy to explain. Have you ever seen *Amadeus*?"

"The movie? Sure."

"Well, sometimes I feel like I'm the Salieri of the saxophone, you know? I mean, I love jazz so much, and I'm so moved by it that sometimes I feel as if it was created just for me.

But as far as being able to play it . . . I can't seem to navigate anything more complex than a three-chord blues."

"Oh, come on. You were great last night. What was that?"

"*That* is called making the most of what you have. I play by ear. I have pretty good phrasing and I use my mouth well."

"I'll say."

I gave her my best lecherous grin and said, "You haven't seen anything yet."

That cracked us both up, and we were beginning to get stares from the tables nearby, but I ignored them. I was having a great time and didn't care who knew it. "Seriously, though, rhythm-and-blues, soul—whatever you want to call it—the music is fun but it's pretty basic and, to be honest, it's not really that creative."

"Damn. Maybe I don't want you to sit in with me after all."

"Don't get me wrong," I said. "I love playing the sax, even if it's only a blues. It's just that the blues is . . . Well, it's just not jazz."

"So do something about it. Can't you study or something?"

"Oh, sure. I could have gone to Juilliard or Cornish. Hell, I could even practice once in a while at home, work on scales and stuff, but I don't. Between work and trying to see my kids, I just don't have the time. And I don't really want to make the time now. So I come down here every couple of weeks—"

"And play at the Owl."

"That, too. But I chose dentistry, and I don't have any regrets."

She made a connection I hadn't thought of and asked me, "So, are you a good dentist?"

I held up my hands like a surgeon freshly scrubbed up for surgery and said, "Madam, they don't call me the Michelangelo of amalgam for nothing." Instead of applause, I received a napkin in the face.

The waitress came around to take our order a few minutes

later. Dinner and Ray Brown arrived at about the same time and I tried not to let my food get cold while I concentrated on the music. The first set was fantastic.

The trio, consisting of Ray on bass, Jeff Hamilton on drums, and Gene Harris on piano, was what I considered to be about the best group of musicians in jazz on their respective instruments. Ray was stunning on his feature, "Put Your Little Foot Right Out," Jeff Hamilton impressively displayed his skills on Dizzy Gillespie's "Night In Tunisia," and Gene Harris was given a standing ovation for his rendition of "Summertime."

Though she seemed to be enjoying it as much as I was, I didn't want Lydia to feel as if I was forcing her to stay for more, so when the set was over I asked her if she was ready to leave. She surprised and delighted me again by practically begging me to stay for the second set. I sipped on coffee through this one and Lydia ordered another Red Hook.

Once again the music was excellent. Lydia had some knowledge of jazz, but confessed that she had never paid too much attention to it before. After what she had heard tonight, however, I was certain that was about to change. It was after eleven by the time I finally paid the check and we left the club. I was beat, but too wired from all the coffee and too high from the music to be sleepy.

I looked across the roof of the truck as I was unlocking my door and simply said, "Home?"

She frowned and shook her head. "Diane'll be there. How about your place?"

All of a sudden the coffee and jazz paled in comparison with what had me wired now. "Works for me."

Once I had parked in the garage beneath my apartment, we ran up the stairs like a couple of teenagers going to a hotel room on prom night. The grand tour consisted of going past the kitchen, straight down the hall, and into my bedroom. Well-rehearsed from the night before, we were both eager to pick things back up again. We stripped off each other's clothes in the dark as we lay on the bed, tossed them to parts unknown, and then dove beneath the sheets.

Things slowed down once we were under the covers. But we'd only been there a short while—exploring each other's bodies and generally seeing how much surface area of one person's skin it was possible to contact simultaneously with another's—when it happened.

Now, I'd been with Janet approximately twelve years, and in all that time it had never happened to me. The only other women I'd had sex with were during high school and college, before my marriage, and it had certainly never happened then. So why, I thought dismally, of all nights, was it happening tonight? The *it* I'm referring to, of course, is that I went limp.

Although my mind was a raging, hormone-drenched sex machine, for some reason—which I was at a loss to explain—my loins were acting as if they'd just been doused with a fire hose. I was hoping Lydia hadn't noticed, and I was trying desperately to get back to my old self, when I realized we were careening recklessly toward the point of entry. Unfortunately, my systems were still on standby.

"Are you okay?" Lydia asked.

I winced in the dark. "I thought I was, but evidently I'm not."

"What? Because of this?" For emphasis she gently grabbed the source of contention.

"Since you put it that way, yes. I don't know what's wrong."

"I don't really see that anything's wrong."

I rolled off her and back onto my pillow, wondering in a vague way what the hell I was going to do if this thing was permanent.

Lydia shook her head. "Are you telling me this has never happened to you before?"

"Not that I can remember."

"Well, I wouldn't worry about it too much if I were you. It's pretty much standard operating procedure."

"What are you talking about? I've read the *Penthouse Forum*, and I don't recall any hot stories where the guy was impotent."

"Take it easy. All I meant was that it's happened to guys I've been with."

"You can't be serious."

"On a first date, sure. You're just nervous, is all. I am, too—it just doesn't effect me the same way. Let me tell you, when you have a war going on inside you between nerves and libido, nerves takes it every time."

"So how come I've never read about this 'standard operating procedure?'"

"The only thing I can figure is that the one-night stand has a great PR man. In my experience, it's usually pretty dismal."

"That's encouraging," I said sarcastically.

"Ah, but there *are* alternatives."

With that Lydia began kissing me again, on the lips at first, but then on my chin and neck, slowly working her way down my chest and eventually winding up at the aforementioned problem area. Miraculously, I was cured. The laying on of hands, or in this case lips, had me performing up to my usual standards in no time.

A few hours later, when we had both reached the pleasure saturation point, I looked at the clock and groaned.

"What?"

"It's quarter to four, that's what. I have to be up in two hours."

"Poor baby," she said, and nibbled on my ear.

"What about you?"

"The hotel, remember? Check out time is at eleven. I don't have to be there until ten-thirty."

I groaned again. "I've got to get some sleep. Can you stay the night?"

"Should I be insulted by that question?"

"Only if you're going to say no. Look, Lydia, I just don't want to take anything for granted. But don't get used to this— once my nerves wear off I'm likely to be very demanding."

"Promise?"

"You can bank on it."

Lydia gave me a kiss and threw back the covers, making her way to the adjoining bathroom in the dark. When the light came on under the door, I sat up and turned on the lamp next to the bed and tried to avert my eyes from the clock. She came out a few minutes later in all her naked splendor and hopped back into bed like she owned the place.

We were in the midst of a little post-coital necking with the light on when Lydia yawned and I noticed the new filling she'd had put in.

"Who does your dental work?" I said. Even with that brief glimpse into her mouth I could tell it was a terrible job.

"Do you use that line on all your women, Doctor?"

"Only the ones I really want to impress. Seriously. I'd like to know."

"Okay. It's this clinic downtown on First Ave. I don't know how good they are, but they're cheap, and with my financial status, and no insurance, that's about the only qualification they need to get my business."

"All right, but if you ever need any more work done, you come to my office when you have a free—"

"Steve! What's that?"

My heart skipped a beat when she shouted and suddenly we were both sitting bolt-upright in the bed. I didn't have a clue what was wrong, but I flopped back down with relief as soon as I saw that Lydia was pointing to my chest, and the rather prominent pink scar over my right ribs.

"Just an old football injury," I said with a laugh. "I meant what I said before, though—when you have a free morning, I'd like you to come in and have me check you out, okay?"

She was frowning intently and rubbing her hand over the raised scar tissue, but it didn't affect her repartee in the slightest. "Oh, I believe you've checked me out sufficiently, don't you?"

"On the contrary, I don't think I've checked you out nearly enough."

Though we did eventually roll over and try to keep our hands to ourselves, I don't remember actually falling asleep the entire night.

15

I didn't get to work until ten after seven the next morning. I noticed Mrs. Keyes in the waiting room as I came in, and nodded to her on my way into the office. Nona wasn't one to glare at watches or feel the need to state the obvious, and at that moment I was truly thankful for it.

"Get on the phone and try to reschedule as much as you can today. I don't know how long I'm going to be able to stay awake."

Nona had picked up the receiver before I'd finished talking. When I turned down the hall I met Laurie head-on. "Are you ready for Mrs. Keyes?" I asked, and she nodded.

"Good. Bring her in and stay with her. I'll be there in a couple of minutes."

I went into my office and collapsed in my chair. Then I rubbed my eyes and almost laughed out loud. I don't know if she'd heard my truck as I pulled into the lot or whether she had been watching me on closed-circuit TV, but there was a mug of steaming coffee on my desk, compliments of Nona.

Now, you have to understand something. If I had thought in any way that I was not up to working that morning, I wouldn't have. Sure, my eyes felt like they had sand in them and my body was craving sleep, but my mind was sharp and I couldn't recall ever having had trouble with my hand-eye coordination, no matter how tired I was. But if I found out after going in that I wasn't up to the task, believe me, I was going to stop.

That said, there were also business considerations to contend with. The seven-to-eight hour is the bread and butter of my practice, and I'm understandably reluctant to do anything to jeopardize it. I'm sure that other dentists' appointment books are solid for the next six months and their four-week vacations in the Bahamas are already blocked out for November. I don't have that kind of luxury. Except during that one hour.

Seven o'clock, the one bright spot on my calendar, was booked through the month of March, and Joanne Keyes was a good case in point why. She headed a large advertising agency downtown and, after putting in her sixty hours a week, still managed to come home and take care of her husband and kids. One of the things she didn't have time to fit into her busy schedule was dental work. But she found that if she got up early a few times a year, I could take care of her and she never missed a beat. I was happy I could do it. What I couldn't do, though, was reschedule her. A root canal was not going to wait until April.

On the upside, my practice was steadily growing, even with the terrible location. I was slowly acquiring new patients, and the ones I had, though small in number, were very loyal. I felt the same way toward them. If I had a seven o'clock scheduled I was going to make damn sure I was there for the appointment, especially if I wanted to pay my bills at the end of the month. So I drank down my cup of coffee, donned my white coat, and did my job.

At least that had been the plan. To put it mildly, Joanne Keyes' root canal was a nightmare. The fact that I felt like one of the living dead only made matters worse, and rationalizing that it wasn't really my fault wasn't going to make it any better. I wound up breaking not one, but two reamers as I was shaping the canal—number twenty-fives, of course, which I swear to

God are made defective to exact specifications right at the factory. When a reamer breaks on me, it's always a number twenty-five.

I lucked out the first time because I was barely able to get a couple of Hedstrom files down in there and tweeze out the broken piece. But with the second one it was nothing doing. I tried for as long as I could, but I knew Mrs. Keyes had to be out of there by eight. Fortunately, I was able to instrument past the broken piece, fill around it with gutta percha, and send her on her way.

Now, there was nothing wrong with that, *really*. In this particular instance the procedure was technically just as successful as if I'd managed to recover the second broken piece. But I never like to leave the operatory feeling that I could have done a better job. I washed my hands again and splashed some water on my face before going out to see how Nona had done with that morning's patients.

"Well?"

"All done. You're free for the rest of the day."

"No kidding? That's terrific."

"But you're going to have to work afternoons all week."

"Not a problem."

From the look on her face I could see that Nona had some advice that she wished to impart to me. And since she'd saved my ass today I figured, what the hell. "Yes?"

"You might want to think about cutting your Monday nights at the Owl down to once or twice a month."

"I wasn't at the Owl," I said, and as soon as the words left my mouth I wanted to go back into the operatory and surgically remove my tongue. But I didn't. Instead, I stood and faced the music. "I had a date," I explained, and shrugged. "I didn't get much sleep."

"Do you want me to call Janet so she can make arrangements to pick up Cathie and Tim?"

Well, that certainly put things in perspective. "Please."

Nona smiled and picked up the phone. In a way I was glad she knew—it felt good to have told somebody. And the more I thought about it, I couldn't have slipped to a better person. One thing I never had to worry about when it came to Nona was confidentiality. Unless I told her differently, she would take what I had said to the grave.

She asked for Janet and then put her hand over the mouthpiece. "Would you have time to sign some insurance forms before you leave?"

I nodded and took them with me back to my office. I refilled my coffee cup and stayed about half an hour doing some paperwork before my eyes refused to stay open any longer.

As I drove home I wondered if Lydia would still be there. She had been asleep when I'd left for work. I'd written a note and set it on the kitchen counter for her, and since I hadn't seen her bring a purse the night before, I'd been tempted to leave her some money for cab fare. But the implications of such a gesture, should it be misconstrued, were potentially disastrous. I'd played it safe and decided that Lydia was a big girl and could take care of herself.

I walked in the door at nine-thirty, an hour before Lydia had to be at work, and I could hear the shower running. The note was still on the counter and I crumpled it up and threw it away. In the bedroom the curtains were drawn but the bathroom door was open, spilling out more than enough light to see by.

I took off my clothes slowly, expecting the shower to turn off any second. It didn't. Standing by the bed for a moment, naked and desperately needing sleep, I looked at the rumpled covers on the bed, then back to the bathroom. The water was still on. Finally, I yawned fiercely, shook the cobwebs out of my head, and ran for the shower.

*   *   *

I crawled out of bed six hours later, feeling like a human being again, and put in a call to Lydia. I was going to invite her back to my place and make dinner for both of us when she gave me the bad news.

"I'm sick."

"How'd you get sick?"

"I don't know. I must have picked it up from Diane." Then Lydia snickered. "She was just getting over it Sunday night when she came out into the front room, remember?"

"Oh, I don't think I'll ever forget that."

"I went home from work early, about three. I took some pain pills and I feel a little better now, but I don't think I'm up to going anywhere."

"Any chance of my coming over there?"

"Well . . . I hate to put it like this, but it probably wouldn't be a good idea."

"Diane?"

"Yeah. But I don't want to give this to you, either. It would be a lot worse for you to miss work than me."

"I suppose."

I think both of us were disappointed, and there was a lull in the conversation. Though I'd been living on my own for a year, the thought of being alone tonight, without Lydia, was dismal. I felt alive again, more than I had since moving out on Janet and the kids. It was way too early to call it love, but it sure looked like it was headed in that direction.

"Call me tomorrow night?" she said.

"What time?"

"Five's good."

"Okay, I'll talk to you then."

"'Bye."

"'Bye."

With the phone hung up I now had an entire evening on

103

my hands with absolutely nothing to do. On a lark I decided to get dressed and go bowling. Leilani Lanes was right across the street from my apartment building, and I walked over and bowled a couple of lines. Afterward, I had a sandwich and a beer in the restaurant and headed home shortly after seven.

With a Diet Coke in hand, I put on an old Dave Brubeck album, *Brubeck Time*, and let Paul Desmond create the perfect unobtrusive atmosphere for reading. My newest paperback was still on the coffee table, and I picked it up and launched into it for the next couple of hours. About ten o'clock my eyes started drooping, so I shut off the stereo and the lights, brushed my teeth, and went to bed.

The rest of the week, as it turned out, was equally anticlimactic. Lydia was sure she had the flu. She said she was exhausted, her back ached, she was throwing up and generally felt like shit. I called her every night after getting home from Medina, and we talked until she was tired out. She still didn't want me to come over, so I stayed home, and with all that time on my hands I was able to do a lot of thinking.

I kept trying to figure out when would be the best time to tell Janet about Lydia, only somehow the best time never came up. My biggest problem was that, no matter how I tried to figure it, I simply had no idea what Janet's reaction would be. There was a chance that it could be drastic—divorce papers on my desk the next day—but as bad as that was there was always the chance that it would be worse. And I'd seen just how bad that could be, close up. The last thing I needed right now was to unwittingly create more turmoil in my life, and I didn't even want to think about how it would effect Cathie and Timmy. So, with my inimitable flair for openness and honesty with my wife, I said nothing.

Saturday after work, when Lydia still wasn't feeling any better, I began to get worried.

"Don't you think you should see a doctor?"

"The only doctor I need to see right now is you."

"I'm serious, Lydia. You could have mono or a viral infection and not even know it."

"I don't have insurance, Steve. I can't afford to see a doctor every time I get sick."

"Can you afford to be missing this much work?"

She sighed. "I don't know what the answer to that is, but if I see a doctor I'm going to owe even more money. And last time I checked, they don't extend credit."

"Look, why don't I just—"

"No. Don't even say it. I'm not your responsibility."

"Fine. Then pay me back. I'm a doctor, and I'm offering to extend credit."

"Come on, Steve. I've had the flu before—everyone has. I've got the same thing that Diane had and she's fine now. I just need to let it run its course. I'll probably be back to work on Monday."

"What about the Firehouse tomorrow night?"

"No way. I already called Bobby."

"I don't understand this. Diane must work. Isn't there any time I can come over and see you?"

"Why don't you call me in the morning? If I feel up to it I can make you breakfast, okay?"

"That's more like it."

"But leave your wallet at home."

"What? And spoil all the fun?"

"I mean it, Steve."

"Okay, I promise."

Work had been fine all week and I was in top form. Getting plenty of sleep every night had helped. But lonely nights were one thing. I wasn't looking forward to spending an entire Sunday without Lydia, and I made up my mind that I was going to see her tomorrow whether she was up to it or not.

16

When the phone rang at nine o'clock Sunday morning the last person I expected it to be was Janet.

"I need you to come over here and stay with the kids for a couple of hours."

I was still in bed, groggy with sleep, and it took me a few seconds to grasp what she was telling me. "You want what?"

"I need you to baby-sit, okay? I have to be in Seattle in half an hour."

"What the hell for?"

"A woman called me—her husband's in jail—look, can you just come over?"

"I kind of had plans."

"Well, break them. I need you. Are you going to help me or not?"

The pitch of her voice had risen about an octave during our brief conversation and I knew I'd better get my ass over there if I wanted to avert a full-scale war. "Okay, okay. Just let me get dressed and I'll be there as soon as I can."

Instead of goodbye I heard a click as Janet hung up. I crawled out of bed and into the bathroom to relieve myself, then I dressed and headed out to my truck, plucking the Sunday *Times-P.I.* from off the doormat and taking it with me.

I couldn't believe it. It seemed like everything was conspiring against me and Lydia being together. First there had been Diane, then Lydia's catching the flu, and now there was my own spineless dealing with Janet. It looked as if Lydia and I would have to settle for another phone call today.

I'd seen my share of Janet's weekend emergencies in my time and it wasn't often that she was back before five. Most likely I'd get a call around noon saying she was at the office going through casebooks and would try to make it home in a couple of hours. Right.

So I consoled myself with the thought that Lydia had to be about over this thing, and that any day now we would be reliving last Monday night. Besides, I had tomorrow off, too. We could always get together for breakfast then. I patted the huge bundle of newsprint on the seat next to me and immediately began making alternate plans. I'd save the paper for tomorrow, pick up Lydia in the morning and take her back to my place, make breakfast for *her*, and then we would read and eat together in bed.

Janet was coming out the door as I pulled into the driveway, and getting into her Mercedes before I'd even had a chance to come to a complete stop. She rolled down the passenger window as she was pulling out and I went over and ducked my head inside.

"They've already had breakfast—make sure Timmy doesn't eat any junk food before noon, and for God's sake make them some lunch, okay? I'll see you in a couple of hours." Her greeting over, she gave me an air kiss and was off.

As soon as I walked in the door the kids were all over their old dad, but it wasn't because they were happy to see me.

"Daaaaaad! Tell Cathie to give me back my horse."

"I don't have it," said Cathie, proudly displaying her hands for me like a magician with nothing up her sleeve.

The floor of the family room was strewn with Lincoln Logs, Tinker Toys, Leggos, and a myriad of toy animals and people. Some incredibly loud cartoon show was blaring on the

TV and the phone chose that exact moment to ring. Suddenly I felt as if I had been transported into a surreal gender-inverted Calgon commercial from the seventies where all I would have to do was yell, *Take me away!* and everything would vanish as I relaxed in a bathtub, neck-high in bubbles.

But that wasn't going to happen, and I was forced to take matters into my own hands. "Cathie, go in there and find Timmy's horse."

"But I said I didn't—"

"Now! And turn down the TV."

When I finally picked up the phone, it turned out to be some guy who wanted to know if Janet was in. On Sunday? I asked him if he wanted to leave a message, but he didn't. I felt a weird tightening in my chest as I hung up, but I didn't have time to ruminate on it. Instead of breaking up a fight, I had inadvertently thrown the two combatants together into the ring, and each of my children was trying to see who could yell louder than the TV.

I stormed out into the family room and shut the damn thing off myself. "Hey!" I yelled at the top of my lungs, and instantly you could have heard a pin drop. I took a second to savor the moment before looking down at the kids, wide-eyed and startled into silence. Then I surprised them. "You guys want to go for a ride to Seattle?"

"Yeah!" they shouted in unison.

"Okay, go put some shoes and socks on, and get your coats."

They were already barreling out of the room as I spoke, all thoughts of stolen horses forgotten. But I couldn't seem to forget that phone call, so I walked back out to the kitchen and put in a call of my own. There was no answer at Lydia's place, even after a dozen rings, and the only explanation I could think of was that she'd unplugged the phone so she could get some sleep. I hung up and tried again, but with the same results.

Though I knew it had nothing to do with her, I suddenly found myself blaming Janet for everything that had happened during the past week. I picked up a piece of chalk and scribbled a cryptic message on the tiny blackboard by the phone, just in case she came back before we did, though I was tempted not even to do that. It might do her some good to sit around and wait on us for a change.

Once I had the kids bundled up we went out to the truck and headed for Seattle. I've never liked zoos—walking around looking at imprisoned animals isn't my idea of a good time—so I took the three of us out to the Seattle Center. Built in 1962 for the World's Fair, the Center has rides, games, and science exhibits designed exclusively for children. And for a few bucks I could always take them up to the top of the Space Needle. The sky was overcast, but it wasn't cold out, and it didn't look as if it would rain.

Four hours and a small fortune later, I had two very full and very weary children on my hands. It seemed as if we'd sampled nearly every franchise in the Food Circus, ridden on every ride, and walked the equivalent of a marathon. Since we were over in Seattle anyway, I gave Lydia a call and waited twenty rings before giving up this time. I thought about just driving over there, but even I was too tired by then, so we just went home.

When I turned into the driveway Janet's car was still gone, and inside there was no message on the answering machine. I wiped off the blackboard with the sleeve of my shirt, made one more unsuccessful attempt to reach Lydia, and then all three of us settled down for a nap, the kids in their rooms, and me on the couch.

I dozed on and off, but it was almost six o'clock when I woke up enough to realize what time it was. And that was only because it was dark in the house. I managed to push myself off the couch and turn on a few lights, and when I trudged upstairs

I found that the kids were already awake. Janet still hadn't called and it was beginning to annoy me—that and the fact that I still hadn't been able to reach Lydia all day.

I called Lydia again from the bedroom, expecting no answer, and getting exactly that. I didn't have my book, I didn't want to watch TV, and the more I waited around the angrier I became. I fed the kids dinner about six-thirty, but it wasn't until an hour later that Janet finally called.

"I just wanted to let you know that I'm on my way home. Did you eat yet?"

"Where the hell have you been?"

"I've been working. What do you think—"

"Look, I have to be in Ballard tonight by nine, and I have to go home first—"

"Don't get pissed off at me, Steve."

I stopped for a moment to keep from saying something I might regret. "Just tell me when you're going to be here."

"I told you, I'm leaving right now. I should be home before eight."

"Well, could you *please* hurry? It's important."

"All right. Goodbye."

She hung up on me for the second time that day, which was fine by me. If Janet did, in fact, get home by eight, I would have barely enough time to make it to my apartment and then out to the Firehouse. I couldn't even call Bobby if I was going to be late, because I didn't have his number with me. I paced the floor for the next half-hour and, just when I was sure she wouldn't show up in time, Janet's car pulled into the garage.

"I'm late," I said, brushing past her at the door. "I'll talk to you tomorrow night."

"Thanks," she yelled as I was getting into my truck, but I didn't answer. I wasn't paying attention to what I was doing, and in my haste to get out of there I accidentally squealed the tires as I backed out. My head was shaking as I drove toward the freeway. I was not looking forward to tomorrow night's confrontation with Janet.

I made it to the Firehouse a few minutes after nine. We wouldn't start playing until nine-thirty, so I'd really had plenty of time. As I climbed up onto the stage Ted nodded hello, and I was amused to see that, aside from him and Bobby, everyone else in the band was different from the week before.

The new drummer was a big guy with a full beard named Bill; the bassist was named Tracy and also had a beard, the same color as his long reddish hair; and Howard, the keyboardist, had half of his blond hair shaved off and wore mirrored sunglasses. But the biggest surprise was the new female vocalist. She looked no more than sixteen and couldn't have stood more than five feet tall, in heels. She had very short, light-brown hair and wore a strapless yellow evening dress. Her name was Cini.

I don't know whether it was the stress of the week before, or rushing to get to the club on time, or just plain worry over Lydia, but I had one of the worst nights playing that I'd had in years. I was awful. As the night wore on I began checking my watch more and more frequently. Between sets I tried to stay away from everyone else. I would walk around outside, cooling off and trying to analyze what was going wrong. But nothing I tried seemed to work.

Finally, mercifully, the last set ended and I packed up as quickly as I could and left. I didn't stick around to collect whatever money Bobby deemed fit to pay me—it couldn't have been much—and I didn't care. There was only one thing I had on my mind and it wasn't likely I was going to get any sleep tonight until it was resolved. That's why I drove straight over to Lydia's.

All the lights were off when I reached her house. There was the definite possibility that Diane would be mad as hell at me for waking her up, especially since tomorrow was Monday, but I didn't care about her, either. I walked to the door with confidence and pounded three times. I waited, expecting a light to come on any second, but nothing happened. I pounded a few more times and began to get the sinking feeling that no one was home.

I walked around the front trying to look in through closed drapes, even going so far as to tap on the windows. When I had gone completely around the house I pounded on the door one more time and then sat on the green steps to think. Diane had been there on Saturday night, the last time I had spoken to Lydia, and unless they had unplugged the phone, neither of them had been home all day Sunday.

After waiting on the steps for twenty minutes, I stood up and walked over to the truck. I fished in my glove box for a pen, then wrote a note on the back of a gas credit card receipt telling Lydia to call me immediately, no matter what time it was, and left it wedged in the door. With that done, there was nothing left to do but go home and wait. My stomach felt twisted in knots with worry as I drove away, and I knew the only thing that would stop it would be hearing Lydia's voice, telling me that everything was okay.

Back home I stripped off my clothes and put on some sweats. Then I turned on the TV, muted the sound, and sat on the couch waiting for the phone to ring. I must have nodded off around four, and didn't wake up until dawn.

With the soft gray of a new morning seeping in the sliding door I sat up a little too quickly, winced, and then tried to rub out the stiffness in the back of my neck. When I could turn my head more than a few inches without sending bolts of pain down through my shoulders, I eased up gradually off the couch and ventured into the kitchen to make coffee. For about half a second I considered not calling—then I picked up the phone and dialed.

I was about to hang up after the twelfth ring when someone answered.

"Hello?" It was Diane, in a barely audible whisper.

"Hi, is Lydia there?"

There was about a five-second pause on the other end before she said, "Who is this?"

"My name's Steve Raymond. I'm a friend of Lydia's. I couldn't get hold of her yesterday and I was getting kind of worried."

Another pause. "I got your note."

"Oh, yeah. I stopped by last night, but you weren't home."

Again there was a long pause before I said, "Is she there?"

Her no was choked off and followed by more silence. My pulse quickened as I waited for more information, but none was forthcoming. "Look, is there any way you can tell me where she is, some way I can get in touch with her—"

"No! I can't!" She sobbed twice and then blurted it out. "Lydia's dead."

17

I felt as if the wind had been knocked out of me. Diane was still crying on the other end of the line, but I couldn't make myself say anything. If this was her twisted idea of a joke, I almost wouldn't have cared, as long as it meant that Lydia wasn't dead. But as I stood in the kitchen, bracing myself against the counter, I knew it wasn't a joke.

"I can't do this," Diane managed through her tears, and I panicked.

"Wait, Diane! Don't hang up."

"Didn't you hear what I said?" She was screaming now. "I can't talk about this on the phone!"

"Then let me come over there. Please."

Her crying had stopped but I could still hear her heavy, labored breathing. She didn't say anything more so I lowered my voice and continued. "Diane, this is very important. I have to talk to you. I need to talk to you. Please, let me come over."

The only sound on the other end was Diane's breathing. She still hadn't said a word.

"Diane?"

"Okay," she said. "Come over." Then the line went dead.

Like a zombie I walked into my bedroom and dressed, my hair still smelling of cigarette smoke from the night before. Halfway through I sat down on the bed. I couldn't cry. I almost couldn't move. I was numb from the shock. The question *why* kept pounding away in my brain, but the only way I was going to answer it was to see Diane, so I forced myself to get back up and finish dressing.

The coffeepot was full, and I turned it off on my way out. I was plenty sober. In the garage the key to my truck didn't seem to fit in the lock, and yet somehow the door opened. I sat for a minute, gazing blankly at the cement wall in front of me, and then I started the engine. My hands felt clumsy on the steering wheel, as though I was wearing boxing gloves, but I was still able to drive.

A steady drizzle fell from the sky and the roads were slick with rain. My wipers kept time like a twin set of metronomes in front of me. I couldn't listen to music. At that moment I never wanted to hear music again. The truck made its way to Lydia's house almost by itself. I don't remember consciously driving there, but before long I was pulling into the driveway. Diane was standing on the covered front stoop.

I stepped out of the truck and shut the door, standing like a statue in the rain. Diane just stared at me. Her eyes were rimmed with red, the lids puffy, her mouth drawn and her cheeks pinched. She was wearing jeans and an oversized ivory cable-knit sweater. Her feet were bare. Her arms were folded across her chest, and in one had she held a cigarette, occasionally bringing it up to meet her lips and drawing in a breath.

We stood there, eyeing each other for what seemed like hours, and finally she said, "Why don't you come up here, out of the rain?"

My feet moved me forward up the steps and I stood beside her. The stoop was covered just enough to keep the rain off, and the front door was wide open. I ran my hands over my head and squeezed the water out of my hair. "You want to go inside?" I asked.

Diane shook her head. "I can't. Not with all her shit still

there." I looked inside again, this time noticing Lydia's music equipment. Had it really been a week since I'd seen her last?

"You're lucky you caught me," said Diane, and she took another lifeless drag off her cigarette. "I just stopped by to get a few things together—I'm staying with a friend. I'm selling the house, too," she said, as though she'd just thought of it on the spot.

We stood there a while longer, not saying anything, watching the rain falling on the grass. I hadn't noticed before, but it needed cutting. "What happened?" I said.

Diane took a last drag and flicked the butt onto the lawn. Then she sat down against the door frame and looked up at me. Fresh tears rolled down her cheeks, but she didn't brush them away. "I went into her bedroom yesterday morning to see how she was doing . . . and she was dead."

"What time was that?"

"I don't know. Seven-thirty, eight?"

"Could you tell how long . . ."

"She was cold, that's all I know. She was fucking cold." Diane tipped her head back, and looked like she was going to break down. Then it passed with a sigh and she began speaking again. "I totally lost it. I ran around the house screaming, and by the time I got on the phone and called 911, I was so hoarse I could hardly talk.

"The ambulance came about fifteen minutes later, along with these two cops who were pretty fuckin' bored with the whole thing. They talked to me for about a minute and left. I must have interrupted their coffee break. Assholes. Anyway, after that I went to the hospital and gave them her mother's name. Lydia didn't have an address for her, not that I could find. I don't know what's going to happen to her music stuff."

Diane stood up and walked into the house, leaving me standing outside. She emerged a minute later with another cigarette and sat down right were she had been before.

"What hospital did you go to?" I asked.

"I don't know. The big one in Magnolia."

"Elliott Bay Medical Center?"

"Yeah, I guess."

We were silent again for a while. Diane took a long drag and exhaled slowly. "She really liked you, you know."

"What?"

The pain was evident in her eyes, and in a strange way it comforted me, knowing that Diane felt the same way about Lydia that I did. Exactly the same way.

"Look," I said. "I don't know what she told you but I never meant to hurt anyone."

Diane was shaking her head. "Don't apologize. I know all about it—she told me everything. Even about last Monday night." Then she smiled for the first time since I'd known her. It was thin and bordered on a grimace, but was a smile nonetheless. "Even about my little performance on Sunday."

"She said you were recovering from the flu."

"And then *she* went and died from it. How does shit like that happen?"

It was a question I'd been asking myself ever since the death of my parents, and would probably go on asking even though I knew just as well as Diane that there's no answer. That's the most frustrating part. I don't think I'll ever fully accept the fact that people who I knew and loved could one day just be gone.

I had watched both of my parents die before my eyes, my mother in the University Hospital from a long, painful bout with cancer, and my father in an accidental explosion that nearly took my life as well. I had seen death up close, and I hated myself for what I was feeling now: relief that Diane had been the one to find Lydia instead of me.

Diane finished her cigarette and said, "I need to get out of here now. I've got some people waiting for me."

"Would it be okay if I looked in her room first?" I wasn't sure why I wanted to, or even that I did. But I'd felt such a connection to Lydia when I was in the house before, and I'd never even seen her room. I knew that the only way her death would be real to me was if I went in there now, said one last goodbye, had one more moment alone with her.

Diane shrugged. "Okay, but I'm going to finish packing."

I followed her inside and she led me to the hallway. I could see the open bathroom door down at the end, and another door on each side of the hall that I figured for the bedrooms. She opened the one on the left and I stepped inside.

The bed was unmade, the covers stretched off the mattress and onto the floor where they'd pulled her body out. It was full-sized with white and gold painted head- and footboards. The bare hardwood floor was littered with throw rugs and dirty clothes. To the right was a dresser and a vanity, both painted to match the bed, and on the left was a cedar chest with a cheap stereo on top.

I walked in. The room smelled faintly of cigarette smoke and perfume, and there were two windows with chintz curtains that let in plenty of light, even on a rainy day. Dust motes weren't visible, but I could feel them tickling my nose. The whole room was dusty, and I almost smiled, wondering if she'd ever cleaned behind her own toilet bowl.

On the wall next to the stereo were pine-board shelves on cinder blocks, that held literally hundreds of cassette tapes, some of them prerecorded but most homemade. Though there were many different styles of writing on the tapes, one style predominated and I knew it must be hers. I picked up one of the empty plastic boxes and just looked at it, thinking back to the night I'd been here and looked at the lyrics scrawled in Lydia's handwriting.

There was a poster of Janis Joplin on the wall, costume jewelry on her dresser, two acoustic guitars in the corner, along with a box full of sheet music and songbooks. A couple of dead, or dying, ivy plants stood sentinel on the dusty window ledge. On her nightstand was a bowl, a spoon glued to the center with dried ice cream, a dirty coffee cup, and some spare change.

Barely visible beneath the wads of Kleenex that littered the stand was a bottle of pain pills and a small white business card wedged beneath the base of the lamp. I reached for the card, noticed it was from the dental clinic where Lydia had gone for that terrible filling, and then put it down next to a glass with an inch of water sitting in the bottom.

"Steve?" came a voice from behind me, and I turned. Diane still had her arms around her chest. "I really have to go now."

"Sure," I said and turned to leave. But I stopped as I reached the door and looked back one more time at her room, its memory, and the memory of Lydia that it had somehow deepened, indelibly etched in my mind.

18

When I reached the front room, Diane was sitting on the carpet trying to untie the knotted laces on a very wet tennis shoe. She wasn't having much luck. Next to her was a heavily scratched suitcase with one lock missing, and a red duffel bag. Never having seen a car in the driveway, I was pretty sure Diane had walked from wherever she was staying.

"Can I give you a lift somewhere?" I offered.

"It's in Wallingford." She sounded almost apologetic as she looked up at me from the floor.

"That's right on my way."

"Thank you." She stood up, stuffing her shoes in the duffel bag, and then walked back toward the hall. "Just a second."

When she returned, she was wearing a black pair of Birkenstock sandals. "Okay, I'm ready."

I helped her with the suitcase and we put everything in the cab, and then she gave me directions. "She told me you're a dentist," Diane said, once we were underway.

"Yes, I am."

"I glanced over at her and our eyes met. "You don't look like a dentist."

"No, I suppose not." I didn't have my earring in, but my hair was loose and I hadn't shaved since the day before. In addition, I hadn't worn a coat, and my clothes were still damp from standing in the rain. Even with Lydia's having told her, I wasn't sure if Diane believed me or not.

She remained silent the rest of the trip, and in that vacuum I found more unwanted thoughts beginning to filter into my mind. I wondered what it would be like to hold Diane in my arms, to cry together, to kiss her. Why was I thinking these things? What was wrong with me? It seemed like a violation of Lydia's memory and I was glad when we finally arrived.

Diane opened the door but told me not to get out, and I watched as a woman in a blue raincoat came out of the apartment building I had parked in front of. She was wearing the hood up, dark hair framing her face, and she took the suitcase from Diane without a word and headed back toward the building. Diane thanked me again as she stepped out, then closed the door and followed the woman inside.

From Wallingford I drove south across the Fremont Bridge, down to Mercer and straight over to Bay Med Hospital. I couldn't go back to my apartment; I couldn't be alone right now. If I didn't stay busy I thought I might lose my mind, a mind that clearly seemed to be thinking on its own. What I needed was to talk, and to take some kind of action that would help me to understand Lydia's death.

Because the dental complex that I work out of is loosely affiliated with the medical center, I hold a staff position at the hospital, and a sticker on my back window lets me park anywhere on the property. In return, I have to be on call one night a month for any dental emergencies. I don't remember which night is mine, though, because thus far I've never been called in.

As I turned off Magnolia Boulevard, Bay Med loomed up before me like a gleaming white tombstone against the gray sky. I drove past the ticket booth, down into the underground garage, parked, and walked into the building. There was no need to take the elevator because Bay Med's morgue, like almost every hospital's in the country, is in the basement.

This part of the building was less familiar to me than the rest of the complex, as I hadn't had the opportunity to visit here during my aborted year of medical school. Guided by the smell of formaldehyde, I eventually located the pathology department and asked one of the lab assistants for Waymon Barnes.

She wrinkled her nose at me and said, "You mean *Doctor* Barnes?"

"Just ask for Waymon," I said, and she walked away with a frown.

For as long as I'd known him, Waymon Barnes had gone by his middle name, Dale, exclusively. He didn't even put a W. in front of it. Dale and I had gone through premed together at the University of Washington and made it into the same freshman class at the Maynard School of Medicine, yet another offshoot of the Elliott Bay Medical Center. Unlike me, Dale had gone on to finish medical school and was now the hospital's Chief of Pathology.

I once asked him why he had chosen that particular area to specialize in, when there were so many other, I thought, more prestigious options. He just laughed and said, "Are you kidding? With what I save on malpractice insurance, I can buy a brand-new car every year." It was a good answer, but it left a lot unsaid. Maybe he was as scared of death as I was, and decided if he couldn't beat it, he'd study it. Whatever the reason, he was happy—Dale loved being a doctor—and in the end, that's all that matters.

A few minutes later a slender black man, almost the same height as I was, came bursting through the inner door with a scowl on his face. He was clean-shaven, with short-cropped hair, and gold, wire-rimmed glasses. He wore a gold Rolex, a class ring on one hand and a wedding band on the other, Gucci loafers, and a suit that no doubt had appeared in a recent issue of GQ—though I couldn't really see it beneath his white lab coat.

It had to have been two years since I'd talked to him last but, God, it was good to see Dale again. Even with everything that had happened this week, the sight of him brought back so many memories that I just had to smile. When he finally spotted me waiting for him, his frown melted away and his big, toothy grin emerged.

"Raymond! You son of a bitch!" He took three long strides toward me and in lieu of a handshake he gave me a bear hug.

"How you doin', Dale?"

"What's with this *Waymon* shit?"

"Well, I didn't want you keeping me waiting, and I knew that would light a fire under your ass."

"Son of a bitch," he said again under his breath, and then, for the first time I think, he really looked at me. Dale's face lost its sunny disposition in an instant. "You don't look so hot, my friend. Is anything wrong?"

"I need to talk, Dale."

"Well, come on. Let's get out of here and go back to my office."

I followed Dale through the lab and out into a hallway.

"You know," he said, "you work, what, two blocks away from here? And I never see you. You're not down here on business, I hope."

"As a matter of fact, I am."

He stopped and turned to me as we reached the door with his name on it. "Right in here."

The office was about the same size as my own, but it had about twenty times the paperwork piled everywhere. Dale took a stack of files off a chair and I sat down; then he moved some more files and lifted himself up onto his desk, facing me.

"What happened?" he said, and it felt good to know the concern on his face was genuine.

"A friend of mine died yesterday morning. I was told they brought her here."

"What was her name?"

"Grant. Lydia Grant."

"Dale hopped to his feet and walked around to sit behind his desk. Then he shuffled through some papers and said, "Here it is. She's being posted today. Oh man, I'm sorry, Steve. Is there anything I can do?"

"This probably sounds weird, but I'd like to ask you if you could do the autopsy yourself."

"Done. What else?"

I took a deep breath and we just looked at each other. "I don't know."

"Any idea why she died?"

"She'd had the flu all last week—nausea, vomiting, fever."

"You're thinking viral infection?"

"Right now I'm trying not to think about anything. I just can't believe it. I guess I just want to know why it had to happen. Why did it have to be her?"

"Man, sometimes we never know that, but I'll give it my best shot. Whatever the cause of death was, though, we'll find out that much out for sure."

"Thanks, Dale."

"Hey, you want some coffee?"

Since there was a half-full pot in the corner and a couple of mugs, I said yes. Dale jumped up and poured me a cup. "So, how's Janet?"

I hesitated, to prepare him, and said, "We separated about a year ago."

"No," he said, handing me the coffee and sitting back down on his desk. "Have you filed for divorce yet?"

I shook my head.

"And this Lydia Grant, you were seeing her?"

"Yeah, you could say that."

"Aw, man. I wish there was something I could do for you. You want to come over to dinner tonight? It's no problem. Hell, you could stay over—"

"No, no, I'll be fine." I took a sip of coffee and steered the conversation away from me. "So, how's Jerri?"

He grinned again. "Real good. We just got back from Mexico a couple of weeks ago, and she looks almost as brown as me."

"So, I take it you've been out hitting all the black-only clubs in town?"

Dale laughed. "Yeah, right."

"Still no kids?"

"Nope," he said, and rapped his knuckles twice on the desktop.

We reminisced a while longer until I noticed him glancing at his watch. I took a last gulp of coffee and stood up. "Thanks for everything, Dale, but I have to get going."

"Yeah, me too. You want me to bring the results by this afternoon?"

"No, I'm not working today. Why don't you give me a call at the office tomorrow morning?"

"I'll bring them over."

Dale and I hugged each other again and promised to keep in touch. After walking back out to my truck, I sat there for a while trying to figure out what I was going to do next; then I turned the key in the ignition and drove home—to my *real* home, in Medina.

19

I wandered around the house for nearly an hour, going in and out of rooms it seemed I hadn't been in for years. Though my parents hadn't built this place until I was in junior high, it felt much more a part of me than our house in Maryland, where I had spent most of my childhood. After my mom had died and my older sisters had moved out, it was just Dad and me. That was the time I remembered best. The struggles of adolescence were over, and my dad and I became close as adults.

Lydia's death brought all of that back to me. I began to think about what was important in my life, what I wanted to accomplish, and it had nothing to do with my career. I had always been interested in science and medicine, and my father had been an M.D. It was a natural evolution. I had never felt as though I was searching when it came to choosing a profession, be it doctor, dentist, or musician; certain careers just seemed right for me. Though I eventually chose dentistry, it had never defined my life; it was a means to an end, that end being my family.

I spent as much time with my kids as I could. I was lucky. I didn't have to settle for one weekend a month. I wasn't just a part-time dad. Janet was another story, though, and I was beginning to have doubts about whether I should have moved out at all. Had I been too hard on her? Was I going too far just to make a point? I wasn't sure anymore. Or was I just feeling this way because Lydia had suddenly been taken from me? Jesus Christ, I hoped not.

The worst part was that I couldn't tell Janet about her. Not now. I was forced to grieve alone, and the only thing I could think of that would ease the pain was to be with my family. Maybe my short time with Lydia had been a sign that I should have been reassessing my life, that I should have been feeling lucky about what I had instead of unhappy about what I thought I was missing. Who knew?

In the end, all that introspection just made me feel worse. I moped around the house for a few hours and then dutifully picked up the kids from school. I met Janet at the door as soon as she came home, and I apologized to her for my behavior the night before.

"Do you feel any better tonight?" she asked.

"Not really."

"Then maybe you should just go home."

She wasn't being mean intentionally; after all, she didn't know what I was going through. But it still hurt.

"I thought I'd stay for dinner."

Her eyes narrowed and she considered me warily. "What's the occasion?"

"No occasion. I'd just like to spend the evening with you, if that's okay."

Her expression softened and her whole body seemed to relax. "It's more than okay—it's long overdue. Why don't you grab a beer and put your feet up. I'm cooking dinner tonight."

The meal Janet prepared was superb, but it was more than just the food. The four of us ate around the dinner table like a real family again, everyone animatedly talking about their day. The kids shared the things they had done in school, and Janet told us about the cases she was working on. There wasn't much I could add to the conversation, and I was content to listen. I didn't think it was that obvious, but after dinner as we were loading the dishwasher, Janet turned to me.

"You were kind of quiet tonight. Is everything okay?"

I finished wiping my hands and hooked the towel over the refrigerator handle. "I had kind of a hard day."

"You didn't work, did you?"

"No." I realized now that I shouldn't have said anything at all. I couldn't explain why I'd had a bad day, and Janet was going to rightly infer that I was keeping something from her.

"So, what is it?"

"I really can't talk about it—"

"Fine." She wanted to be mad, but she didn't seem to hang on to it very long. "Do you want some coffee?"

"Decaf would be great."

I watched her pour water into the coffee maker and put beans into the grinder and was quietly heading out to the family room when she called me back. "Steve? Can I talk to you for a minute?"

"Sure."

She had finished grinding the coffee and was dumping it into the filter when she said it. "I wanted to ask if you'd have any objections to my going out once in a while."

I stood silently for a moment trying to get my bearings. "What do you mean by *going out*?" I asked, almost positive that I didn't want to know the answer.

She wouldn't look me in the eye, busying herself putting the filter over the pot and flipping on the machine. "Just what I said, going out."

"What, with other men?"

The embarrassment was killing her, but I wasn't going to let her off the hook. I didn't like what I was feeling, and I glowered until she finally turned to face me. "Yes."

"Jesus Christ, Janet. I don't believe this." I was being the quintessential hypocritical asshole, and I didn't give a shit.

After all, this was my wife. "Is this about the guy on the phone?"

Her eyes widened. "What guy?"

"Sunday, while you were out. Some guy called here and wanted to talk to you. Wouldn't leave a message."

"Well, then how do you expect me to know who it was?"

"Oh, so there's more than one?"

"This is ridiculous. Didn't you even hear what I said? I'm asking you if it's okay. I haven't done anything yet."

"Yet? So, you've got your eye on some guy down at the office and what you're really asking for is my permission to fuck him?" She threw her hands up and so I gave her an answer. "No, then. If you're going to ask me, the answer's no."

"Why not?"

"Because you're my wife."

Without warning, her embarrassment turned to anger. "Is that what you call it? Because it sure as hell doesn't seem that way to me."

I leaned against the counter and tilted my head back until it reached the cabinets above the microwave oven. My neck felt stiff. When I looked back toward her again she was still staring me down. "What do you want from me, Janet?"

"I want what I've always wanted. I want you to move back in here so we can be a family again. Barring that, I'd like to get on with my life. I'm tired of feeling like I can't make decisions for myself, that I always have to consider how you're going to feel. I'm tired of you treating me like shit."

"What are you talking about? I've never interfered in your life. I've always left you alone. I've never asked you what you do when I'm not here."

Her lower lip was quivering slightly, and though I hadn't seen it often, it looked as if she was going to cry. "That's exactly what I'm talking about, Steve."

This was not what I wanted to happen tonight. It was

unbelievable. "I thought I was doing the right thing," I finally said. "I thought it was what you wanted."

She was shaking her head. "I never wanted this. What I want is a husband, and I don't really know whether I have that anymore. But what I need most of all, Steve, is a decision."

"Tonight?"

"Why not? It's been over a year. How much more time do you need?"

"It's not that simple. I've just been—"

"You haven't been doing anything. This is killing me, and it doesn't look like things are ever going to change. I think you're perfectly happy to let me go on living here, being your absentee wife. You spend more time with your kids than you do with me."

"And just whose fault do you think that is?"

"God *damn* it, Steve!" she yelled at me. "I fucked up, okay? If you want me to go around wearing sackcloth and flagellating myself, that's fine—as long as I know you're going to come back afterward. But I don't see that happening. I don't think you want to. And I can't let you keep punishing me forever."

"So what are you saying? You want a divorce? Is that what you want?"

"No. I want you to come upstairs with me right now so I can fuck your brains out, and then I want us to grow old together." A tear broke loose from her left eye and rolled down her cheek. She quickly wiped it away.

"And if I don't?"

"Then I'm going to file for divorce."

I walked past her out of the kitchen, took my coat from the hall closet, and left the house without saying another word. I drove back to Seattle in a daze wondering how I was even going to be able to function at work in the morning.

When I reached my apartment I couldn't bear to go inside, and drove a few more blocks east, to Carkeek Park. The gate was closed but I pulled into the lot anyway, and hopped over it on foot. It was an extremely long walk down the cement path, past the picnic tables and down the stairs to the beach, but I felt better than I had all day. Standing there with the water lapping at my feet, I could breathe again.

A bit to the south I could just see the lights on Bainbridge Island across Puget Sound. I walked up and down the beach for a while, picking up small stones and throwing them in the water. Later, I worked my way back to the grass and sat down.

Janet was right. I had to make a decision. Being with Lydia would have been an easy way out, but I didn't have that option anymore. And maybe that was for the best. I had to decide for the right reason and not because I thought I was in love with someone else. It had been more than a year and I didn't want to go back now any more than I had when I'd moved out.

What I'd been doing wasn't fair to Janet or the kids, or to myself for that matter. It was time to own up to the truth and do the right thing. I knew then that Janet and I were going to be divorced.

I brought my legs up and wrapped my arms around them, my chin resting on my knees. I hadn't cried since my father died eight years before, but I cried now. Only it wasn't for Janet and my lost marriage. It was for Lydia.

20

I was glad to be busy Tuesday, after the emotional upheaval of the previous two days. My mind was on automatic pilot as I became increasingly absorbed in work. It was getting close to lunch and I had one more patient to go, an onlay that I'd made myself and was anxious to see in place. Out at the reception desk, Nona motioned to me before I went back.

"Dr. Barnes is here to see you. He said it was urgent so I had him go into your office."

"How long has he been here?"

"Just a few minutes."

"Good. Thanks, Nona."

When I walked into my office Dale was standing behind my desk, scrutinizing my diplomas.

"Not so close," I said. "I don't like nose prints on the glass."

Dale turned around, his face serious, and pointed to my bachelor's degree. "This is a forgery, isn't it? There's no way they would have let you graduate."

"Sit down," I said, and I heard him laugh as I shut the door. When I looked back he was relaxing in my black leather chair, his face beaming. Shaking my head, I took the chair in front of my desk.

Dale turned serious immediately. "Man, your friend was in a bad way."

"What do you mean?"

"Advanced hemolytic anemia. The blood samples I took were ugly—almost nothing but plasma and hemosiderin. She had some cerebral hemorrhaging, but it didn't look to me like the loss of blood in her brain was enough to cause the massive red cell destruction I observed."

"What do you think caused it?"

"It could have been any number of things, Steve—some medication she was taking, plant poison, exposure to a toxic chemical—or it might have been a secondary reaction to some type of infection. I honestly won't know until we get the blood chemistry results back. Whatever it was, she'd had it for several days."

"How did she die?"

"My guess is she passed out in the middle of the night from lack of oxygen—there just weren't enough blood cells left for transport. And since she couldn't get up or tell anybody, she lapsed into a coma and died."

I looked away from Dale. My throat felt constricted, and I couldn't make myself speak. After what seemed like several minutes, my head in my hands, I said, "I wanted her to see a doctor, on Saturday. If I'd made her go, she'd still be alive."

"And if somebody had told Kennedy not to go to Dallas, he'd be alive, too."

I looked up at Dale.

"You're not responsible," he said sternly.

"I had an opportunity—"

"And that's all you can say." He sat up and leaned forward, planting his forearms firmly on my desk. "Do you know how many suicides I get where the relatives had hundreds of opportunities to prevent the death? They don't realize that it doesn't matter. If a person wants to kill himself bad enough, he's usually going to do it anyway. Once the decision's been made, nobody can stop it."

"You're not trying to tell me that she committed suicide?"

"No. What I'm saying is that it was her responsibility to get to a doctor, not yours. When the type of anemia she had starts destroying blood cells, and the loss exceeds production of new cells, the onset of death can happen fairly rapidly—two to four hours. That's an awfully small window of opportunity to seek emergency treatment, and that's why I think it happened while she was sleeping."

"But you still don't know what caused it?"

"Not for sure. Not yet. I sent out the samples yesterday, though. I put a rush on it and I should have something for you late next week."

I nodded.

"The way I see it now, it looks pretty cut and dried. I don't think I'll have any problem finding out what it was."

"Thanks, Dale, for everything. I really appreciate this."

I figured the conversation was over at that point, and I was preparing to show Dale to the door when he leaned back in my chair and rubbed his chin. "There is one thing I'd like to ask you about, though, something I ran across during the autopsy. It may or may not be important."

"What's that?"

"Did she ever complain to you about a toothache?"

"Toothache? Why?"

"The girl had a bad mandibular abscess. Now, I'm not making any guesses, but depending on the type of infection, it could be significant."

"The cause of the anemia?"

"Possibly."

"That doesn't make any sense. I know for a fact that she had a dentist appointment just last week."

Dale looked skeptical. "Are you sure it was that recent?"

"Positive."

"That's strange. You'd think that the dentist who put in her filling would have spotted it."

"Not necessarily. An early abscess can be tricky to spot. Sometimes they don't even show up on the x-rays. Most of the time the best warning we can get is when a patient complains of sensitivity. Was the swelling on the same side as the filling?"

"Yeah, the new filling was what tipped me off. I was doing the oral examination, and she had about half a dozen fillings, but I spotted the shiny one right away. I figured it had to be a month old, at least—any more recent and the dentist would have spotted the swelling that I noticed on the right side of her jaw. It wasn't major, but asymmetrical enough that I checked it out, and that's when I found the abscess."

That made me angry. "She was going to some cut-rate dental clinic. God damn it. I should have taken a look at her myself. I could see they'd done shitty work."

"Wasn't the dental school, was it?"

"No, no, this was downtown, some private clinic."

"And she never mentioned the abscess to you?"

"The last time I saw her was a week before she died. I talked to her all that week, but no, she never mentioned it."

"Man, I always thought those things were supposed to hurt like a mother."

"It depends. Most of the time they do, but like a lot of things, you can have it for months and not even know it. I know she was taking pain pills, too, and that might have masked the pain enough for her not to notice."

"Well, I just thought you should know about it. You want me to call you next week when I get the lab tests back?"

"Please."

I walked Dale out and then went back to my onlay appointment. The procedure went smoothly and the onlay was a perfect fit. By eleven-thirty I was done, and as I went back into my office I began to put together some of the vague thoughts I was having about what Dale had told me.

There was the fact that the dentist could have misdiagnosed

her, that the tooth should have received root canal therapy. That was the logical assumption, but it was only one possibility. I kept running the information over and over in my mind, and one question always emerged: what if Lydia had been infected with an unsterile instrument—a dirty probe or drill bit?

The image that sprang to mind was of a medieval surgeon doing dental work, his instruments consisting of a chair on a dirt floor and a pair of pliers, with farm animals in the corners and children dressed in rags running between his legs as he worked.

Even though no modern dentist's office could even remotely resemble that image, it didn't mean that Lydia couldn't have been contaminated with a septic instrument. In fact, there were more sloppy dentists out there than I cared to admit, and I knew I'd have to see the one who had worked on Lydia for myself. The old joke about doctors could just as easily apply to my profession: somewhere out there is the worst dentist in the world and, right now, someone has an appointment with him.

If I found out some quack was responsible for Lydia's death, I was going to make damn sure the son of a bitch paid for it. I pulled out the Seattle Yellow Pages and looked under dentists, but there were several clinics listed downtown. I'd only glanced at the business card and the pain pills on Lydia's nightstand, and I certainly couldn't remember what they'd said.

Since I had almost three hours before I had to be in Medina, I could run over to Lydia's house right now. It was hard telling if Diane would be there, though. Most likely not. But the alternative was to do nothing, and I didn't like that at all. I notified Nona that I wouldn't be back after lunch, leaving her to lock up when she was through, and drove north toward Green Lake.

As I had suspected, Diane wasn't home, and the front door was locked. It wouldn't be as easy walking around the house in the daylight. There were other houses alongside, and if someone looked out and saw me trying to get in a window, I could very easily wind up in the back of a squad car trying to explain myself to the cops. I circled the house quickly, stopping only to try the back door—also locked—and I could see that none of the windows was cracked. Lydia had probably been worried about her musical equipment being stolen.

I was about to climb back in my truck and give up when I stopped and ran back to the front door. A hidden key. Nearly every house had one, and this seemed like a prime candidate. I exhausted the obvious possibilities right away: the doormat, above the doorframe, and under the scruffy potted plant on the stoop. Now it was time to think creatively.

I'd heard of people burying the spare key in the flower bed, but when I looked at the weed-choked row of dirt that skirted the house I knew I could dig around forever and not find it in there. A loose brick was an idea, but there was no brickwork anywhere around. Now I was stuck. I sat down on the steps and peeled back the Astroturf where I could. Still no key. I was all out of ideas.

Hell, maybe they didn't need an extra key. I backed up a few steps from the stoop and just looked at it for a while. Two flat hooks jutting out from the bottom of the mailbox held a yellowed newspaper. It obviously hadn't been delivered recently, so I bounded up the steps and pulled it out. The rotted rubber band broke before I could get it off, and I unrolled the paper. The date was from January, but there was no key inside. I was putting it back when I began to take a closer look at the mailbox.

Though it had once been black, it was now a weathered, rusty orange. It stood vertically on the wall with a little door in the top that squeaked as I pried it up. Inside were two envelopes, both bills, one from Puget Power and the other from US West. I took them out and peered inside, but the depth of the box and the lack of sunlight prevented me from seeing anything. So I pulled back and stuck my hand inside.

The hinge of the rusted top was such that I could only get my arm in at an angle. The box was narrow anyway, and as a result I couldn't touch the bottom. I pulled my hand out and had to bend the top forcibly, rusted metal flaking off into the box. Now the top wouldn't shut all the way and looked like an open mouth, but I could reach all the way in. Bingo. I'd had to feel around for a few seconds but it was there. Tweezing it out with my first two fingers I brought forth the key to Lydia and Diane's house.

Wasting no time, I unlocked the front door and went inside. It didn't look as if Diane had been back since yesterday, and I walked directly to Lydia's room. The bottle of pills was there on her nightstand and it was the first thing I picked up. I was shocked to see it was Demerol. That seemed like an extremely excessive painkiller for a filling. But while it didn't make sense, but it sure as hell explained why she hadn't noticed an abscessed tooth.

I slipped the vial into my pocket and rooted through the wadded Kleenex until I found the business card. First Avenue Dental Clinic, it read—a Carl Thompson, D.D.S., was listed as the clinic's head dentist—and I pocketed that, too. Then I glanced at my watch and saw that it was only twelve-thirty. I still had two hours before I had to be in Medina—just enough time to pay a visit to Dr. Thompson.

21

The southern end of First Avenue in downtown Seattle is home to numerous pawnshops and adult bookstores, but the address on the card was up in the north end. Where a few years ago the area was mostly run-down buildings and vacant lots, it was now filled with upscale apartment buildings and condos, along with trendy restaurants and businesses to serve the recent influx of residents. I had made my way out to Aurora and driven south into town, right onto Denny Way and left onto First. Two blocks later I was there.

The clinic was housed on the second floor of an old, two-story brick building, the first floor of which still had its windows boarded up. The dirty glass door on the end of the structure had the words General Dentistry, 9:00 a.m. to 5:00 p.m., painted on it, and I pushed it open onto a set of sagging wooden stairs. Each step squeaked as I made my way up, no doubt to let the receptionist know when a new patient had arrived.

I was surprised to find a fairly comfortable-looking waiting room when I reached the top. There were no carpets, but the wood floors were polished and several large potted plants added color to the area. The ceiling was at least fifteen feet high and paneled in dark wood, the plaster walls painted in a pastel green. A dozen upholstered chairs lined the perimeter, and the requisite outdated magazines were strewn on tables for perusal.

I walked up to the enclosed reception desk, much like the one in my own office, and a round-faced black woman who looked about forty slid open the glass window and gave me a smile. "May I help you?"

"I hope so. I'd like to see Dr. Thompson."

"Do you have an appointment?"

"No," I said, and handed her one of my business cards. "But I'm a dentist, and I wanted to talk to him about a patient he referred to me."

"Okay, Dr. Raymond. If you'll just have a seat I'll be back with you in a minute."

Pleasant enough, I thought. I took a seat opposite the desk, across from a man in a blue suit that had become shiny with wear. A few chairs down to my left was a rather fat woman in a taut, floral dress with three small children swarming around her. And on my right was a beautiful young woman with long dark hair who was dressed entirely in black.

The door opened and a man holding a clipboard called out, "Ms. Friesen?" The woman next to me stood up and followed him into the hallway beyond. I waited another fifteen minutes and glanced through as many copies of *Sports Illustrated*—with stories in them about the Houston Oilers and the Los Angeles Raiders when the inner door finally opened again.

"Dr. Raymond? Dr. Thompson will see you now."

As soon as I was through the door, the receptionist opened another door to my left and I walked into one of the most opulent offices I'd ever been in. It was twice as big as the waiting room, the far wall completely covered with windows and displaying an impressive view of the waterfront. The vast expanse of light-brown carpet felt thick and bouncy under my feet and was only broken up by a cozy-looking tweed couch and chairs on the left, and a huge solid-wood desk to my right.

Behind the desk were perhaps thirty framed certificates and civic awards, as well as two large diplomas, but I was too far away to read them. To the left of the diplomas was another door, and to the right were a couple of glass-enclosed bookcases filled with medical and dental texts. A series of oak file cabinets, set off by framed prints by Elton Bennett above them, lined the only remaining wall.

A white-haired man in a gray pinstripe suit was sitting at the desk reading some papers, and when I entered he casually took off the reading glasses he was wearing and flipped them onto the desk, then stood up and walked around to greet me.

"Dr. Raymond. Come in."

His features were distinctly Italian—dark, watery eyes, olive skin, a prominent nose, and a wide smile. He was about five-ten, late fifties, and smelled of cologne as he offered me a hand of thick, stubby fingers. We shook hands and then he motioned toward the couch. "I think we'll be more comfortable over here," he said, but I wasn't in the mood to be seduced.

"That's okay—I'll only be here a minute."

Now that he was standing nearer to me, I could see that his face, though closely shaved, would never be rid of the blue tinge caused by his thick beard. He had large pores, and I could see plenty of gold dental work when he smiled.

"My receptionist tells me that I referred a patient to you, but I can't recall that we've ever met."

"No, we haven't, but I am seeing a former patient of yours—Lydia Grant." He continued smiling at me but said nothing. "Do you remember her?" I asked.

"Dr. Raymond," he said, walking over to gaze out the window with practiced ease. "We have several doctors on staff here and quite an extensive patient base. It's not really possible, or practical, for me to remember every patient's name."

"But she was just in here last week."

143

When he looked back at me his smile had turned condescending. "As I said, we have quite a few patients."

I took the bottle of pain pills from my pocket and flashed it. "Then you probably don't remember writing this prescription for her, either."

Instead of taking it from me, Thompson headed for his desk and picked up his glasses. Then he walked back and squinted through them as I held the bottle. He didn't touch it.

"Ah, yes. This is one of our prescriptions."

"Our?"

"Yes. I have six other full-time dentists on staff here, but they're not my partners. They work for me. My business is incorporated and my name appears on all of the relevant documents." He went over to his desk again, picked up a prescription pad, and handed it to me. "Though the individual doctors initial the form, I personally review the files before signing for any prescription. Just a precautionary measure, I assure you.

It sounded absolutely ludicrous to me. What dentist would want to work for somebody else, especially this guy?"

"So which of your dentists was it who did the work on Ms. Grant? I'd like to talk with him."

"I'm afraid that's privileged information—you know, doctor-patient confidentiality."

"That's ridiculous. I'm not the police."

"Still, it is within our legal rights to withhold the files of any patient."

"Yes, but since I am her new dentist, I think it would be in the patient's best interest to let me at least look at her treatment record."

He was already shaking his head. "I'm afraid that would fall under the same category."

"You're kidding?"

He held out his hands with a shrug.

"Well, would you mind telling me what this dentist was doing prescribing Demerol for a filling?"

Thompson's exasperation was beginning to show, and I could tell he was starting to size me up, in case I didn't go away pretty soon. He walked over to one of the file cabinets and said, "What was the name again?"

"Lydia Grant."

He pulled a set of keys from his pocket and unlocked one of the drawers, leaving the keys dangling in the lock. I watched him riffle through the files, select one, peer inside, slide it back, and lock up the cabinet again. Only then did he say, "I show Ms. Grant to have had a final appointment for root canal therapy on February twenty-second, last Monday."

"Root canal?"

"And I believe that, depending on the severity of her discomfort, and the discretion of the dentist, the use of Demerol could have been indicated. So, if there's nothing else, Dr. Raymond, I have patients to attend to."

"Now that you mention it, there is something else. My patient has been having some problems due to what I consider inferior dental work that she received here. And unless I can talk to the dentist who did the work and he can explain his procedure to my satisfaction, I'll be forced to seek other avenues of redress."

I had a feeling I had hit the right button on that one, but before Thompson could answer the door behind his desk began to rattle in its frame as someone pounded on it from the other side. Though the voice was muffled, and I was hearing it through the pounding, it sounded like the person on the other side was yelling, "Dog turd! Dog turd!"

I knew Thompson wanted to get me out of his office first, but he wasn't going to have the chance. He ran over to the door and opened it. Standing there was a small, East Indian in a white coat. The man was wearing glasses and sweating profusely, and I could see spots of blood on his smock. He was wringing his hands and going on about some sort of emergency, and his Indian lilt sounded like everyone's imitation of Ghandi. Thompson was frowning intently and then looked over at me.

"Please wait here, Dr. Raymond. I'll be right back." Then he shut the door and was gone. That's when I realized what it was that the Indian must have been shouting: Doctor.

The first thing I did when he left was walk over and try the file cabinets. Every one of them was locked. This place was weird. Did the receptionist have to come in here with a key to get to them? Or did she have to get Thompson to open them for her? It didn't make any sense.

I made my way over to Thompson's desk. It was neat and clean with nothing on top but a blotter, a small calendar, and a pen and pencil set. The papers he had been reading looked like junk mail. There were three drawers on each side of the black leather chair, and one in the middle. I tried them, and only the lower right one was locked. The drawer just above the locked one had some interesting-looking papers and files in it, but I didn't dare take a closer look in case he came back.

I could hear noise now that I hadn't heard before from the other side of the room, and sauntered over to the door. I pressed my ear against it, but it wasn't any more distinct. What the hell, I thought, there's no law against opening a door. I turned the knob slowly and eased it open. It wasn't the medieval surgeon's sod hut—not quite, anyway. It looked more like a nineteenth-century dental sweatshop.

The view afforded from the door in Thompson's office was obviously something that had been intentional; I could see everything in the entire room from here. It was bigger than the office and had the same polished wood floors as out front, but was divided into ten different sections. The partitions were only four feet high, and from where I stood I could see into every one of the cubicles.

Each one contained a reclining dental chair and overhead lights, a station for air, water and drills, a sink, and a couple of stools. Three rooms on the far right appeared to be set up with x-ray machines and were currently not in use. Thompson had said there were six other dentists working for him, but I counted eight chairs currently in use, each with two white-clad people bent over the open mouth of a patient.

Of the eight dentists I counted, four of them were Asian, two were black, and only one was white. None of the assistants was white, as far as I could see. The East Indian was in the far corner and, oddly enough, Thompson had donned a white jacket and was working on the patient himself while the Indian assisted. It looked like Thompson was going to be there a while.

I shut the door as inconspicuously as possible and ran back to Thompson's desk. It probably broke every professional ethic in the book—not to mention laws—but I knew he was being dishonest about something. The top drawer on the left contained nothing but junk—an empty glasses case, some broken instruments, toothpaste samples, and the like. The next drawer down looked to be personal correspondence, and the bottom one was full of American Dental Association journals and other magazines.

I heard a voice on the other side of the door and slammed the bottom drawer shut, then practically jumped over to the other side of the desk. My heart was pounding so hard that I put my hand up to my chest and started to laugh at myself. God, that had scared me. Nobody came in, so I walked over to the door and took another peek out. Thompson was still bent over the patient, and so I went back to his desk.

The drawer in the middle contained office supplies and I was becoming increasingly curious about what was locked in that bottom right drawer. The top right was full of dental gold, models and assorted appliances. The next drawer down, the one with the interesting papers, was now the only one of interest, but I had no idea I was about to hit the jackpot.

Among the legal papers I found there—letters of incorporation, business licenses, and insurance policies—were two thick files that somehow didn't surprise me at all when I discovered they were malpractice suits. One was two years old, and the other six. I went back through the other papers until I found a deed. It turned out that Thompson had bought the whole building eight years before, and started the clinic two years later. A lawsuit on your first year out—not a very propitious start.

I had just finished putting everything back and was gently closing the drawer when I heard the voice behind me. "What do you think you're doing?"

I jerked around to find Thompson glowering at me. His face was red and he was pissed. I didn't say anything. There wasn't much to say. I walked around to put the desk between us.

"Of all the nerve. First you come in here and threaten me, and now this. I should call the police and have you arrested."

"Look, why don't I just leave—"

"Better yet, I should call the State Dental Board and have your license revoked for unethical behavior and wanton disregard for patient confidentiality."

I tried to keep a calm exterior, but inside I was trembling something fierce. Had he really said "wanton?" All I wanted to do was leave, but I'd fucked up and he'd bagged me on it. I had a feeling I was going to pay for my stupidity.

"I don't know what kind of long-haired hippie types they're putting through dental school these days, but just looking at you I should have expected as much. I want you out of here right now, *Doctor* Raymond. And I don't ever want to see you in this office again. Do you understand me?"

I was so stunned I almost couldn't answer. "Yes," I managed to croak out.

"And if you ever have any business to discuss with me in the future you'll do it by mail. Now, get the hell out of here."

He followed me to the door and it was difficult for me not to turn around to keep my eye on him. I was sure he was going to clobber me. He didn't stop at the door, though. He followed me all the way out to the top of the stairs and watched as I descended to the street.

Once outside in the cool air, my legs turned to rubber. Jesus, that was a stupid move, I thought, as I walked back to my truck. But the further I got from the clinic, the better I felt, and soon I was smiling. Thompson had unwittingly confirmed for me, like nothing else could have, that I was on the right track. Though he'd threatened to call the cops, he hadn't.

In my mind that could mean only one thing: Dr. Thompson had something to hide. I was a dentist, too, and if it had been me catching someone going through my desk, the guy's ass would be sitting in jail right now. No question about it. But Thompson probably didn't want the cops anywhere near his place. And I knew I was going to have to find out why.

22

I apologized as soon as Janet walked in the door Tuesday night. She said she wanted to talk to me and we went up to the bedroom. There was no strip tease this time. Janet undressed and showered in the bathroom, and then came into the bedroom wearing her robe.

She sat on the bed and pulled her legs up under her. "What would you think if I had an associate at the office start drawing up papers?"

"I wouldn't object."

"That's a rousing endorsement."

I sighed.

"I'm sorry," she said. "I'm sorry for last night, too. I shouldn't have forced you into making a decision right then."

"Please, Janet, don't apologize. You were right, and that's all there is to it. I was being an asshole."

"I sure wish I'd been wrong."

She stood up and began drying her hair, relieving me of the obligation to respond. There were other things I needed to say. "I've been doing a lot of thinking about us, even before last night. Things have been happening in my life that I haven't been able to tell you about. I haven't been totally honest. And if I can't be honest with you I shouldn't be married to you. And I certainly shouldn't force you to stay married to me."

She turned to me and said, "Are you seeing someone else?"

I'd been waiting for that question, and thinking a lot about what I would say when she asked it. Of the two ways I could answer, one was cruel and would serve no purpose. Sometimes honesty isn't the best policy. I shook my head. "No, there's no one else."

She climbed back up on the bed next to me and I held her close, hugging at last with no reservations.

"I love you so much, Steve."

"I love you, too," I said, and I meant it.

"And you really think this is the best thing for us?"

"What do you think?"

"Probably." Janet sat up and looked at me. Her eyes were brimming with tears, but the relief on her face was evident. The uncertainty was over. "You can have another lawyer look over them if you want."

"No. I trust you. You're the only lawyer I need."

"Am I ever going to see you again?"

"Hey, you're the mother of my babies. I should hope to hell I'd get to see you, not to mention them."

"Okay, but you just might get roped into making dinner."

"How about tonight?"

"Are you serious?"

"Sure. Tonight *you* can put your feet up and have a beer."

Janet laughed and started pushing me off the bed. "You're on."

I cooked up some pasta and fresh spinach that I found in the fridge, and though the kids were a little more distracted than the night before we had a fine time again. I begged off staying any longer and put in a call to Dan Lasky, asking if I could come over and talk to him. He said that was fine and I left the house shortly after seven. Janet and I said our goodbyes much more civilly than we had yesterday, and I had to admit that I felt a lot better, too, knowing that the situation had been resolved.

* * *

Dan lived in West Seattle and I didn't envy his having to cross the West Seattle Freeway every day to get to work. It was one of the many notorious spots of congestion during Seattle's considerable rush hour. Once I'd passed over the Duwamish Waterway on the south end of Harbor Island, I turned right onto Harbor Avenue and continued up the hill to the Lasky's red-brick, two-story home.

I shook hands with Dan and he showed me into his den, a small room with two opposing couches, a desk and a computer, and his police commendations framed on the wall. As soon as we were seated I excitedly began to tell him about my visit with Dr. Thompson.

"Aw, Christ," he said, interrupting me as soon as I came to the part where Thompson walked in on me. He pushed himself up off the couch. "I don't even want to hear any more of this shit. Do you know who this guy is?"

"Yeah, some low-rent dentist who thinks he's hot stuff."

"For your information, he just happens to be hot stuff. Are you really telling me you don't know who Carl Thompson is?"

Dan was pacing the room now, still in the brown slacks and white shirt he wore when he was working. He had taken a certain measure of comfort, however, by removing his tie.

"No," I said. "Why don't you tell me?"

"For one thing, the guy's loaded. Who do you think owned all of that property on the north end of First Ave.?"

"So he's rich. Is there some reason I should care?"

"They guy's also a member of about every damn civic organization there is, and he donates heavily to the police department."

"I suppose now you're going to tell me his real name is Carlo Thomasetti, and that I should be thankful I'm not sleeping with the fishes."

"For Christ's sake, he caught you going through his desk."

"Exactly. And yet Dr. Police Connections didn't even call the cops."

Lasky stopped pacing and just stared at me for a second. Then he sat down heavily across from me.

"Just hear me out, Dan. First, his files were locked up tighter than Fort Knox."

"The guy has a right to privacy."

"Then, he has any number of dentists working for him—he said six, but I counted eight—like employees."

"Doctors work for hospitals all the time. What about Group Health?"

"*And* they're all minorities."

"So he's an equal-opportunity employer. Just listen to yourself, Steve. You used to be a nice, respectable dentist. Where the hell did these paranoid delusions come from?"

I'd thought I might have trouble convincing Dan Lasky about Thompson, but eventually convincing him had always been part of the plan. I had hoped I wouldn't have to bring Lydia into the picture, and now it looked like that was the only thing that would do it.

"Let me at least tell you how I got on to Thompson in the first place, okay?"

"Be my guest."

"A couple of weeks ago I met this woman and, not to put too fine a point on it, we started dating." If he was surprised by this revelation, it didn't register on his face. "A week ago yesterday she went to Thompson's office, and someone there finished doing root canal work on her. Then, last Sunday, she died."

"Steve . . ."

"Wait, that's just the beginning. A friend of mine happened to do the autopsy on her—"

"Happened?"

". . . A friend of mine did the autopsy on her, and he found an abscess in her jaw. Well, that's just not right. You do a root canal to prevent abscess. If he'd done the procedure correctly the swelling should have been going down that whole week, not getting worse. At first I thought he might have infected her with an unsterile instrument, but more and more I'm beginning to think that he just didn't get all of the root pulp out, or worse yet, operated on the wrong tooth."

My voice was beginning to shake with emotion and I took a deep breath to calm myself down. Dan leaned forward, but didn't interrupt. "On top of all that, he prescribed pain pills that, if not directly contributing to her death, masked the pain enough that she didn't seek additional treatment in time.

"I think that whoever worked on her caused the infection that killed her. But when I asked Thompson, he wouldn't tell me who it was. For all I know *he* did the work. Somebody at his little dental sweatshop is responsible for this woman's death and I want to find out who it is."

Dan leaned back and rubbed his five o'clock shadow while he thought. Even though it was probably due to the naturally circumspect nature of his job, his discretion was one of the things I valued about Dan's friendship. He wouldn't mention Janet unless I brought her up first.

"What was the cause of death?" Dan asked.

"Anemia. Her blood cells had all broken down."

"And you think this abscess caused the anemia?"

"It could have."

"Tell me how."

"All right. You do a root canal when the tooth pulp becomes infected. If it's not treated right away, the infection has nowhere to go but down the roots and out into your jaw. If the infection continues unchecked, it can eat away the whole bone structure under your teeth. Obviously it's important to catch it well before then.

"The problem is, the infection isn't always easy to detect

in the early stages, and sometimes it doesn't even show up on the x-rays, so you have to depend on your patients for clues. But if someone doesn't go to the dentist regularly, they might not come in until they already have an abscess. By that time the pain is so great that they can't ignore it any longer."

"Is that what happened to this . . ."

"Lydia Grant."

"Is that what happened to Grant?"

"I don't think so. I think she must have been having some sensitivity, either to pressure or temperature, and that's what brought her in to the dentist. She seemed fine the day before her appointment, but for her to be so swollen a week later, the dentist should have easily been able to spot an infection that advanced on the x-rays.

"Now, once the treatment had started, the dentist would have removed the infected pulp, filled in the empty chamber with inert material, and the infection would have begun to subside. The day after her appointment Lydia got sick. I wasn't able to see her then so I don't know what the progression was, but the pathologist noticed swelling on her face and traced it to an abscess."

"So you're saying it got worse instead of going away like it should have?"

"Right, which can only mean one of two things—either he left some of the infected pulp in the root, or he operated on the wrong tooth. And because nothing was done about the infection, it eventually began to break down her blood cells and caused her death. As far as I'm concerned, the guy killed her."

"And that's all you have?"

I was stunned. How could he not find the evidence as overwhelming as I had? "Isn't that enough?"

"Unfortunately, no. Not right now, anyway. First off, you don't even know who it was that operated on her. I suppose you could probably find out if you sued Thompson, but that seems like an expensive way to obtain information. And second, you have absolutely no hard evidence that links this guy to the cause of death. By the way, does your pathologist friend agree with your theory?"

"He doesn't know about it."

"Why not?"

I shook my head, knowing how this was going to sound, but I had to say it anyway. "He's not positive that there is a link between the abscess and the anemia."

He held out his hands. "If the pathologist doesn't even know, how can you be so sure?"

"It can't be anything else, Dan."

"But when will you know for sure?"

I sighed. "When the blood tests come back."

"Look, Steve, I know you came here looking for support, and I'd like nothing better than to give it to you, but I can't. What you've got here may wind up being malpractice or wrongful death, in which case you'd want to file a civil lawsuit, or report it to the state dental board. Even if you could convince the police—which you can't—the most we could charge this dentist with is involuntary manslaughter. It's certainly not murder."

I nodded thoughtfully, trying to hide my intense dejection. This thing was taking an emotional toll on me that I hadn't expected. What I needed right now was to get rid of the anger I was feeling toward Dan. It wasn't his fault. He was just doing his job. "Ah, you're right, Dan. I guess I got a little carried away."

"Nothing wrong with that. Someone dies, it has an effect on you. People do funny things. I'm just glad you came and talked to me about it, before you went and did something you'll regret."

"Like storming in there and making a citizen's arrest?"

Dan winced. "Don't even say that. Christ, don't even think it. You're going to give me an ulcer."

"Don't worry. I just went a little crazy. I'm okay now."

"Good. Say, do you want something to drink, a beer or anything?"

"No thanks. I have to get home pretty soon. Where's Rena?"

"My wife has decided to leave me every Tuesday and Thursday night, if you can believe that. She takes a class up at the U."

"I believe it. What's she taking?"

He smirked. "Creative writing."

"Hmm, a budding author in the family?"

"Yeah, she's showed me some stuff, except I don't go in much for that slice-of-life crap."

"Don't talk like that. This is probably just what you need. Broaden your literary horizons."

"Sure, I'm lucky if I can get past the sports page every night, let alone read a book. How's things on the home front with you?"

I shook my head. "It looks like Janet and I are going to go ahead and get a divorce."

"Damn. That's too bad."

Neither of us had much to say after I dropped that bomb, and I made the first move to get up. Dan followed and walked me to the door. "If you need anything, Steve, you let me know."

"Thanks, Dan."

"And the same goes for Janet. You tell her that, okay?"

"Okay."

He handed me my coat and I walked out to the truck, but hesitated before getting in. Dan had said I could file a suit against Thompson to find out who had done the work on Lydia, but dealing with red tape would be like stepping in quicksand. I could just see Thompson after being served with papers or after notification of a state board investigation. He'd have some of his indentured servants hauling files and other incriminating evidence out of his office at midnight and stashing it all over town. The guy was slick and oily in a way that had nothing to do with his ethnic stereotype.

The thing that made me angriest was that I should have to do anything at all. The medical profession had been getting a lot of bad publicity over the past few years, with rising fees, more malpractice suits, insurance scams and the public's perception of just plain insensitivity toward patients on the part of the medical community. But I'd always thought of dentistry as being above all that.

The association of pain with dental work had rapidly diminished over the past decade, thanks to increased emphasis on patient comfort and advances in technology and techniques. Where doctors had been acquiring the same money-hungry reputation as lawyers, dentists, I believed, had been living up to their responsibility to make people feel better, by improving their appearances and alleviating their pain.

From what I'd observed, Thompson was only in it for the bucks, and his entire operation bothered me. Lydia's death was still an open wound, and though I didn't know where it would lead me, there was one thing I was certain of: I couldn't just let this thing go. Dan had said the police would need proof. Well, all right, then, that was exactly what they were going to get.

23

I drove straight home from Dan Lasky's and changed into a pair of sweatpants and a blue Seahawks sweatshirt. Out in the living room I paced for a while, then put on Grant Green's *Idle Moments*, and began to think.

The first thing I needed to do was talk with one of Thompson's dentists and find out what their working arrangement was. I couldn't imagine why a good dentist would want to work for someone else. One of the reasons a person became a doctor or a dentist, I always assumed, was so they wouldn't have to punch a clock. And how much was Thompson paying them? Even considering overhead, it couldn't possibly be as much as they would be able to make in private practice.

But that presented another problem. How could I be sure I wouldn't inadvertently talk to the one who had done the work on Lydia? I thought of Thompson in his white jacket hunched over the Indian's patient this afternoon. Did they have many emergencies like that? And the possibility that Thompson himself might be personally responsible made me more determined than ever to nail him.

Another thing that bothered me was the number of minorities working there. It would be nice to think, as Dan had suggested, that Thompson had hired them for altruistic reasons, but I had a hunch it was more along the lines of exploitation, though exactly how, I wasn't sure.

From the patients I had seen in the waiting room and from what Lydia had told me, it was clear that Thompson was discounting his dental work. But there didn't seem to be any reason for that, either. It was common knowledge that if a person was short on cash or insurance, or both, they could always go to the dental school clinic and have their work done at a reduced rate. The dentists were unlicensed students, true, but they were fully supervised by the licensed professors. What dentist would voluntarily lower his prices to compete with the dental school for patients?

Getting answers to all of these questions hinged on talking with one of Thompson's employees, but that posed some logistical problems that I wasn't sure could be solved. Monday through Friday at five I had to be with the kids in Medina, waiting for Janet, and with Thompson keeping bankers' hours I'd never get back to Seattle in time to catch any of them leaving work. The only other option was to go there during lunch hour, or in the morning coming to work, but if I didn't want it to interfere with my own work, I'd have to wait until Monday.

That left the night. I could always go around back and take a look in Thompson's Dumpster, maybe root through saliva-soaked gauze, discarded rubber dams, and used dental bibs for scraps of incriminating evidence, but for some reason that didn't sound very inviting. And knowing Thompson, I also had a feeling that all I'd find in the way of papers would be eighth-inch strips produced by a paper shredder. The next logical step was breaking and entering.

Logical? I shook my head. If going through Thompson's papers while he was in the other room had been idiotic, I didn't even want to know what breaking into his clinic at night would be. Illegal for one thing, and I was getting a little shaky just thinking about it. It didn't have to be like that, though. I didn't possess the knowledge or the initiative to jimmy a lock or break a window, but it wouldn't hurt to just go down there and take a walk around the building. There was nothing wrong with that, was there?

I turned off the stereo so I could concentrate. It was almost eleven o'clock. I'd be home in bed by midnight. I could just drive down and have a look, that's all. Maybe I'd take a peek in the Dumpster, but that was it. Hell, they couldn't arrest you just for looking.

I went into my bedroom, a little giddier than I ought to have been, and put on a pair of black jeans. I didn't have a black pullover, so I slipped on a black dress shirt over my Hawks sweatshirt. Likewise, I had no black sneakers, but I did have some black dress shoes with crepe soles. With those and a pair of black socks I was in business.

Once I was dressed, I went into the bathroom to take a look at myself in the mirror. Dark hair, dark clothes—except for my pink-white complexion, which was sure to stand out like neon, it was perfect. I removed my earring, lest the glint of metal give me away, and since there was a clock in the truck, I left my watch behind as well.

Out in the hall closet I found my flashlight. The batteries were weak, but I probably wouldn't need it anyway. Then I went back into the bedroom and took my Kodak 35mm auto-flash camera out of the bottom drawer in my nightstand. It wasn't exactly standard equipment for industrial espionage, but I remembered some pictures Janet had taken of me in my office right after she gave me the camera for Christmas; you could read the fine print on the diplomas behind me. And besides, I seriously doubted I would even find anything worth photographing. After all, I wasn't going inside.

Ten minutes later I was parked on the east side of the street, half a block down from the First Avenue Dental Clinic, hours, 9:00 a.m. to 5:00 p.m., Carl Thompson, D.D.S. and all around sleezebag, proprietor. The street was generously lit but from my vantage point, at least, it made the alley in back of the building that much darker.

I stepped out of the truck and, since I didn't have any pockets to put them in, I stuffed the camera and flashlight down the front of my shirt. It was cold out but I was comfortable in my extra clothes. A car drove past me, and I could see one or two pedestrians in each direction, but they were several blocks away. Other than that, I was alone. I took one last look around, and then set off down the street, *away* from the clinic.

I circled the block and came up Western Avenue until I hit Clay Street, which ran alongside the clinic, and ducked into the alley. I could make out the windows of Thompson's office clearly, the wall of the one-story building to the west at my back. Farther down there were more windows, the ones in the giant honeycombed operatory. And at the end of the building . . . a fire escape.

I walked the length of the alley without stopping. The pavement gently sloped down from both buildings toward the middle, metal drainage grates in the center. There were also three Dumpsters, two along the clinic side and one on the opposite wall. For the most part the alley was fairly clean; there was some litter and old newspapers but, more importantly, there were no people around. When I emerged at the other end of the block, I circled back along Western and reentered the alley on Clay.

I flipped up the lids of the clinic Dumpsters and all I saw were bundles of neatly tied plastic bags and some wet cardboard, but they stank all the same. I decided then that I wasn't in the mood for Dumpster diving and closed them back up. The windows, upon closer inspection, all appeared to be shut tight, with one very important exception. On the far side of the fire escape was a small square window that looked like it was cracked open a couple of inches. Not having remembered seeing one while I was in the waiting room, I had a good idea that it was a restroom.

By taking a running jump, I was barely able to reach the bottom rung of the sliding ladder on the fire escape. I hung onto it and had planned on letting my weight pull it down, but the screech in the alley as it began to descend was deafening. I released my grip immediately and walked as fast as I could out of the alley, scared shitless.

I took two turns around the block this time before I was calm enough to go back and try again. I knew better what to expect now. But before I went into the alley again, I walked back and forth between Western and First a few times to make sure there was no one approaching. When I was as certain as possible that I wouldn't be caught, I ran as fast as I could into the alley, jumped up, and pulled the screeching ladder down. I scrambled up to the first landing, hauled the ladder up after me, and then I laid down on the grated metal deck.

I remained there, motionless, for about ten minutes. I waited long enough to see a couple walk by along Clay Street, and even for someone to walk the length of the alley, peeking into the Dumpsters as he went. By then I was breathing regularly and I sat up to check the contents of my shirt. The camera and flashlight seemed okay, so I put them back and turned my attention to the window.

The fire escape went up another flight to the roof, but I was just where I needed to be. I stood up and walked to the end of the landing. There was an emergency exit door, but it had no knob on the outside so I ignored it. I was about three feet from the window, and it was definitely open. From the heady scent of Pine-Sol emanating from the three-inch crack, I knew I was right about its being a restroom, too. I leaned over as far as I could against the railing and was barely able to get the heel of my left hand under the window frame. Then I gave a mighty push. It didn't budge.

I was at an awkward angle anyway, so I wasn't really getting that much pressure on it, and even standing on my tiptoes didn't help. Now I was faced with yet another decision: head down the ladder and go home, or climb up and stand on the railing, bracing my hand on the window frame, my body stretched out in an inverted V, and pull up the window with my free hand.

Normally, a one-story fall would not have been that frightening a prospect—ten or twelve feet at most. This building, however, was anything but normal. With fifteen-foot ceilings inside, another couple of feet for the foundation, three more feet for the fire escape railing, and the fact that I would be above that by another three feet, I was looking at no less than a twenty-three foot drop to the tilted pavement below. I glanced at the window again, and then down at the alley.

The tiny ridges on the soles of my shoes were all I had in the way of traction. If it had been raining, forget it. The railing was squared off instead of round—another vote for going—but if I didn't make up my mind pretty soon, it wouldn't matter; eventually someone was going to walk into the alley and see me standing here deliberating. Fuck it, I thought, and went for it.

I put one foot up on the rail, reached out as far as I could and grabbed the window frame. Then I pulled myself up until both feet were on the thin strip of iron, and walked my hands out to the far edge of the window, my body leaning against the building for support. It wasn't until I was all the way in position that I realized I had made an egregious error in judgment. With both arms fully extended, and my center of gravity some twenty-odd feet above the alley, I wasn't sure I could get back onto the fire escape if the window didn't open.

Though the night air was cool, I now found myself sweating freely, and wishing I had not worn the sweatshirt. Hell, as long as I was wishing, I might as well have wished myself off this fire escape and back home in bed. Enough already, I thought; my arms were starting to get tired.

Tentatively, I released my right hand and found I could brace myself just using my left. Then I cupped my right hand under the window, and just about herniated myself trying to pull it up. Nothing. A drop of sweat trickled down and dripped off my nose. With another Herculean effort I pulled again, and this time the window gave.

There was a loud snap as the right side of the window moved up about a quarter of an inch. It almost caused me to lose my balance, but I managed to hang on. More sweat was running down from my forehead and stinging my eyes. I could feel the muscles in my left arm beginning to burn, and I knew I was in trouble. Since only one side of the window had moved, that meant it was now crooked in the frame. Old windows were a bitch to open even when they weren't sticky.

I had to stretch out even further now in order to pull up on the other side. The new angle on my left arm eased some of the muscle strain and I was thankful for that. I reached my free hand over as far as possible, and yanked twice for all I was worth. It wouldn't move. One more try and I was going to be spent. Using all my reserves I gave one last mighty heave, and I heard a satisfying snap accompanied by about a half-inch of movement.

Just knowing the window was free gave me newfound strength, but I still wasn't finished. I had to seesaw the window several times before there was enough room to climb through. When it was open a little over a foot, I grabbed the inside of the sill and let my legs slip off the railing. I hung there for a moment, relying mostly on my right arm for support, my left being about one second away from useless. Before my shoulders had a chance to tighten, I hoisted myself up, bicycling my legs in an attempt to gain some purchase against the brick wall with my toes, and pulled myself through.

I was in.

24

I must have stayed on the floor for about five minutes, and it wasn't just from exhaustion. I'd suddenly realized that the only way I was going to get out of there when I was done was by dropping from that window. When I finally hauled myself up from the floor I could see I was in a one-person restroom—a toilet and a sink, and not much else.

I pulled the flashlight out of my shirt and walked over to the window, putting my hand over the bulb to shield the beam. I turned it on, and nothing happened. I shook it a couple of times, but still nothing. It wasn't until I had taken my left hand off of the bulb that it flashed on and nearly blinded me.

With my hand cupped over the beam, it let out just enough light for me to verify what I had suspected: the window had been painted in place. The snaps I'd heard had been the paint giving way. That was probably why it had been left open—that and the obvious reason assaulting my nostrils.

I turned off the flashlight and walked over to the door; then I turned the knob slowly and pulled it open. There was nothing but a blank wall before me and I stuck my head out. To the right was the emergency door to the fire escape, and to the left a small hallway that I quietly stepped into. The sign on my door said MEN, and the next door down said WOMEN. I only had to walk a few more paces before I was at an archway to my right that opened onto the partitioned operatory. My eyes were immediately drawn to the door in the far corner of the room, Thompson's office. Then a nasty though hit me: what if it was locked? Damn.

A sudden noise froze me in my tracks, but as it continued I gradually began to place it: a refrigerator in the room at the end of the hall. In the quiet of the building it had sounded as loud as the ladder in the alley. I walked over and looked in the room. It was just an employee lounge—a sink, a fridge, a couple of tables and a dozen molded-plastic chairs.

When I turned my attention back to the operatory, I could see as I walked through that it wasn't as bad as I'd first imagined. There was a lot that was hidden below the partitions. Each station had its own sink, and a chest of drawers with basic dental supplies: impression trays, syringes, amalgam pellets, and sterile cotton—everything neat and tidy. There were no instruments in the cubicles, but I had a pretty good idea where they were.

Over against the outer wall of Thompson's office, three autoclaves stood atop a long bank of drawers. I pulled a few out to verify the contents: enough instruments for an army of dentists. It was nice to see a couple of hand-pieces among the other instruments being sterilized in the autoclaves. I wouldn't have thought it possible, especially with the threat of AIDS, but even today some dentists were resistant to heat sterilizing their hand-pieces, as if there were no possibility that they could pass on the virus with them. At least Thompson was doing something right.

I took a look inside one of the three x-ray rooms and everything seemed to be in order there, too. The drawers were filled with bitewings and periapical film. The last room, however, unexpectedly contained a panoramic radiograph, a machine that takes a single x-ray of your entire mouth, and I began to gain some respect for Dr. Thompson's little sweatshop.

Though it didn't look like much, it was a very modern and workable clinic.

They weren't exactly second thoughts I had at that point. There was still the fact that Lydia's dentist had probably done something wrong, and Thompson's secretiveness that made me think he had something to hide, but because I hadn't managed to uncover the evil health hazard I'd imagined the place to be, I did feel somehow less justified in being there. Still, I was there, so I might as well finish what I'd started.

There was plenty of illumination in the operatory because of the windows, but in the dark hallway that led to the waiting room I had to turn on the flashlight again. I wasn't worried, though. Without windows here, no one would be able to see it from the outside. Just off the entrance was a door I hadn't seen on my first visit. It said LAB on it and, when I looked inside, sure enough, it was a lab. I flashed the light around and could see another door inside labeled DARKROOM. Then I shut that door and walked down to the reception desk, purposely saving Thompson's office for last.

Inside I was surprised to find a huge bank of extra-wide file cabinets, again, just like the ones at my office. Two sets of files? I'd heard of two sets of books before, but what possible reason could Thompson have for two sets of dental records on every patient? The cabinets were unlocked and I raised the face of the F-G-H section, sliding it back up into the top. It only took a few seconds to find Lydia's file.

There was the root canal and a couple of fillings before that—she'd been here before. There was no doctor listed, and every one of the entries looked as if it had been written by a different hand. There was no mention of payments, either, and that's when it hit me: the files in Thompson's office were financial records, and it was only the treatment records that were kept out here.

I hadn't thought of it before, because all of my billing records are kept on computer; it takes up less space than a traditional paper filing system, and generates bills automatically. The same program takes care of my employees' wages, making automatic deductions, and Nona can easily access all the information at tax time. The software doesn't cost that much, and I figured if I could afford it, certainly Thompson could.

So why the extra set of files? What was on them that he couldn't trust to a computer? Maybe he *was* cooking the books, or maybe he *did* have an insurance scam going. There was only one way to find out, so I walked across the hall and twisted the knob. Locked.

The door was rock solid, hinges on the inside, and when I shined the flashlight on the doorknob I didn't have even the vaguest idea of how to go about picking it. Oh, well, there was only one door left, and then I was out of there. I turned off the flashlight and walked out to the operatory. The door there was locked, too, but it felt different. I tapped on it lightly. It was hollow. I was also pleased to find that the hinges were on the outside, though that would have to be a last resort. But it was the lock on the doorknob I was most interested in.

It had a nice, wide slot where the key went in, and looked to be the type commonly used for bathroom doors. This was one lock I knew how to pick. I was pretty sure that if I stuck a screwdriver in there and twisted, it would pop open. I ran over and looked in the drawers below the autoclaves. There were no screwdrivers, but I found a wide bevel that would probably do the job nicely. It did.

The door must have been added later when Thompson had found he was too far away from the action, probably after the first malpractice suit. With bevel in hand I walked straight over to the file cabinets. On closer inspection I found it would never work. The keyholes were the kind shaped like the Greek letter omega, and my flat bevel would be useless. So much for the financial records—on to the desk.

As I was walking over to Thompson's desk, I heard a strange noise and I stopped, straining to see if I could hear it again. Probably just the fridge shutting off, I thought, and continued. I knew there wasn't much in the other drawers, so I went straight for the one on the bottom right—the one that was locked.

I pointed the flashlight at the crack above the drawer and could see that the lock was a simple tongue in groove, a strip of metal that seated into the frame to prevent the drawer from opening. By taking out the drawer above and sticking the bevel in the crack and prying up, I was able to bend up the frame of the desk enough to get the bottom drawer out.

I couldn't keep the smile off my face as I turned the flashlight on the contents. There were three or four dozen slim files inside and I started pulling a few out at random. Each was an employee file, but as I began going through them more methodically, one particular feature became alarmingly clear: the people in these files were *all* dentists. I went through them again, making a more detailed inspection, and this time I noticed termination dates on most of them. Still, that seemed like an awful lot of dentists in just eight years.

The files on all of the other employees must have been in the cabinets against the wall. As far as the dentists' files were concerned, the eight in front were evidently the only ones still in Thompson's employ—eight, not six, as he had told me earlier today.

I picked one of those out for scrutinization. Cham Bui was a Vietnamese immigrant who had only been in the U.S. for five years. He was thirty-eight and married, and lived on Capitol Hill. He hadn't received his citizenship yet, but in the file was a copy of his green card and his work permit for Washington State. There was also a ratty photocopy of a Vietnamese certificate, which I took for his dental degree, but I couldn't find record of a U.S. degree, or state boards results.

That made me curious, so I began to go through the other current files, looking for the same thing. I found two with valid U.S. degrees, only one of which, a Dennis Keith, had a valid license to practice. But the license in Keith's file was from Arizona, not Washington. Son of a bitch. I couldn't believe it. That was why these people were willing to work for Thompson, and that must have been why Thompson's name was on all the prescription pads. None of his doctors had a license to practice in Washington State.

I felt for the camera in my shirt, and then I stopped myself. There was nothing to take pictures of. You couldn't very well photograph the absence of something. I pulled open the top right drawer, found a pen and a prescription pad, and began to write down the names of the dentists still working for Thompson. As I finished writing down each name, I put the file back into the drawer in order.

The slanted light cast by the flashlight as it lay on the carpet had dimmed considerably, and I knew it wouldn't last much longer. I was already thinking about the fall I was going to have to take out the window when two loud snicks from behind me almost made my heart stop. I whipped my head around and found myself looking down the barrels of two guns, each of them manned by one of Seattle's finest. Shit.

25

"Freeze!" yelled the cop on the left, as if I needed any more incentive.

The next few minutes were ones I'm not likely to forget for the rest of my life. One of the cops walked up to me and planted the barrel of his gun on my temple. The other came around behind me and pushed me facedown onto Thompson's plush carpet. My hands were unceremoniously wrenched up to the middle of my back, and handcuffs placed on my wrists. Only then did the one cop remove the gun from my head.

While on the floor I was carefully frisked, and my camera removed from my shirt. That and my flashlight were placed in a plastic bag as evidence. After holstering his piece, the cop took out a radio and informed his buddies that they were going to check around for any other would-be burglars. I could have saved them the trouble, but I doubted that they'd have appreciated my help.

Once the place had been secured, I was hoisted up off the floor, Mirandized, and guided down the steps and out the front door. Three police cars were parked at various angles to the curb, their lights silently rolling. The back door of the closest one was opened and a hand was placed over my head, lest I bump it on the doorframe as I was getting in. After that, it was just two quick minutes down to the Seattle City Jail, where I was ready for booking.

The only thing that saved me from a complete breakdown was knowing what I'd found. Not only would someone from another country have to take the state boards, but even someone who was fully licensed in another state would have to pass them before being able to practice in Washington. Apparently, Thompson was grabbing these people right off the boat, so to speak, and promising them work—not a bad offer for someone who doesn't speak the language and might require years of study to get a license in the States. I wondered how many of them knew they were breaking the law.

My only knowledge of the booking procedure was from the cop shows and movies I'd seen on TV, but it was clear that Hollywood had done its homework. The real thing resembled an assembly line more than anything else. First I was booked: the officers read the charge to the desk sergeant and I, in turn, gave him my full name and address, and surrendered my wallet and keys. Then I was fingerprinted, a quick and methodical procedure at the hands of the female officer who performed it. At last, I was taken over for a portrait sitting. It wasn't Olan Mills, but then it didn't have to be. Two shots, front and profile, with no choice of background.

One of the officers asked me if I wished to have my attorney present during questioning, and I said yes. He took me to a phone without my asking, but I did have to request a phone book because I couldn't remember the number. It was nearly midnight, and I hated to call this late, but I didn't have any choice.

The phone rang three times, each ring increasing the tension, and making me less sure of myself. "Hello?"

It was Rena. Christ, I hadn't thought of that. They probably received calls in the middle of the night all the time, but for some strange reason I didn't want her to know it was me.

"Hello?" she said again, and I knew I'd better say something.

"Lieutenant Lasky, please." I was just wondering if cops said please, when Dan came on the line.

"Lasky."

"Dan, this is Steve Raymond."

"Steve?"

"I'm sorry to wake you up like this, but I was arrested tonight. I'm downtown at the jail and I need to talk to you."

"Did you call Janet yet?"

"No. I need to talk with you first."

"Okay, I'll be there as soon as I can."

I hung up the phone, and then they threw me in jail. More accurately, they threw me in the drunk tank. There was a ragtag assortment of men in the cell with me, none of whom looked as though they'd paid any rent in a while. Most of them were sleeping on the floor; the rest kept to themselves, as did I. Twenty minutes later, an officer called my name and I was out.

I was taken to a room down the hall from the jail and Dan was waiting for me when I walked in. He was wearing his brown suit and didn't look very happy.

"I see you took that little talk we had to heart. What the hell was that all about?"

There was a table and a couple of chairs in the middle of the room, but I didn't sit down. "Listen, Dan. I found out what Thompson is up to."

Dan just stood there as I recounted my suspicions about the clinic, and added to that what I had discovered about the dentists who worked there. When I had finished, he was silent for a minute and then said, "Have you called Janet yet?"

"Janet? Didn't you hear what I just said? All the doctors at Thompson's clinic are practicing without licenses. He's breaking the law."

Now he smiled. But it was only briefly, then he was all business. "Steve, the only one who's broken any laws tonight is you. You're in trouble, and I think you'd better put in a call to Janet so she can get you out of it, at least temporarily."

"I was counting on you to do that. Can't you get me out of here? Don't you realize what I found?"

"You didn't find anything. The police found you. Christ, I don't know if I'd get you out of here even if I could. But that doesn't matter because I can't."

"Why not?"

"You watch too much TV. You broke the law, for starters, and right now Thompson's out there with his lawyer pressing charges."

"His lawyer?"

"Yeah. The desk sergeant had to get out another sheet because they couldn't get them all on one. He's going to slap you with everything in the book—breaking and entering, destruction of private property, libel, slander, endangering the public health—"

"Public health?"

"Yeah, he says you contaminated his operatory. Let's see, there was defamation of character, invasion of privacy, disturbing the peace—"

"How'd I do that?"

"He was sleeping and the phone call woke him up."

"I don't believe this shit."

"Go easy on the righteous indignation, Steve. This is nobody's fault but your own."

I walked around the table and pulled out a chair. This seemed like a good time to sit down. "What about charging Thompson? He broke the law, too."

"Maybe, but you don't have any proof—the lack of something isn't proof of anything. And even if you did, it wouldn't be any good to us if it was obtained illegally."

God damn it. The list was still back at Thompson's office. He'd probably already seen it and now he knew I was on to him.

If he hid his records and his dentists went to ground, there would be no way to dispute that he was the sole practitioner of his clinic. Even if they interviewed former patients, Thompson could say that the dentist who'd seen them wasn't working there anymore.

I was in big trouble.

"How'd the cops know I was there?"

Dan raised a hand and rubbed the back of his neck. "Silent alarm. A motion detector in the operatory set off a silent alarm at a private security company. If it doesn't go off in five minutes, they call the police."

"How'd they get in? I didn't even hear them."

"They had a key."

I gave Dan a questioning look, but he had no sympathy. "I tried to tell you about Thompson, but you wouldn't listen."

"So, what happens next—"

"Call Janet."

I had planned on Dan being able to get me out if anything went wrong. Calling Janet wasn't on my agenda. Though I had been dreading it, it turned out that she was very understanding, once she was over the initial shock.

"It's probably going to take me about an hour to get there," she said. "I'll have to call Kim so she can stay with the kids. I can't leave until she gets here."

"All right. I'll see you in an hour."

It was the longest hour of my life. I didn't want to sit down, and there was no real room to pace. I was forced to stand against the vertical bars of the cage and think, for thirty-six hundred ticks of the clock. Most of my other cellmates stunk of urine, vomit, body odor, and alcohol. In addition, I was beginning to feel the lateness of the hour. I had to be at work in less than five hours, four by the time Janet arrived. Another night without sleep—great.

"Is this the part of your life you can't tell me about?" Janet asked when I walked into the interrogation room again.

179

"Not exactly. What's going to happen?"

"Well, I already told the police you're not going to answer any questions. You're lucky we have a night court now, or you'd be spending the night in jail."

"I feel like I already have."

Night court was nothing like the TV show. Oh, I was processed right along with the hookers, the winos and the other petty thieves, but there was very little levity during the proceedings. I pleaded not guilty, and with my sterling record Janet was able to have me released on my own recognizance, over the strong objection of Thompson's lawyer. Thompson, who was nowhere to be seen, must have gone back home to bed.

Then Janet drove me back to my truck on First. "We'll talk tonight," she said. "Okay?"

"Okay. I'm really sorry—"

She put a finger over my lips and shook her head. "Tonight."

As I watched her drive away, I began to think about how much I owed Janet. She had been with me all through school, she was a wonderful wife, a caring mother, and an exquisite lover. Was it fair of me to hold a grudge this long? What was I afraid of? Did I really think it would happen again? To be honest with myself, I didn't. But I could never be sure, and that's what had kept me at a distance.

As much as I'd felt for Lydia, and as angry as I still was about her death, we hadn't had enough time together. I'd had feelings for her, but they seemed nebulous now, something intangible that I felt had all but slipped away. I had liked Lydia, but I would never know where that might have led. With Janet there could be no doubt. I loved her.

My breath hitched in my chest and I fumbled for my keys before I unlocked my truck and climbed inside. I had to sit there for a minute to regain my composure, and then I drove myself home.

26

By setting my alarm as close to seven as possible, still allowing myself time to get to the office, I managed to catch a little over three hours of sleep. I was dragging ass Wednesday morning, but I caught my second wind about nine-thirty and coasted the rest of the day. It's funny how differently the body reacts to sleep deprivation depending on the situation. After my night with Lydia, I'd been exhausted, but my little sortie at the clinic and run-in with the cops had left me with some energy to go on today.

Nona kept my mug full and I managed to burn through my patients, and the coffee, in record time. At eleven-thirty I was walking out to my truck and I had an idea. Instead of heading toward home and an eagerly awaited nap, I drove south into town. There wasn't time to talk to Janet first; I wanted to catch Thompson before he'd had a chance to simmer too long.

Oh, sure, I was going to turn him in to the authorities eventually. There was little doubt in my mind that one of Thompson's quacks had been responsible for Lydia's death, and I'd be right up there on the stand testifying against him if it came to that. But until then . . . I was going to eat crow. I was going to apologize, crawl on my knees, beg—whatever it took to get Thompson to drop the charges. If I could perform onstage at the Firehouse, I could certainly put on a show in his office.

I left my truck parked on Western, and walked past the infamous alley to the front of the clinic. After a couple of deep breaths, I bounded up the stairs and headed right for the reception desk. The receptionist looked at me as if I'd just offered to extract her wisdom teeth, sans anesthetic.

"Hi," I said, flashing her my best Colgate smile. "I'm Doctor—"

"I know who you are. The doctor don't want to see you. I'm supposed to tell you to go away."

About this time the lone Caucasian dentist, Dennis Keith, walked in behind the reception desk and began to hunt for a file.

"Look, I just need to talk to him for a couple of minutes. We had a little misunderstanding last night that I wanted to clear up."

Arms crossed beneath her substantial bosom, she moved her head in a slow wag the entire time I was talking. "Doctor says no."

There were two other women behind the desk, both Asian, and they were looking back and forth between me and the receptionist with rapt fascination.

"I know that's what he told you, but things have changed. Believe me, he'll want to see me when he finds out what I have to say. It'll only take a minute."

Now I had Keith's full attention, too. Great.

"Doctor says no," she repeated.

"Yes, I *realize* that, but I have something important to tell him. I know he'll want to see me—"

Her head went down and she began to rearrange the files on her desk. "Mr. McInnis," she said over my shoulder, and walked out to the door. A little gray-haired man shuffled past me and into the land of dentistry-without-a-license.

I stood at the reception window being ignored for a few seconds more, and said, "Fine. I'll just show myself in."

I walked over and opened the door, but before I could reach Thompson's office, Keith stepped in front of me. Now, I'd seen him the first time I'd come to the clinic, and I hadn't paid him more than cursory attention. Close up like this, however, I could see that he was another four inches taller than I was, and had a good fifty pounds on me, all of it appearing to be muscle.

He bent down so close that our noses were almost touching, and in a soft but intense voice that smelled of Listerine he said, "I don't think the doctor wants to see you right now, so why don't you get the fuck out of here?"

I thought about telling him to take his Arizona license and stuff it up his ass, but Janet would probably refuse to defend me after that, even if I was her husband. Oh, well. So much for my hot idea. I didn't want to give the impression that I was hightailing it out of there, so I took my own sweet time. The result was the same, though. I left.

*　　*　　*

That encounter had drained the last of my reserves, and when I walked into my apartment the only thing I wanted to do was fall into bed and take a nap right there. Instead, I forced myself to change my clothes and drive over to Medina. I didn't want to fight the traffic from Seattle to pick up the kids after just waking up.

I was on the way out when the blinking light on my answering machine caught my attention. The message was from Ted Aykroyd, and since he'd left his number I gave him a call.

"Ted? This is Steve. I just got your message."

"Hey, Steve, thanks for calling back. I wanted to let you know that I've got a bass player and a drummer coming over tonight. Are you still interested in playing?"

"I'm afraid I can't, Ted, as much as I'd like to. It's just bad timing right now."

"No sweat. Thought I'd ask anyway. Well, you take it easy, and let me know if you change your mind."

"Okay, I will." I was about to hang up when a thought struck me. "Listen, Ted, before you go, could I ask you something?"

"What?"

"This is kind of a strange question, but I was wondering if you'd ever been to the First Avenue Dental Clinic."

Ted was silent for a moment and then said, "That is a weird question. Why do you want to know?"

"I need some dental work done and I'm asking around for recommendations, but I can't seem to find anyone who's ever been there."

"Stay away from that place—that's my recommendation."

"Why?"

"My wife, back before the divorce, spent three hours in the chair getting her lower wisdom teeth pulled."

"Were they impacted?"

"Nope. She said the guy who worked on her was breaking off roots and had to drill them out, or something like that. I'm not sure what all happened, but I know it was a mess. She looked like a chipmunk for a week, and it hurt like hell for months. The only reason I took here there was that it was so cheap."

"What did they charge you?"

"Fifty bucks."

"That's all?"

"Yeah, and they even knocked off ten bucks because it took so long. The price might sound good, but believe me, it ain't worth it."

"Did they charge your insurance?"

Ted laughed. "You're joking, right?"

"Sorry."

"I have insurance now, through my job, but back then I was on a strictly cash basis. I must have called twenty places, and since this place on First Ave. was only charging half the going rate, that was all it took to convince me. I'd never go back there again, though, not after what happened to my wife. Like I said before, take my advice and find another dentist."

"Will do. Thanks, Ted."

"Don't mention it."

After I'd hung up, another piece of the puzzle fell into place. Cash payments well below the going rate—was that the reason Thompson had his billing files locked up? It was the most likely explanation, especially if he was taking money under the table, and it certainly fit with what Lydia had told me. Now that I knew Thompson's dentists were unlicensed, Ted's story didn't surprise me at all.

To keep myself awake on the trip over to the Eastside, I forced myself to put in order the knowledge I had about Thompson, and how Lydia fit in. I tried to think back to the last night I'd seen her. She hadn't even mentioned to me that she'd had a root canal, and I'd been so worried about her reaction to my being married that I wasn't sure I'd given her the chance. I knew she hadn't finished her dinner that night, but for the life of me, I couldn't remember how much she'd actually eaten. After having a root canal, it couldn't have been very much, but my attention had been focused on the music instead of her.

Then there was the Demerol, which made matters even more complicated. For Thompson to prescribe something that powerful, Lydia would have to have been in dire straits, but when I saw her, she had seemed perfectly fine. There were only five of the original thirty 100mg tablets left in the bottle I found on her nightstand. Under that kind of heavy sedation it was no wonder she hadn't mentioned anything about pain all week.

Dale said that her face had been swollen, but I hadn't noticed anything of the sort. Had I missed it? Had it already started Tuesday morning? She had complications late on Tuesday that brought her home, and when she took her pain pills, she obviously felt well enough to ignore my urgings to see a doctor. And, ultimately, that's what had allowed the infection to spread throughout her entire body and eventually kill her.

The only theory that explained everything to my satisfaction was that the dentist had made a mistake, either leaving part of the infected pulp in her tooth, or operating on the wrong tooth. And then it hit me: the tooth. God, how could I have been so stupid? Dan said he needed proof and all the time it had been right there in Lydia's mouth.

I would need to call Dale as soon as I reached the house, and ask him to pull Lydia's tooth. Once we had the proof of malpractice it would be a simple thing to present it to the state board and ask them to investigate Thompson and his dentists. If I was lucky, Thompson might even do some prison time. In any case, his license would be revoked. I wasn't sure what would happen to the others, but when I found out which dentist had killed Lydia I was going to do everything in my power to make sure he paid. Everything short of killing him myself.

27

Seeing the Porsche as I pulled up to the house reminded me that with all that had gone on during the past few weeks, I hadn't had it out on the road in a while. Maybe this weekend, if I had time. Once inside, I gave Dale a call. He was out so I left a message with one of the assistants for him to call me back as soon as possible. After that there was nothing left to do but sleep. I decided to hell with the couch and crashed up in the bedroom after setting the alarm. It was only a couple of hours, but it went a long way toward reviving me.

Janet was late coming home, which was fine by me. It gave me another hour to work on my story. If she was going to defend me I was going to have to mention Lydia at some point—there was no way to get around that—but I would simply say that she had been a patient of mine. Her previous dentist hadn't done a very good job and I'd wanted to talk to him about her treatment. Then, after I'd been given the bum's rush by Thompson, I'd had Nona call Lydia back to verify another appointment, and that was when I learned she was dead. It was simple.

Until Janet came home.

"Sorry I'm late," she said, and kissed me lightly on the lips as I held the door for her. "You'll have to stay for dinner. We can talk afterward."

As I watched her walk toward the stairs without a look

back, I felt the familiar pull of sexual attraction that had always existed between us. But I wasn't fighting it this time, and it made me smile. This was the Janet I'd known and loved, self-assured, confident, and in control.

Though neither of us had been in a position of emotional dominance in our relationship, I realized that during the past year I'd had her at an unfair disadvantage. Instead of being her own person, the woman I loved, she was the woman who was trying to get me back. She was trying to be alluring, trying to make things comfortable for me at home, trying to be a good wife and mother—things she never had to work at before.

At best it was an artificial situation—at worst it was outright dishonesty. And that's when it dawned on me: it was all my fault. I had forced Janet to be dishonest for the past year. She was afraid to lose me and, because I could sense her fear, I didn't want to go back. It wasn't too surprising that we weren't able to work on regaining any kind of trust.

During the past couple of days I'd seen Janet in a new light or, more exactly, in an old light. Lydia had just been Lydia, herself, and *that's* what had attracted me to her. Now that Janet was back to her old self, I could see that's what had been missing all along. Now my leaving seemed idiotic. We had always worked out our problems in the past with total honesty and there was no reason we couldn't have done it this time, too. I felt like a fool.

When Janet came back downstairs she was dressed in jeans and a flannel shirt, and it took all the restraint I could muster not to attack her right there in the kitchen. The four of us cooked spaghetti together and it made me incredibly homesick at the thought of having to go back to Seattle. After dinner Janet chased the kids upstairs to their rooms, I put on a pot of coffee, and we settled down in the family room to talk business.

"I never had a chance to thank you for last night," I said, "for bailing me out."

"That's what I'm here for." She took a sip of coffee and then picked up a yellow legal pad and a pen. "I'm going to need to know everything about why you were in that clinic last night."

I nodded. "I know."

"If you tell me everything, I'll be in a better position to work with Thompson's lawyer and we might be able to reach a settlement, get him to drop the charges."

I had thought we were going to work on my defense. I couldn't believe what I was hearing. "You mean pay him off?"

"Whatever you want to call it, but there's really no other way. You were caught in the clinic illegally, Steve. You're guilty. The only sure way to win the case is not to try the case."

I had been all set to launch into my prepared statement, but the look in her eyes changed my mind. If I was really serious about wanting her back, the one thing I couldn't afford was another lie. And yet the truth threatened to destroy any chance we had of resuming our marriage. In the end, I didn't really have a choice. There was only one way it could work.

"All right," I said, "but there's something I need to tell you first, before we get into this, and I'd like to do it all at once. Could you not say anything until I'm through with the whole story, including the break-in last night?"

Janet had been leaning sideways against the couch with her arm across the back, and now she sat up straight. We were about a foot away from each other, our knees almost touching. I picked up my coffee mug to give my hands something to do and started in.

"I don't know how far you've gone with the divorce papers yet, but I've reconsidered. I don't want a divorce anymore."

Her eyebrows furrowed and her mouth dropped open

slightly. When I saw that she was about to respond, I shook my head. "Please. You need to hear everything.

"We've always been honest with each other in the past, and I made a big mistake by leaving you without talking things over first. I should have believed you when you said it would never happen again. I was stupid. I should have trusted you and I didn't. That was my fault, and I'm sorry.

"What it comes down to is that I want my family back. But more importantly, I want you back. I love you, Janet. And though I don't expect you to understand it, I think that in some screwed-up way, it's only because of what's happened in the last few weeks that I finally realize what I've been doing, why I've been lying to you. I'm tired of living alone, and I want to come back, if you'll have me."

Though she was trying for my sake to repress it, her face was absolutely radiant. I wished to God I could have stopped right there. But it was too late for that. Things had gone too far, and knowing that tonight might be the last time I ever saw her like this didn't make it any easier.

"I just wanted you to know that before I tell you the rest." I hesitated, like a convict reaching the end of the gangplank. Then I stepped off. "About two weeks about on a Sunday afternoon, I got a call at the apartment from a guy named Bobby Stutz. He has a band and he wanted me to play that night at the Ballard Firehouse . . ."

By the time I arrived at Monday night, something like rage was flickering in Janet's eyes, but that softened as I explained about the following week. When I told her of Lydia's death, the anger changed to confusion. Once I was into my suspicions about Thompson's office she began writing notes on her legal pad. Her face was expressionless now; she was all business.

Afterward we were both silent. My coffee was cold. I hadn't taken a sip the entire time, so I set the cup back down. Janet tossed her legal pad on the table and leaned back. Her jaw was clenched and she wouldn't meet my eyes. I didn't know what else to say and just sat there dumbly. I wasn't going to be the first to speak.

After what seemed like an eternity of sitting in silence, Janet finally stood up. She walked around the other side of the coffee table and picked up her pad. Her head was shaking as she grimly chuckled. Then she looked me in the eye and said, "Get yourself another lawyer."

She was heading out of the room and I had to run to get in front and stop her. "Wait. Janet, please. I need your help on this."

"Tough shit."

"Come on, Janet. Don't do this to me now."

"Why not? You sure as hell did it to me, for a solid fucking year, or have you forgotten already?"

She made another move to leave and I grabbed her arms. "Get your fucking hands off me!" she yelled, and shrugged out of my grasp. She didn't leave the room, though.

"Look, all I'm asking for is that you help me get out of this trial, and that's all. I don't want to have to get another lawyer."

She took a step back and rubbed her forehead, her other arm across her chest. She wasn't crying, nor did she look likely to. Then she locked eyes with me again. "You son of a bitch. You stood right there in the kitchen and made me feel like shit for asking to go on a date. And the whole time you were fucking someone else."

"She'd died the day before."

"Oh, what do you want me to say, I'm sorry you lost your girlfriend?"

"No." I backed off and paced around a few steps. "Jesus, I'm trying to say I'm sorry about what happened. I'm sorry about everything. But that doesn't change the fact that I need you right now, more than I ever have before. Maybe I don't deserve it—hell, I probably don't—but I'm asking for it anyway. If you still love me . . . if you ever loved me, please help me."

We were over near the table and Janet pulled out a chair and sat down. I remained standing. There was another long stretch of silence before she said, "You never told me exactly why you wanted to come back to me."

I wasn't sure what to say to that, so I took a deep breath and walked over to the table. "Because I love you."

"So you said."

I was going to snap back when I realized what she was really asking. "You're different now, Janet, and I was too stupid to see what was going on before. After I left, you were tying so hard to get me back that you'd lost your . . . I don't know, your vitality. The person I'd been with the last ten years wasn't there anymore, and I realize now that it was my fault. Instead of facing things, I decided to run away. Well, I'm not running away anymore. I want to be with you, and I want to stay married to you, and I'll do whatever it takes."

She let out a sarcastic grunt and then sat there thinking. She looked up at me a couple of times, and a few minutes later she stood. The vaguest of smiles played at the corners of her mouth, and there was suddenly something dangerous in her luminescent blue eyes.

"All right," she finally said, and nodded to herself. "I'll represent you on one condition."

"What's that?"

"You'll see in a minute. I'll be right back."

She walked by me toward the stairs, and then I heard her go up. I sat down at the table, not caring what it was that she wanted me to do, because I knew I'd do whatever she asked. As long as she was still representing me, everything would eventually work out. I was sure of it.

Janet came back downstairs in minute later with her briefcase. She set it on the table, snapped open the locks and opened it up. Then she went through it, pulled out a legal file, and slapped it down in front of me. "I'll just need your signature on these."

I looked in disbelief as I turned the cover to see my own divorce papers. "Didn't you hear what I said? I don't want a divorce."

"I heard everything you said, Steve, and you're right. I have been walking on eggshells for the past year, and it's about time I stopped. If you want my help, you're going to have to sign those papers."

"And what if I don't?"

"Then you really will need another lawyer. Not only for your little escapade last night, but for the divorce, because I'll take you to court."

This was definitely not the way I had envisioned things going. "So the only way you'll defend me is if I give you a divorce?"

"I didn't say that. I only want you to sign the papers."

"Why?"

"Because then *I* get to decide. I still don't know how I feel about all of this shit, but once these are filed, I'll have three months to think it over before I have to set a court date."

"I don't understand why you want me to sign these then. If you want more time I'll give you all you need."

"That's not good enough, Steve. These are drawn up for a no-fault divorce, so you won't even have to be there. Once you've signed them I can appear in court any time after the three-month waiting period and have them finalized on my own. You'll have nothing whatsoever to say about it."

"God, is that really the way you want it?"

"You've had me on edge for an entire year, wondering what you were going to do. I was a wreck. Now it's my turn. You should feel lucky—I'm only asking for three months."

I flipped through the sheaf of papers and said, "What's the agreement?"

"You get the house, I get the kids. Our money's been separate the last year so there's no problem with that, and you sure as hell don't need to pay me alimony."

We both managed a smile at that, and though it scared me, I figured it was the least I deserved. "If that's what you want, I guess I'm in no position to argue. Where do I sign?"

"At my office tomorrow afternoon," she said, and scooped up the file from out of my hands. When I looked up at her the radiance was back. "I want them to be notarized."

28

I don't know what time it was when I opened my eyes that night; I'm just damn glad that I did.

When I came home from Medina Wednesday evening, it was about eight-thirty. I was beat, so I went right to bed. It could have been the combination of the nap I'd had that afternoon and my early bedtime, or maybe I'd actually heard something, but whatever the reason, I woke up in the middle of the night and saw a man standing over my bed.

There are only two things I remember about him from the instant that I actually saw him. One, he was wearing a black ski mask, and the only part of his face that was visible was his eyes. And two, he was holding a syringe, poised above me in a pencil grip, and was about to stick it into me.

Within the single second during which these observations took place, my adrenals came to the rescue and dumped about a gallon of adrenaline into my bloodstream. My covers were loose—I've always hated feeling tucked in at night—and I brought my legs up almost instinctively and kicked out at the intruder's chest.

Because of my angle to him, it was only a glancing blow, but he hadn't been expecting it and I was able to spin him away toward the head of the bed. I was out of the covers in the same motion and heading out of the bedroom. My feet, however, were still tangled in the sheets, and I went down.

I was kicking and scrambling, trying to get the covers off my feet and get out of the room at the same time. To put it mildly, I was in a panic. By the time I had finally managed to extricate myself from the bedspread I was almost in the hall, and I reached up for the doorknob. Once I was on my feet, I slammed the door shut and had about two seconds to decide my fate.

There I was in the hallway, gripping the doorknob for dear life, and in addition to hyperventilating and sweating, I was standing there stark naked. I would have preferred to be dressed but, since I always sleep in the nude, my first option, running down the hallway and shouting to the neighbors, was out. I could try for the phone in the kitchen and dial 911, but if my guest had a gun I was dead. So I did the only sensible thing I could think of and locked myself in the bathroom.

It probably wasn't the smartest decision under the circumstances. After all, what's a little immodesty in a matter of life and death? But let me just say this: when you wake up with a killer—which is what I assumed he was—hunched over your bed, that's just not how your mind works. When you come from a society which is still struggling with the legacy of Puritanism and Victorian prudishness, and the horrors of the naked body jump out of your subconscious and start running the show, you head for the only place people are allowed to be naked: the bathroom.

Now, if he did have a gun he could have easily shot through the bathroom door but, as I said, I didn't have a lot of time to think things through. I had the door locked—and from my venture into Thompson's office I knew just how effective that would be—and my body braced against it. My heart was galloping in my chest and I was breathing so heavily that I couldn't hear anything from out in the hall.

Jesus, I thought, if this was one of Thompson's goons, I was in big trouble. Was there a Mafia in Seattle? If so,

Thompson would certainly be my choice for the Don. I kept waiting for someone to kick the door down, not sure how well my 180 pounds would be able to resist. But nothing happened. The muscles in my legs were taut, the bottoms of my feet precariously gripping the vinyl surface of the bathroom floor, and my finger was firmly depressing the button on the doorknob. But still, nothing happened.

It must have been two minutes—although it seemed longer—before I reached for the light switch. I stopped myself instantly. If he didn't already know where I was, the light under the door would tip him off. What was he doing out there, or had he left by now? Was he trying to kill me, or just scare me? He'd certainly succeeded in the latter.

It was a long time afterward, maybe an hour, maybe longer, before I slithered down to the floor. The sink was to my right, and I opened the cabinet underneath so that I could brace my foot against the vanity, keeping my back against the door. Still I waited, and nothing happened. I was sure he had to be gone by then, but there was no way I could really be sure. There was no way to know.

He could be waiting for me, standing to one side of the door so that when I poked my head out to look he could stick me in the neck with his syringe of potassium cyanide, and that would be it. I'd be the late Steve Raymond. So I sat and waited. I could sit there as long as he could. By then my eyes had adjusted to the dark. I was in the half-bath between the bedrooms, and thankful I hadn't run into the bathroom adjoining my bedroom. At least this one had a window.

Not that it would do me much good three floors up. I could yell out of it, but trying to be heard over the traffic on Greenwood Avenue wouldn't be much better than jumping out. Which I couldn't do anyway, because the thing was only six inches tall and two feet wide. At one point, though, I did have to get up and use the toilet—but I went right back to my post.

It seemed like days later, and I think I'd nodded off a couple of times, before I heard it. The sound was muffled, but it was there: my alarm. It was five-thirty, not quite daylight, but I could see the beginnings of light through the window. The guy couldn't possibly still be in my apartment. Now I did turn on the light. It blinded me at first, but my eyes adjusted quickly. Then, quietly, I eased the door open. No one jumped me, so I took a few tentative steps out into the hall. Nothing.

Next I walked toward the kitchen. The front door was wide open, and I left it that way. I went over every inch of the apartment, opened every closet, looked in every cupboard, still buck naked, until I was sure he wasn't there. Only then did I shut the front door and lock it. As soon as I had my robe on I went to the telephone in the kitchen and made a call.

"Jesus, Steve, why do you always have to call *me*?"

"You're the only cop I know."

"How'd I ever get so lucky?" Dan said with a sigh.

"So, are you going to help me, or not?"

"Help you? Right now I'm going to get into my car, cuss all the way across the West Seattle Freeway, and go to work."

"Don't you think someone should investigate this?"

"Steve, that's not even my precinct. There's not a damn thing I can do. From what you've told me, I don't think there's much anybody can do. Keep your door locked next time."

"My door was locked! Didn't you year anything I said? The guy broke into my apartment in the middle of the night. He tried to kill me."

"But he didn't. So consider yourself lucky, and be prepared next time."

"How do I do that? Keep a sawed-off shotgun under my pillow?"

"If that's what it takes, then yeah. Look, Steve, if you want to call the police up there, fine. You can get them to come in and take a look around, but I don't think they're going to find anything."

"You're damn right. This guy was a pro. He's working for Thompson and the son of a bitch hired him to kill me."

I must have made Dan's morning with that one because he had to put the phone down he was laughing so hard. There wasn't much left to say after that, and when the conversation was over I called the Greenwood Precinct. The dispatcher said she would send a car out here right away.

I ran to the bathroom, took the world's fastest shower, and was almost dressed when the cops arrived. They took a statement from me, dusted for prints on the front door and the inside of my bedroom door, didn't find any, and as they left said to keep in touch. Wow, I felt safer already.

As I drove to work the only thing I could think of that would have precipitated an attack like this was my visit to Thompson's office yesterday. There was no way it could have been random violence. It had to be Thompson. Including dental school, I'd been in the dentistry business for eight years. There was no way to mistake the syringe the guy in my room had been holding.

It wasn't the short kind made of plastic that people associate with taking blood or shooting up. This one was made of stainless steel and was about six inches long. It had an open breech, designed to accept a cartridge containing a specific amount of a drug, and could be prepared by an assistant while you had your hands in the patient's mouth.

It was a Novocaine syringe.

29

"Did you call the police?" Janet was pacing the floor behind her desk.

"I called Dan, but he said he couldn't do anything. Then I called the cops and they came in and dusted for fingerprints, but the guy hadn't left any."

The view from the window in Janet's office was nothing short of spectacular. I could see all of downtown Bellevue, and across Lake Washington to the skyline of Seattle in the distance. Though she was only an associate, Janet had been number two in her law school class and highly recruited. There was little doubt in my mind that she would eventually make partner.

"Well, I hate to be the bearer of more bad news," she said, still pacing. "But listen to this. I called Thompson's lawyer as soon as I came in this morning. I told him what we had, what you'd found last night, and he didn't care. He said it wasn't true."

"No way."

"Just wait, it gets worse. After much haranguing and arm-twisting, I was finally able to get a couple of investigators from the state board to come with me over to Thompson's office. We met there shortly before noon today—he didn't eve have his lawyer with him—and he proceeded to produce eight valid Washington State licenses for the dentists who were there."

"That's impossible! Did they I.D. all of them?"

Janet nodded. "And when the investigators called in the licenses for verification, and they checked out, that was it."

"I don't believe it."

"The two men from the state board were very embarrassed and apologetic with Thompson, and very pissed off at me."

This was not good news. The one piece of leverage I'd had against Thompson was gone. "Remember I told you I also found valid licenses for people who weren't working for him anymore?"

"Yeah."

"Maybe he had phony I.D.'s made up ahead of time to match them. I don't think this is the first time he's been through this."

"Maybe, but it would take a long time to prove it, even if it was true."

I scratched my head. "What are we going to do now?"

"We're all right. The court date's not for a couple of weeks yet. There's still time to dig up something on him."

"The malpractice suits?"

Janet was already nodding. "I went down to the courthouse after I finished at Thompson's office. Both of the cases were settled out of court, the day before the trials were set to start."

"Shit."

"No," she said. "That's a good thing. I'd be willing to bet he won't go to trial with us either. He's just going to take it down to the wire, sweat us out, so that when the offer comes we'll take it."

That perked me up. "And we will."

"Exactly."

Janet pulled out her chair and sat down. Our eyes met in mutual admiration. I think if I'd had any other lawyer but her, I would have been scared to death. As it was, I knew that Janet would do anything and everything possible in my defense.

"That's why this whole attack at your apartment doesn't make sense," she said. "Thompson must figure he's got us over a barrel—why try to kill you?"

"I can't be positive that's what it was. But it sure seemed that way."

Janet was frowning, not looking directly at me, and muttered, "Doesn't make sense." Then she shook it off and looked back up.

"Are you doing all right?" I asked.

"Considering that roller coaster ride you took me on last night, I think I'm doing pretty well."

"That's good."

"Why couldn't you have had your revelation a month ago?"

"I wish I had, believe me."

"Ah, well. Anyway, that reminds me." She pulled out one of the drawers in her desk and brought out a file. "Now, for the real reason you're here."

"All right," I said, trying to keep the reluctance out of my voice. "Let me have 'em."

She took out the papers that needed signing, pushed them across her desk, and handed me a pen. "Don't we need the notary public in here?" I asked.

"Technically."

"What does that mean?"

"We almost never have papers that are signed in the office actually witnessed. I'll give it to the notary later. You'll need to sign the petition, and I'll file that tomorrow. The final papers and joinder have both been postdated. If I decide to go through with the divorce after the three-month waiting period, I'll have them notarized then, and present them in court."

"Is that legal?" I asked, only half serious.

"It's the way were going to do it."

I picked up the pen and made one last plea. "You know I don't want to do this."

"Your objection has been noted for the record, Dr. Raymond. Now please sign."

I laughed. "You're a hard woman, Janet."

She grinned. "You wouldn't want it any other way."

I couldn't argue with that, and I signed. When I was finished Janet looked them over, and then I stood up to leave.

"There's one more thing before you go," she said.

"Yeah?"

"I want you to stay at the house tonight."

"Janet—"

"I don't want any argument. Unless you're planning on installing a security system at your apartment this afternoon, that place isn't safe. I don't know what that guy was trying to do, but he's not going to get another chance."

"You're sure?"

"I'm telling you, aren't I?"

"I guess I would feel safer at the house."

"Good. Do you have time to get your clothes and still make it back to the school? I can pick up the kids if you don't."

"No, that's okay. I'm sure I can make it."

Janet stood and came around to walk me out. We were silent going down the hall, and in spite of all that had happened, I felt good about having told her everything. She went all the way out to the elevators with me and we hugged before I stepped on.

"See you tonight," she said, and gave me a kiss just before the doors closed.

I took the 520 Bridge to Seattle, knowing that if I didn't hit any traffic on the way back I'd be in Medina with plenty of time before school let out.

The hallway in my apartment building seemed ominous as I walked down to my unit, and as I reached out my keys to unlock the door, my hand began to shake. Get a grip, I told myself. This time I tried the knob first. It was still locked. I couldn't believe I was scared to go into my own apartment, but that's how I felt. It was a relief to know I would be staying with Janet and the kids tonight.

After I let myself in, I took a quick look around, and everything appeared to be in order. I changed out of my suit and into some jeans and a plaid dress shirt. Then I picked out a suit for work the next day and threw some underwear, socks, and dress shoes into a small leather travel bag. In the bathroom I finished loading the bag with everything else I would need and then headed out the door.

*　　*　　*

Kids are funny sometimes. Most of the time, it seems, they take you for granted, expecting you to take care of them, and love them, always be around to smooth out the rough edges of life. All of which I do gladly. But every once in a while they surprise you. When I told the kids I'd be staying at the house, they both squealed with delight. Then Cathie climbed up on her knees in the cab of the truck and kissed me.

"I love you, Daddy."

I wrapped her up in my arms and hugged her tight. "I love you, too, sweetie."

Timmy, though just as excited, was a bit more pragmatic. "Does that mean you can make us breakfast in the morning?"

"It sure does," I said. This was followed by more squeals, and then I pulled out of the school parking lot and drove us home.

That night after dinner, I broached the subject of where I was going to sleep. "I can stay down here on the couch if you want."

"There's no reason that you shouldn't sleep with me."

"You're sure it's not too soon?"

"Not for sleeping."

Janet let me read to the kids and tuck them in, and when I came back into the bedroom she was already in bed reading. That

205

sounded like a good idea, but since I'd left *The Rainmaker* at the apartment, I had to go out into our small library and find something else. I eventually chose a book of short stories by Hemingway, and then crawled under the covers on my side of the bed.

An hour later Janet put her book down and turned off the lamp on her nightstand. I wasn't sure what to think when she scooted over next to me and rested her head in the crook of my arm. While I buried my face in her hair and took a deep breath, she ran her hand lightly over my chest and said, "You don't mind, do you?"

"Oh, I think I'll manage."

"I'm so mad at you, Steve."

"I know. I'm sorry."

She moved herself closer to me and I could feel her naked breasts against my skin, and her leg as she moved it up over my own. We'd been together long enough that I knew she wasn't trying to arouse me.

"I've missed you," she said softly. "I've missed the times like this."

"Me, too." I rubbed my cheek against her forehead and she turned and looked up at me. Then we kissed.

I moved out from under her and rolled her on her back. Then we hugged and kissed for a long time. Everything was slow and easy, thoughtful and appreciative. I was excited and scared at the same time. I could feel her heart beating against my chest as we were on the verge of making love.

I still wasn't sure if it was what she wanted and I looked closely at her beautiful face. Tears were rolling out of her eyes and down across her temples. "I will if you want to," she said. "But I don't think I'm ready."

I kissed her softly and wiped away the tears. Then I shook my head. "I want us both to be ready."

We fell asleep a few minutes later, still wrapped in each other's arms.

30

I did make breakfast on Friday morning, but it wasn't quite the family experience it was on the weekends. I wound up making French toast at six in the morning, while everyone else was in bed. I put the plate of toast in the oven on low, and the bottle of syrup on the stove in a pan of warm water, and left for work at six-thirty, with the knowledge that no one would be up for another half-hour.

I didn't even attempt to cross the lake on the traffic-choked four lanes of the Interstate 520 Bridge, opting instead for the seven roomy lanes of I-90. Traffic was a little sluggish through town, but I made it to work on time. Friday is a light day anyway, with Julie using one of the operatories all day for her hygienic work, so I only need one assistant. Susan and Laurie alternate, and I had Laurie today.

My nine o'clock patient had canceled out on me and I was in my office looking through the day's mail when Janet walked in.

I stood up immediately. "What's going on?"

"Don't worry. Everything's okay. I had to come down to the courthouse to file some motions, so I thought I'd just come and talk to you in person." She shut the door behind her and sat down. "Thanks for breakfast."

"I promised Timmy." I walked around and leaned against the front of my desk facing Janet. "So, what's all this about?"

"The Nation's case."

With everything that had happened since Lydia's death, I'd completely forgotten about the late Rick Nations and his lovely widow Pamela.

"Yeah?"

Janet looked up at me with amusement on her face and said, "It looks like you were right."

"About what?"

"Pamela Nations."

I didn't say anything, but nodded for her to continue.

"When I walked into my office this morning, two police detectives were waiting for me. They had the chemist's report on Rick Nations' autopsy."

I smiled. "What did he overdose on?"

Janet gave me a funny look. "No, you don't understand. The police were there to find out where Pamela is."

Now it was my turn to be confused, but Janet continued. "I thought I was taking the case in order to determine the circumstances surrounding Rick's death, but I was operating under the false assumption that Pamela was a grieving widow."

That caught my attention. "Are you saying she's not?"

"The chemist's report showed he was poisoned."

"You're kidding. What was it?"

Janet pulled a slip of paper out of her jacket and handed it to me. It had the word "ricin" printed on it. While Janet continued, I took down the Merck Index from my shelves to check it out. "The detectives are pretty sure that she killed her husband."

"That's incredible. Do you know where she is?"

"She's disappeared. The detectives wanted to know if I had any information on her whereabouts."

"How did they know she was your client?"

"I was on the list for the lab results on the autopsy."

"Right. My God, I figured her for a gold digger, but not

208

a murderer. What was the motive? She told me her husband didn't have any insurance."

"That's what she told me, too, but it turns out he did have a ten thousand dollar policy paid by Lacroix Chemicals."

"I don't believe this."

Janet grinned at me and nodded. "I called off our man inside last week, because we hadn't found anything, but with what the police told me today it's easy to see why not. Far from being negligent, Lacroix backs up their safety program with an insurance policy for every employee. They underwrite it themselves, which makes sense—not very many people are going to die while they're working for you. After a year, which was about how long Nations had been with the company, they automatically set up a ten thousand dollar accidental death policy. Nations had signed his about a month before his death, with Pamela as the beneficiary."

"Before he decided to file for divorce?"

"That's what the police think. They figure that Pamela did receive a copy of the divorce papers, came up here to talk to him, and then slipped him the poison to collect the insurance."

"How did she know about it in the first place?"

"No one's sure. Rick must have told her at some point."

"Did she collect it?"

"You bet. She showed up at Lacroix's headquarters in Tacoma the day after she talked to us, presented them with a copy of the death certificate, and walked out of there with a cashier's check for ten grand."

"And now she's gone."

"The police have had the lab results for the past two days, and they've pieced together most of the case since then. The hospital had given her all the possessions Rick had on him when he died, including the keys to his apartment, and the day after she picked up the check she went there and cleaned everything out. She left the furniture, but she took everything else that wasn't nailed down. The manager didn't even know she'd been there—he didn't even know that Rick had died, because his rent wasn't due until the fifth. Pamela's apartment manager down in Glendale says she moved out a week ago, and the bank where she worked says she quit. Neither place has a forwarding address."

I walked back to my desk and sat down. I chuckled and I could see Janet smiling back at me. In a way, it was satisfying to know that I'd been right about Pamela Nations from the start. If only I'd somehow known what she was up to. Then I remembered her visit. "Wait a minute. There's one thing that doesn't fit."

"What's that?"

"When she came to see me, she said it was to find out why Rick had *really* died. Wouldn't that have given her away?"

Janet was shaking her head, and moved to the edge of her seat. "No. She was just pumping you for information. My guess is that after seeing your name on the police report, she thought she could get a line on whether anybody had discovered the poison. If she'd gone to the police, or the coroner, and *they* suspected—"

"She might have been arrested."

"Exactly. But this way, if you found out anything that looked suspicious, she could have disappeared right then."

"So why'd she go to see you?"

"That was a smoke screen. She probably figured that poison was poison, and wanted to make sure that if any was found in his body, the finger would already be pointing to the chemical plant."

"Instead of her. Damn, that's cold-blooded. Do the police have any leads?"

"They said the FBI has been called in. They'll trace the check and find out if she has any family, things like that."

"Wow, you just never know about people."

"Well," Janet said as she stood up. "I thought you'd find that interesting, seeing as how you were there from the start. I'm sorry I didn't take your suspicions more seriously."

"Ah, forget about it." I stood and met her at the door. "Are you going to be in town for lunch?"

"No. I have to get back this morning."

"How about tonight?"

"Oh, yes," Janet said seriously. "I think you should stay the whole weekend. It's still too dangerous at your apartment."

We both laughed. "I was just talking about dinner," I said, "but that sounds good, too."

"Okay, I'll see you tonight."

We kissed and Janet left. I went back to my chair in disbelief. It was almost eerie to think that a murderer had sat right across my desk from me. Jesus.

I only had a couple of checkups after Janet left, and I took a short lunch at eleven-thirty. It was a few minutes before one when Nona came back to the lab to tell me I had a telephone call. I walked down to my office and sat at my desk before picking up the line.

"Hello?"

"Steve! I'm glad I caught you before you left." It was Dale. So much had happened the day before that I'd forgotten all about Lydia's tooth.

"Did you get my message?"

"Yeah, but I have something to tell you first. I just got the lab results back on Lydia Grant yesterday afternoon, but before I could call you back, I had to turn right around and give them to the medical examiner's office."

"Why?"

"It looks like your lady friend was poisoned. A protein called ricin caused the hemolysis."

"What?" I shot up in my chair so fast it nearly pitched me

forward against the desk. The Merk Index was still open in front of me, and I stared down at the pages, unable to speak.

"Steve? Are you still there?"

"Yeah," I muttered. "What the hell happened, Dale?"

"I went over the file again myself and I still don't have a definite method of introduction. There was nothing in her stomach when she came in, but there wouldn't have to have been. My best guess is that she ate some castor beans and fully digested them by the time she died."

I looked at the page in front of me and Dale's assessment was correct. There didn't seem to be any way to get ricin poisoning other than eating castor beans. Death wasn't immediate either, and could occur up to twelve days after ingestion.

"I'm sorry I had to call you like this, man, instead of coming over, but it's been a madhouse around here the past couple of days."

"That's all right."

"What was it that you called me about?"

"Nothing. It's not important anymore." That was the understatement of the year. If Lydia had been poisoned, it was no wonder Thompson hadn't flinched when Janet had spilled what I suspected. And if Thompson wasn't responsible for Lydia's death, then who was? "Listen, Dale, do you keep copies of all your autopsy reports, even the ones you sent to the medical examiner?"

"Sure. For a while, anyway."

"Would you be able to look up another file for me?"

"Absolutely."

"Great. This would have been about two or three weeks ago." I turned back the calendar on my desk to the previous month. "The sixteenth or seventeenth of February. The name is Rick Nations—I need the lab results."

"You want to hang on, or—"

"I'll hold."

While I waited for Dale, I finished reading the entry on ricin in the Merk Index. The substance, though natural, was one of the deadliest known. It was found only in the bean of the castor plant, which was used in the production of castor oil. Once the oil was extracted, the remainder of the bean contained all the ricin. As few as four or five beans chewed up, with or without the oil, could be fatal.

The Nations case was one thing, but where in God's name could Lydia have possibly come across castor beans and eaten them? Though the plant was native to tropical regions, it could now be found growing wild in the U.S. But even so, it still seemed impossible.

The longer Dale took, the longer I sat there thinking about Rick Nations and Lydia. And the longer I thought about them, the darker my thoughts became. I couldn't believe what I was thinking.

Both of them were musicians, and both of them had been involved in open-mike playing situations. Rick had been playing at the Owl, but it was conceivable that at some point he could have played with Lydia at the Lion's Lair. And as much as I didn't want to believe it, it was just as likely that they could have wound up in bed together. If Pamela Nations had found out about it, could she have killed Lydia, too?"

I was breaking out in a cold sweat when Dale came back on the line, and he startled me. "Hello?"

"Right here, Dale."

"This is weird. Did you already know that this guy died of the same thing?"

"Yeah, but I wonder if the police have connected it to Lydia's death."

"They will. I had to send the body over to the medical examiner the next day. I have the toxicology here, but I hadn't looked at it since it wasn't our case anymore."

"Could you take a look through your notes and see if

213

there's anything unusual about that case, compared with Lydia's death?"

"Okay. But I'm curious. How did you know about his guy?"

"It's a case Janet's working on."

"Well, do *you* know how they're connected?"

Unfortunately, yes. "Unfortunately, no. That's why I wanted you to take a look at them side by side. Can you tell me how they compare?"

"Sure, let's see . . . Hemolysis was still in the initial stage when Nations died. It looks like he had the CVA before his blood had time to break down." Dale paused. "That's probably the only difference. They even made the same mistake about the abscess that I did on the Grant case. There's no sign of—"

"Whoa. Wait a minute, Dale. What mistake about the abscess?"

"Well, it turned out not to be an abscess after all. The sections taken in both cases had high concentrations of the poison. Whatever form they ingested the beans in, some of it must have been lodged down between the dental ridge and the cheek after eating. The reaction to the toxin caused the redness and swelling that we mistook for an infection."

"Hmm. Anything else?"

Another pause. "Not that I can see. The reaction time seems to be the only variation—that and the cause of death. But that's not unusual—every person would react differently, anywhere from two hours to two weeks. Other than that, they're exactly the same."

"All right. Thanks for the call, Dale."

"Sure. You mentioned the cops putting these two cases together. Do you know if they've found anything out about Nations?"

"Yeah," I said. "And they're pretty sure it's murder."

Dale's only reaction was a low whistle.

31

As soon as I'd hung up with Dale, I called the police. The dispatcher said that Lieutenant Lasky wasn't in, so I left a message for him to call me as soon as possible. Now what?

On a whim, I picked up the phone again and dialed Diane's number, but I had no idea whether she'd be home. I gave it a couple rings and was about to hang up when she answered.

"Hello?"

"Diane. This is Steve Raymond."

"Hi, Steve."

"I didn't expect to catch you at home."

"Yeah, well . . . this is where I live." I was trying to figure out how to broach the subject of Lydia's poisoning when Diane continued. "Say, you wouldn't happen to need any guitars or amps or anything, would you?"

"Why?"

"I'm trying to sell some of Lydia's stuff so I can make the mortgage payment."

God, it was hard to believe she was dead. "What's going to happen to her half of the house?"

"I wish I knew. I still haven't been able to reach her mom. It's like she dropped off the planet. I've resorted to taking out a personal ad in the Santa Cruz paper. Hopefully, if anyone knew her mom down there, they'll give me a call. Sure you don't need any music equipment?"

"I'm not in the market for anything right now, but I do need to tell you something about Lydia."

"Yeah?"

"I don't exactly know how to put this, so I'm going to give it to you straight. I've been in touch with the hospital where Lydia was taken after she died. A friend of mine did the autopsy and he called me today when he got back the tests that were done on her blood."

"What did he say?"

"He said it looked like Lydia had eaten something poisonous."

"What the fuck . . ."

"Do you know if she was in contact with anyone who could have given her something poisonous?"

"Wait a minute—you just said she ate something poisonous, and now you're saying that somebody *gave* it to her, that somebody *killed* her?" The keen in Diane's voice told me the tears would be along soon. I tried to hurry.

"Please, Diane, you have to try and remember. Did she see . . . Was she seeing anyone who could have done something like this?"

There was no answer for the moment. Diane was going to take her own sweet time on this, and I was going to give it to her. "What was it?" she finally asked.

"Hmm?"

"What was it that killed her?"

"Oh, they said she ate some castor beans—they're extremely toxic. But she wouldn't have had to eat the actual bean—it could have been ground up and mixed into anything. I guess what I'm fishing for here is if you remember somebody you didn't know very well who might have cooked for her or given her something they had cooked, anything that Lydia might have eaten."

I heard the first sob. "She was in bed all week. We didn't see anybody."

"She would have eaten it before that—before she got sick."

"Ah, I don't know, Steve." She spoke very quietly. "We hadn't been doing much together for the past six months or so. She was busy with her music thing, and I had my own stuff going on. I don't know."

I took a deep breath now. "Diane, I hate like hell to ask you this, but you have to believe me that it's only because I'm trying to find out who did this to her."

"You don't think she ate this bean thing accidentally?"

I tried to think of how to answer and then said, "No, I don't."

"All right. Ask."

"Was Lydia seeing any other men right before she began seeing me?"

"Jesus, you go right for the jugular, don't you?"

"I'm sorry, but I really need to know," I answered, and she was quiet for a long time.

"Ah, what the hell. It doesn't make much difference now. Yeah, she was. You weren't the first. I mean, after me."

"What do you know about them?"

"Not a damn thing. She never brought them over here, though, so I wouldn't. You were the first for that, if it makes you feel any better."

It did, but I let it slide. "Did she tell you anything about them, anything at all?"

"I don't know names or ages, if that's what you mean. Like I said, I never laid eyes on them. The only thing I do know for sure is that they were both like you."

"How's that?"

"Musicians."

We said goodbye a few minutes later, but I couldn't get my mind off what Diane had said. Though there was no way to prove it at the moment, I was sure. One of the musicians Lydia was seeing could easily have been Rick Nations, and if Pamela had killed her husband, it only took another small step of logic to deduce that she could have killed Lydia, too."

And as horrible as that was, it also meant that I was in deep shit. Jesus, I'd been stupid. I hadn't taken pictures in Thompson's office because I'd known that the mere lack of licenses in the files wasn't proof, and yet that very same lack of evidence had had me convinced that Thompson was responsible for Lydia's death. That left me high and dry with a breaking and entering charge over my head, and absolutely no room to talk my way out of it.

The more I thought it over, the more I was sure that the charge would stick. I was not fond of the idea of doing jail time. In the end, everything came down to putting my faith in Janet. It wouldn't be the first time. She was the only one who could get me out of this, which was good. I didn't think she was too hot on my being locked up, either.

While my thoughts were on the future, a knock on the door brought me back to the present. "Come in."

Nona opened the door and poked her head inside. "Are you still going to pick up the kids from school?"

I sat up straight and looked at my watch. Damn, it was already after two. "Yeah, thanks for reminding me."

She shut the door and I kicked myself for not having planned things better—the story of my life. I wanted desperately to talk to Dan before I did anything else, and he'd be calling me here at the office. There was only one thing to do if I was going to be able to stay here, and that was call Janet and ask her to pick up Cathie and Timmy.

"Sure," she said, when I'd finally made it past the receptionist and Janet's secretary. But she hadn't said it right away. She'd made me sweat a little first. "What's going on?"

"It's unbelievable."

"Tell me anyway."

I wasn't sure how Janet would react to news about Lydia, but it was too late to worry about it now. "I have every reason to believe not only that Pamela Nations killed her husband, but that she also killed Lydia Grant."

"My God, Steve, how in the world did you come to that conclusion?"

I briefly outlined what Dale had told me about the same poison being found in both bodies, and then about the one thing that connected the two of them: they were both open-mike musicians. Everything else was circumstantial, but had the distinction of fitting perfectly with the known facts.

"I really hate that bitch," Janet said, and for a moment I wasn't sure who she was talking about. "Does she really think she can just murder people and then go on with her life? That's one trial where I'd like to be on the other side, prosecuting."

"If they find her."

"Speaking of which, have you talked to the police yet?"

"That's kind of why I need you to pick up the kids. I'm waiting for a call from Dan."

"I still have the card from the detectives who were in here about Rick Nations. Do you want their names?"

"Yeah, that would be great. I can tell Dan and then he can contact them." Janet gave me the names and a phone extension at the downtown precinct.

"I still don't understand how Rick Nations could have been out playing the night he died if the same poison kept Lydia bedridden."

"The cause of Rick's death was a CVA, remember?"

"You mean the bleeding in his brain?"

"Right. This poison breaks down the capillaries as well as the red blood cells. In Nations' case he must have had a weak vascular wall in his brain to begin with, and that was the first thing to go."

"Okay."

"Besides, for all we know, he could have been sick the whole week before."

"No, he wasn't."

"How do you know?"

"When I was first checking into the case for Pamela, I went down to the plant and took a look at his work record. We were thinking that if the chemicals at work had caused his death, he might have had a pattern of staying home sick."

"And he didn't?"

"Nope. The guy never missed a day of work. In fact, he even worked on the day he died. Another couple of weeks and he would have been eligible for a week's vacation. The only time he'd taken off work was for two hours the Friday before his death."

"What was that for?"

"A dentist appointment."

A chill began to creep up my spine and I was silent for a moment.

"Steve?"

"Yeah, right here."

"I should get going if I want to get to the school on time. I'll see you tonight. I'm anxious to hear what Dan has to say."

"Sure, okay. I'll be home as soon as I can."

The second I hung up I went to the door, and when I'd caught Nona's attention I asked her if Dan had called. She shook her head. "If he calls, I'll take it immediately, even if I'm on another line." She nodded and I closed the door and went back to my desk.

I was stunned, and my hand trembled slightly as I reached for the phone. Pamela Nations was a gold digger and a snob, and I had no problem believing she was cold-blooded enough to murder her husband for a mere ten thousand dollars—and

Lydia, too. But now I only needed one piece of information to put her in the clear.

The card was still on my blotter and I pulled it out and dialed. It rang once before the familiar voice answered. "First Avenue Dental Clinic."

"Hello," I said. My throat felt dry and constricted. "I just had some work done a few weeks ago, but my tooth is still giving me trouble. How soon could I get in to see the dentist?"

"Your name, please?"

"Rick Nations."

"One moment."

My palms were sweating as I waited. The entire scenario was clicking into place. There was just one more thing I needed, and a minute later the receptionist at Thompson's office came back on the line and gave it to me.

"Okay, Mr. Nations, I have your file right here."

32

I had to get hold of Dale again. Now that it was straight in my mind exactly what had happened, he was the only person who would be able to confirm it. I picked up the phone and punched in the number to the Elliott Bay Medical Center—if I dialed his direct line I knew I'd get voice mail. Once I'd run the gauntlet from the main reception desk through the hospital reception desk and on to the pathology lab, I was able to ask for Dale directly.

"Dr. Barnes is busy at the moment. May I take a message?"

"No, this is an emergency."

"I'm afraid Dr. Barnes is working right now, but if you'll give me your name—"

"Listen to me," I said, my patience gone. "I want you to go into the autopsy suite and tell Dr. Barnes that Dr. Raymond is on the phone and that it's an emergency. I don't think his patient will mind, okay?"

I could practically hear her frowning through the phone line.

"Just a minute."

I'd been right all along, in a way. Whichever dentist had worked on Lydia had certainly killed her, but it hadn't been an accident. After learning that Rick Nations had gone to the very same clinic only days before his death, I knew it had to be murder.

If Dale had what I needed, I would have the method. If Lydia and Rick had been treated by the same doctor, I would have the means. The one thing I lacked, for the time being, was a clear motive. But there were a lot of things I didn't know about the dynamics of the First Avenue Dental Clinic, and I wasn't going to be surprised if, under police investigation, a motive eventually presented itself.

"Hey, Steve, I'm really busy here, man."

"Dale, I need you to get the files on Nations and Grant for me again." When there was no response I said, "Dale?"

"I'm here. Tell me first what the emergency is."

"I think something was overlooked in Rick Nations' autopsy, and now the police are looking for the wrong person."

"Say no more. They're in my office. I'll put you on hold and pick up in there." A couple of minutes later Dale answered. "Okay, what do you need?"

"Remember how you said that the new filling in Lydia's mouth tipped you off to what you thought was an abscess?"

"Yeah."

"I want you to look over Nations' file and tell me where the abscess was. I'm willing to bet there was also a new filling right above it."

"Let's see . . ." I could hear him flipping through pages and reading an occasional word out loud. "Hey, here it is. Just like you said."

I wasn't sure whether I should be happy about that or not. On its own, it still wasn't enough. There was only one way to prove who the killer was, and after what Diane had told me about not being able to get in touch with Lydia's mother, I knew there was only one chance left.

"There's one other thing I need to know, Dale. Is Lydia's body still there?"

"Let me see." More shuffling of papers. "Yeah, for a couple

more hours, anyway. Nobody claimed the body, and when we need the space—like now—they get cremated."

"Don't, please. We need to pull Lydia's tooth—the one with the filling—and take a look inside the pulp chamber. If I'm right, I think I've found the method of introduction of the poison."

"What's that?"

"I'm pretty sure the poison is in her tooth, beneath the filling. The abscess wasn't caused by irritation on the outside of the gums—it was from poison being absorbed through the roots."

"Are you telling me a dentist did this on purpose?"

"Unfortunately."

"Ah, man. As if I didn't already have enough reasons to stay away."

"So, maybe it's time you switched dentists."

"And go to you? No, sir. When you bailed out of med school I had to do all the lab work in biochemistry myself. Some partner you turned out to be."

"You're still mad about that?"

"Damn straight," he said, and then laughed.

"All right. But can you at least get that tooth for me?"

"No way."

"Why not?"

"Evidence, man. You haul that tooth out of her and it's useless. I'm going to have to call the medical examiner's office and get them to come and pick her up. Then, if you're right, they can nail the bastard."

I hadn't thought about that. "How am I going to know what they find?"

There was a moment of silence. "Should I be insulted?"

"Sorry. I wasn't thinking."

"I'll let you know as soon as there's something to know."

"Thanks, Dale."

"Hey, thank you. If what you say is true, I'm going to come out smelling like a rose on this one."

"I assume that means you'll be taking all the credit?"

"You'll get an honorable mention."

"Great. Listen, can you take care of this as soon as possible?"

"The second I hang up the phone."

"Okay, look, I have to go now. I'm expecting another call—"

"I'll take care of it."

"Thanks, Dale."

The door to my office opened the instant the receiver hit the cradle. It was Nona.

"I forgot to tell you," I said. "I called Janet and she's going to pick up the kids."

Nona smiled. "I just wanted to tell you that Julie and Laurie left a while ago, and I'm leaving now. Are you staying?"

I looked at my watch and couldn't believe it was already four o'clock. "No call from Dan Lasky?"

She shook her head.

"All right. I'll see you tomorrow."

As soon as Nona was gone I tried Dan's number again.

"Lasky."

"Dan? This is Steve."

"Hey, I got your message. Sorry I didn't get a chance to call you back."

"Do you have time to talk for a few minutes? It's really important."

"Sure. Go ahead."

I gave him the full rundown, everything I'd learned that day in exactly that order. Dan listened silently the entire time, and when I was finished he said, "Why don't you give me the names of the two detectives in homicide." I did, and he continued. "They're going to want to talk to you, I'm sure, and you'll probably have to go downtown and give them a statement. I'm going to give them your home number if that's all right."

"Sure, but you'd better make it Janet's number. I'm staying there for a few days."

"Hmm. Is that as promising as it sounds?"

"I sure as hell hope so, Dan."

"All right. Well, good luck. I hope things work out between you two."

"Thanks, Dan."

"Okay, I guess that's it. Someone will be talking to you in the next couple of days."

"Wait a minute. A couple of days? What about right now?"

"This isn't my case, Steve."

"I know that, but shouldn't somebody go down to the clinic and arrest this guy?"

"What guy? Come on, Steve. Not only don't we have the proof yet, but we don't even know which dentist it is."

"Dan, the clinic closes at five. You won't have another chance to nab this guy until Monday, and that's assuming he doesn't catch on and skip town."

Dan sighed. "Nab him? Skip town? Listen, Steve, do me a favor, okay? Go home and have dinner with your family, play with your kids, make love to your wife, and let the police handle this."

"Dan, we have to go down there and make Thompson tell us who did the work on Lydia and Rick Nations. They have to be the same guy."

"Hold it right there. *You* aren't going anywhere but home, and if I find that you've been within a mile of that clinic, I'll come down there and arrest you myself. Understand?"

I leaned back and rubbed the five o'clock shadow on my chin. "Steve?" Dan said, with emphasis.

"Yeah, I understand."

"If I hear anything, I promise I'll let you know. Now go home and forget about this thing."

"All right. I'll talk to you later, Dan."

I leaned forward with my elbows on my desk and my face in my hands. There was no way I could let it go. It had been bad enough when I thought it was slipshod work that had killed Lydia. But to learn that it was premeditated murder . . . It was damn frustrating to sit here and think that the son of a bitch was probably working on someone right now.

Why had he done it? Why had he selected those two people, or were there more that nobody else knew about? What if the cops didn't get around to questioning Thompson until Monday? They still had to check out Lydia's tooth. What if they didn't even get to *that* until Monday?

I pushed myself up from my desk and walked out to the front door. My coat was in the closet and I took it out and slipped it on before locking up and heading for my truck. As I sat in the cab I hesitated for a minute, then I looked at my watch. It was quarter to five. Finally, I put the key in the ignition, started the engine, and pulled out of the parking lot onto Magnolia Boulevard. I looked both ways, and then turned my truck south toward downtown.

33

I pulled up right in front of the clinic this time. I walked in the front door and up the stairs, not even bothering to acknowledge the receptionist, though I could see from the corner of my eye that she had definitely recognized me. With supreme confidence, I opened the inner door, walked through, opened the door to Thompson's office, and shut it behind me.

"You got a lot of fucking nerve coming in here unannounced."

He was sitting behind his desk and I walked right up to the front of it. "We have a problem here, Dr. Thompson."

"You're going to be the one with the problem, pal, if you don't get the hell out of my office." He stood up now, to even the sides.

"Do you remember that patient I told you about the first time I was in here, Lydia Grant? She's dead, and I think one of your dentists killed her."

Now he flashed me his slick grin. "Is that what all this bullshit is about, the state board and everything? I don't believe this. If you're not out of here in about ten seconds, I'm going to call the police."

"Please do. I've been trying to get them down here all week but I haven't had much luck."

His hand stopped on the receiver when I said this. He lost the grin. "What do you want?"

"One thing," I said, "and then I'll leave you alone. If I'm wrong you can feel free to prosecute me to the fullest extent of the law for breaking in here the other night. But if I'm right, you have a murderer working for you."

"What is it?"

"Two weeks before Ms. Grant died, a man named Rick Nations, also a patient of yours, died from the very same thing: ricin poisoning. Both of them died approximately a week after having work done here in this clinic. And, in both autopsies, the method of introduction was confirmed to have been via the open ends of the tooth roots and a pulp chamber full of poison." The part about the autopsies was a lie, but I was desperate.

Thompson was eyeing me warily but with increasing unease. "Now, let me get this straight—"

"There isn't time." I looked at the clock behind his desk and it read two minutes to five. "I have to know whether the same dentist worked on those two people during their last appointments here. And if he is the same, I need to know who he is."

Thompson regarded me for a moment. It was clear he had questions about why I was here and not the police, but I could also tell he'd just remembered something. "And if he's not?"

"I'm out of here."

As soon as he reached in his pocket for the keys, I knew I had him. He headed for the file cabinets, but as I moved toward the door behind his desk he became alarmed. "Where are you going?"

"Nowhere. I just need to see who's still here."

"They all signed release forms, you know. All of them. I'm not responsible."

Even though I was nervous as hell, I managed a small chuckle as I took hold of the doorknob. "There are ways to get around release forms, Dr. Thompson."

I opened the door and looked out into the operatory as

Thompson fumbled with the locks on his file cabinets. All of the stations were still full. They must have been running behind. I knew only Dennis Keith by sight, and he was easy to recognize beneath his mask. I couldn't tell which of the two East Indians was the one who had panicked the last time I was here, and I had no idea which of the Asians was Cham Bui.

"What were those names again?" I heard from across the room.

"Lydia Grant and Rick Nations."

"Grant, Nations, Grant, Nations . . ." He was chanting it like a mantra as he pulled out drawers and looked through them.

When I turned back to the operatory, my heart jumped up to my throat as I saw Keith staring directly at me. He must have just looked up, because he proceeded to look down the hallway and around to the other stations. As composed as I could, I shut the door and walked over to where Thompson was seemingly frozen next to the file cabinets.

"Did you find them?"

When I reached him I could see that his face had gone as white as the hair on his head. "This doesn't prove anything, you know."

"Come on, Thompson. Who is it?"

"They're the same," he said, and for the first time I think he really believed what I had been trying to tell him. "They're the same."

"Who is it?"

"You say the autopsies confirmed that the poison was in the tooth?"

"Yes, beneath fresh fillings that had been put in right out there." He didn't even seem to notice as I pointed toward the operatory. "Now, who is it?"

"Keith," he breathed.

Why didn't that surprise me? I walked back to the rear door

231

and looked out. Keith was gone—the cubicle was empty. Shit. I had wanted confirmation that I was right, and I had wanted Thompson to know it, too. What I hadn't wanted was for Keith to take off before the cops could get here.

My heart was pounding as I scanned the room. I took a couple of steps out, but there was still no sign of him. Then I thought of the fire escape and started running. I didn't know what I was going to do if I caught him, but I knew that if he got away, I'd have that hanging over my head, too.

I was barreling full-speed toward the hallway, preparing to hang a left around the last cubicle toward the rear of the building, when I collided head-on with Keith, who had been running up the hall from the reception desk. His arms came up immediately into a football lineman's position across his chest, and he sent me sprawling.

Keith, on the other hand, hadn't budged. He had been able to pull up just enough that my body simply caromed off his. The additional shove was all it took to shoot my feet out from under me. Then I slid along the polished floor until I hit a tray full of instruments. The operatory had still been busy, but the resulting cacophony silenced the room.

As soon as I was able to push myself up to a sitting position, I could see Keith hunched over the drawers in his empty cubicle. Beyond him, Thompson was just coming out the back door of his office, and to my left, amazingly enough, two uniformed police officers were walking toward me down the hall.

I jumped up as fast as I could and ran to meet them, but before I could even reach the archway to the hall I saw the receptionist pushing her way past the officers. She pointed at me and screamed, "There he is!"

Christ, this was the last thing I needed. The officers never took another step. Each of them pulled out his service revolver and one of them dropped to one knee. Both guns were trained on me and I though I was going to pass out.

I might have, too, if not for the arm that suddenly snaked around my neck and held me up. It was a powerful arm with fine blond hairs on it. Once I felt steady enough to stand on my own I tried to release myself from its grip but, like a boa constrictor, it only tightened. In a panic I twisted around to try and see who it belonged to, and came face to face with a stainless-steel hypodermic . . . held in a pencil grip.

34

At the time, I had thought that the cops catching me in Thompson's office was bound to be the most terrifying moment of my life. I was wrong. This was number one—with a bullet.

My legs felt like rubber, and it took all my strength to remain standing and not let Keith's arm around my neck strangle me. I knew it was Keith when he whispered in my ear. The faint mixture of Listerine and body odor was exactly what I'd smelled the last time he'd spoken to me. Maybe that was what had awoken me that night in my apartment.

"Tell them to back off," he said. "This isn't Novocaine— it's mercury."

Beads of sweat had emerged on my forehead and were beginning to coalesce and drip down my face. My bowels felt hot and loose, and I wasn't sure I would be able to hold them back much longer. At the same time, I was surprised I hadn't pissed my pants already. The mercury he had in the syringe could kill me instantly.

In spite of what *60 Minutes* says about the risk, there is no way you could put enough mercury in conventional dental amalgam to harm someone, the reason being that while mercury vapors and mercury compounds can be extremely dangerous, straight metallic mercury, when ingested, is nontoxic.

But I could be in a hospital emergency room, surrounded by a crack ER staff, and that same metallic mercury *injected* into my bloodstream would kill me instantly. There would be absolutely nothing that anyone could do. With that in mind, I gulped down a breath of air and said, "Back off. He can kill me with what's in the syringe."

The cop who was standing up pulled his gun back so that it was pointing at the ceiling and walked back toward the reception desk. He was met in the hallway by Thompson. They talked for a moment, then the two of them went into Thompson's office.

The other officer was motionless, his revolver trained, I assumed, on Keith. Though there were other people in the operatory, they were separated from us by the partitions. The rear door to Thompson's office opened slowly and the other officer motioned for the patients and doctors still in the room to come toward him. Keith didn't do anything about it, because he couldn't. He didn't have a gun. The only person in the room he could kill was me. After all of the people had filed through the office door, we were alone.

"What's in the hypo, Keith?" asked the cop, once he was back behind his partner.

Then I felt the needle press against the skin of my neck. At the rate my heart was beating, it wouldn't have taken more than a few seconds for the mercury to kill me.

"Tell them," Keith whispered in my ear.

"It's mercury. If he injects me, I'm dead."

The cop who was standing walked back down the hall again. He returned a minute later and said, "Let the hostage go." Gee, why hadn't I thought of that?

"No," Keith yelled, and the sound of his full voice startled me. I'd only heard him whisper before. "The two of us are leaving together."

"You can't get out of here, Keith."

"Then the doctor dies, too."

Evidently Keith knew more about me than I'd given him

credit for, but then again he'd been inside my apartment and tried to kill me. There was no telling what he knew.

With all the time that had gone by since I'd been taken hostage—maybe five minutes—I half expected the place to be swarming with SWAT teams, guns trained on Keith from every possible angle, and superiors telling their men, "Shoot him as soon as he makes a move." But there were only the two uniforms. Dan was right. I probably watched too many cop shows.

"We're leaving," Keith yelled, and began to move me forward.

"Wait, Keith. What do you want to let the hostage go?"

As fascinated as I should have been by what Keith would have been willing to swap for my life, I couldn't pull my attention away from something my shoe had just hit: the foot control for the drill. I listened closely and I could still hear a generator in another part of the building. The air pressure that ran the drills and aspirators was still on.

"My car is in the lot across the street. The doctor and I are going to get in and drive. I'm not letting him go."

I tried to relax my neck as much as possible. I couldn't feel the tip of the needle against it anymore, and that was good. My face had worked up a good sheen of sweat and I knew that I could use that to my advantage if what I was planning managed to work.

Conventional wisdom says that I probably should have done everything Keith said, and let the cops handle my liberation. But Keith was a cold-blooded killer. It didn't matter that his methods were more meticulous than most; the results were the same. I had made up my mind that I was not going anywhere with Dennis Keith.

With his arm around my neck, the surface area where he could jab me had been greatly reduced, and I was betting that even if he did manage to stick me with the hypodermic, he wouldn't be able to depress the plunger. Everything had to happen at once, though, and it had to happen perfectly. I had no doubts that Keith would kill me if I fucked up. He had nothing to lose.

I lifted my foot and pressed down as hard as I could on the speed control. We were only inches from the chair, and in the silence of the operatory, the whine of the drill sounded like the turbines turning at the Grand Coulee Dam. Keith immediately jerked his head around to see what had happened, and in the same instant I tucked my chin and twisted my head, relaxing my legs and letting gravity pull me down.

My head popped out from underneath Keith's arm. I was looking up as I fell, and I could see the needle sink into the headrest of the dental chair, inches above my face. In the next instant, just as I hit the floor, two shots rang out. One caught Keith in the chest and the other in the shoulder, and then he collapsed on top of me.

I was having trouble breathing. My lungs couldn't draw enough oxygen through my constricted throat, and I was floundering, trying at the same time to remove Keith from on top of me. Blood was spewing from his wounds, slicking my hands and matting my hair. I couldn't get him off of me.

Then there were cops everywhere, dozens of them. They finally pulled Keith away. Stretchers were wheeled into the room, people were shouting. I heard the squawk of police radios as I tried desperately to catch my breath. Just when I thought I wasn't going to make it, someone pressed a plastic mask to my face. I sucked at the pure oxygen. It felt wet in my lungs.

I was breathing so fast now that I began to hyperventilate, and I felt powerless to stop myself. Then my mouth started to water and the back of my throat tensed up. I ripped the mask off my face, my stomach hitched once, and I leaned over behind the dental chair and threw up.

35

On Monday Dan Lasky called me at home in Medina and said he had something he wanted to show me, and asked if I would mind coming over to the station house. This was about eleven in the morning and I said fine, I'd be right over.

I reached the Magnolia Precinct about a half-hour later, and was led to a glass-enclosed office on the second-floor squad room. Dan shook my hand when I entered, and offered me some coffee. I accepted, but what I received was a paper cup containing black swill that I couldn't drink after the first sip. Dan threw his back in two gulps and sat down at his desk.

"I just got a copy of the report on Dennis Keith this morning and I thought you'd be interested in what it says, seeing as how you broke the case yourself."

Yeah, I was some kind of crime buster all right. After I'd lost my lunch, the paramedics had insisted on taking me to the hospital. I went to Harborview along with Keith—different ambulances, of course—except that I'd been released an hour later. As far as I knew, he was still in critical condition.

"Has Keith's condition been upgraded yet?" I asked.

"This morning: serious."

"So, he might pull through?"

"Nobody's predicting that yet, but if he does, some district attorney is going to have a field day in court. Homicide found a complete chemistry lab in the house he was renting in

Wallingford. There were dozens of those castor plants all over the place and he was extracting a powder from the beans that was about fifty-percent pure ricin."

Lasky was sitting behind his desk flipping through a fat folder, and he stopped to look up at me. I nodded for him to go on. I was content just to listen.

"You were right about Grant's tooth. The medical examiner pulled it and when they cut it open it was practically hollow. The stuff on the inside exactly matched the purity of the stuff Keith was producing in his home.

"All of that happened Saturday. Yesterday one of the detectives made some phone calls down to Scottsdale where Keith had been before he moved here. Guess what the M.E. down there had to say? Five cases of unexplained ricin poisoning within the last two years. They never checked teeth on any of the victims, just like we missed Nations' up here.

"We won't be able to make a case against Keith for Nations without the body, but we've got him solid on Grant, especially with your testimony."

"You figure I'll have to testify?"

"This is a pretty healthy statement you gave here—I can't imagine they wouldn't want to have you on the stand."

Ah, yes. When it was clear I wasn't going to die, I'd been taken from my hospital room at Harborview Medical Center back to the downtown precinct, where I had been previously incarcerated, to tell my tale. I had called Janet from there and barely managed to keep her at home. If it hadn't been for Cathie and Timmy, I knew she would have been sitting next to me for the grueling four-hour interrogation, er, I mean, statement.

I hit the high points with Janet when I finally made it home, and fell asleep the instant I climbed into bed. At work the next day it seemed as if no time had passed. I felt like a raw nerve. All I wanted to do was forget that I'd ever known Dennis Keith. I wasn't having anything like flashbacks, but he was never very far from my thoughts. And now I was going to have to testify against him in court.

"If he lives," I thought out loud.

"Right," said Lasky, and he flipped through a few more pages. "The statement from Thompson's receptionist is interesting. Thompson had given her instructions to call the police the next time you showed your face in the clinic. That's where the two uniforms came from.

"We don't know this for sure, but we suspect that the reason Keith went back into the building was that he saw the patrol car pull up. The receptionist said that when he walked out he told her to have a nice weekend, and that he would see her on Monday. She was a little surprised to see him running back up the stairs, but she just figured he'd left something behind. Two seconds later the uniforms showed up and she forgot all about him.

"It's funny when you think about it—Keith could have walked right past them and they wouldn't have given him a second look."

Yeah, that Keith was a barrel of laughs, all right.

"Anyway, she took the uniforms on back and then she pointed you out, but what the patrolmen saw was Keith coming up behind you with the syringe. That's when everything came down, and the rest you know.

"We also interviewed all of the dental assistants, and while none of them could specifically recall working with Keith on Nations or Grant, they did remember times when he would send them, in the middle of a procedure, on some errand or another. We figure that's when he placed the poison in the teeth.

"Of course, the illustrious Dr. Carl Thompson himself is quoted here as saying that he knew nothing about what Keith was doing."

I grunted and Lasky smiled. "Yeah?" he asked.

"Saturday," I said, "while I was at work, Janet called Thompson and forced him to meet with her. Considering everything that had happened, and the fact that I had really been after Keith, he magnanimously decided to drop all charges against me for the breaking and entering."

"I tried to tell you, Steve. He's quite a guy."

I actually laughed then, briefly, and it felt good. I was glad I could count Dan Lasky among my friends.

"What about Lydia's family? Any luck there?"

"Yeah. They found her mother living in Freemont, California, recently married and living under the name of Worthley. The body is being sent to a funeral home there today."

Dan and I looked each other in the eye for a long moment, neither of us uncomfortable in the silence. "You know Keith was the one who broke into my apartment and tried to kill me," I finally said.

"Any idea how he got in?"

"Not really, but I had been at the clinic that afternoon and I did speak with him. He could have followed me home and figured a way in. I don't know."

"Well, it's all over now."

"Why did he do it, Dan? Why Lydia?"

He shrugged. "They didn't find any diary or scrapbook of the killings in his house, if that's what you mean. The medical examiner in Scottsdale did remember the cases he'd had down there and it seemed to him that all of the people who were poisoned were living at or just above the poverty level. The same could be said for Nations and Grant.

"What we did find, were some books and articles at his house about doing away with welfare and taxes, anarchist kind of stuff. Our guess is that he felt these people were a drain on society, and so he decided to get rid of them, his own social

Darwinist crusade. It's a theory. I suppose we'll just have to wait and ask Keith when he recovers."

"*If* he recovers," I amended.

"Right. There's always the possibility we may never know."

"I'm not sure I want to know, Dan, not really. What about the rest of Keith's patients?"

"We're looking up all of the patients Keith has had in the past week to see if they're okay. So far, so good."

"What about before then?"

"That's going to take longer."

We talked for ten or fifteen minutes more, about our wives and kids, and made tentative plans to get together for another barbecue once the weather was nice enough. After depositing my paper cup full of cold coffee surreptitiously under my chair, I rose to leave.

"One more thing," I said, as Dan placed his hand on the doorknob. "What about your prime suspect in the Nations case, Pamela Nations?"

Dan walked back to his desk and flipped through a few more pages. "It says here they finally located her in San Francisco. Apparently she landed a job at a bank in Oakland but didn't tell her previous employer. She used the insurance money to put a down payment on a house, and now she's living there with some guy. And this should interest you—it says here he's a drummer."

It started slowly at first, just a giggle that spread out from my stomach. That soon turned into a full-fledged laugh, and in seconds I was forced back into the chair. Tears were streaming down my cheeks, the days of pent-up emotion finding their release in laughter.

Dan stood watching me with a bemused grin on his face, and when I had finally calmed down enough he asked me, "What?"

All I could say was, "You had to be there."

36

It was three weeks to the day after Dennis Keith died at Harborview Medical Center, from complications due to gunshot wounds, that I moved the last of my belongings back into the house in Medina. In that time the four of us had taken a couple of Sunday drives to the mountains in the Porsche—the kids were still small enough to ride comfortably in the pseudo-backseats—and Janet and I were working on regaining the trust we'd once had in each other.

Though they never said it in so many words, subtle changes in the kids' behavior told me that they were glad to have me back. And I was damn glad to be back. Janet and I eventually made love, and for the most part hadn't missed a beat.

I had done my best to put the whole Keith business behind me, and being back home helped tremendously. I was also beginning to listen to music again, for the first time since Lydia's death. My stereo was back in the front room, and I put on a King Pleasure disc and cued it up to his vocal version of Charlie Parker's "Parker's Mood."

I'm feelin' low down and blue; my heart's full of sorrow.
Don't hardly know what to do. Where will I be tomorrow?

The sorrow was almost gone, and I was far from blue, but somehow "Parker's Mood" always comforted me, and I walked back out to the family room feeling pretty good about life in general. A few days after I had moved in I'd bought a pair of wireless speakers to hear the stereo in the family room. I adjusted the volume so that the lyrics were clear, but the music wasn't loud enough to be distracting.

I was just coming back to the kitchen when the next song on the disc began, and I wrapped my arms around Janet's waist and sang along with King.

What can I say, dear, after I say that I'm sorry?
What can I do to prove it to you, that I'm sorry?

"I'm glad you're the one singing that now," she said. "I was getting a little tired of my rendition."

I pulled her close and she turned back to kiss me. Dinner was almost ready and the kids were nowhere in sight, but I could give them a yell before we sat down to the table. Janet was boiling up a pot of wild rice and I was given the task of cutting up the vegetables for the stir-fry. I looked up at the knife rack next to the stove and it was empty. There were no knives on the counter and I knew they must all be in the dishwasher, in varying states of encrustation.

When I began pulling out drawers, Janet asked me what I was doing.

"I'm looking for a knife. I thought we had a bunch of . . ."

I had just opened a drawer that did indeed have a knife in it. The blade was about nine inches long with a sharp point on the end, maybe an inch, inch and a half in width. It had a black handle and I took hold of it and removed it slowly from the drawer.

Janet stood mute by the stove and watched me, her face intensely serious. When I looked down to see what her eyes had been drawn to, I saw that my hand had gone unconsciously to the scar on my ribs.

The cut hadn't been very wide, but it had been deep, and would have gone deeper if the blade hadn't become wedged between my ribs. I had only needed four stitches, but after I was sewn up it seemed as if Janet had suffered the most trauma from that night.

It all started with the case she'd been trying in Olympia. She hadn't been home much and I was doing the best I could to pick up the slack. We were both frazzled, we were both tired, and we'd both said some things we shouldn't have that night. But I suppose I was the one who was really responsible; I was the first one to get physical.

By the time the argument had escalated, Janet had decided she'd heard enough and pointedly began ignoring me. She walked out to the kitchen and I followed, haranguing her all the way. She was cutting something at the breadboard when I grabbed her by the arm and twisted her around. The next thing I knew I was pulling a knife out of my chest. It wasn't exactly Ozzie and Harriet.

Looking back on it now, I know we could have made it past that. We could have worked it out. Instead, I chose to run, and things went downhill from there. I was just so grateful now to have another chance.

"I'm sorry," she said. "I stuck it in that drawer and forgot about it. I didn't mean—"

I shook my head and she stopped talking. Then I walked over to the sink, opened the cupboard underneath, pulled out the garbage bin, and dropped in the knife. "I think that's one knife we can do without. Don't you?"

Her eyes were sparkling blue, on the verge of tears, and I stepped over and hugged her as tightly as I dared. When we released she smiled at me and walked out of the room. The rice only had another minute to cook and I knew I'd better get the vegetables done fast, but before I had the chance to root in the dishwasher for another knife, Janet came back.

She was holding the divorce papers I had signed, and flashed them at me so there could be no mistake. Then she walked past me and deposited them into the garbage on top of the knife. "I think that's something else we can do without. Don't you?"

"Yeah," I said, and nodded for emphasis. "I do."

E.B.O. / December 15, 1991, Issaquah, WA
/ October 28, 1992, Bellevue, WA

Lying Through Your Teeth

A Steve Raymond, D.D.S. Story

This story first appeared in *Alfred Hitchcock's Mystery Magazine* in March of 2005.

I

"Ah, bite me!"

What? I was just passing by the x-ray darkroom in my office, heading toward the reception desk, when I heard the exclamation followed by a rattle of dental instruments. I poked my head inside the door and said, "Excuse me?"

"Oh, I'm sorry, Dr. Raymond." It was Susan, one of my assistants, cleaning up at the end of the day. "I've been trying to get this autoclave to shut for ten minutes and I can't figure out why in the world it won't go."

I stepped inside the small space next to Susan and said, "Let me have a look at it."

There are two autoclaves in my office, large stainless-steel cylinders used for sterilizing medical equipment. Baskets full of instruments go into a pan of water where they are steam-heated to kill off not only bacteria but the more tenacious viruses as well. Sure enough, the door would almost close before seeming to bind up at the hinge and not quite sealing. I squatted down to take a closer look at the hinge.

"I looked at the hinge, but nothing's there."

"Does it close without the basket?"

"Yeah."

I stood up and held out my hands but she was already shaking her head.

"I tried all the baskets and it still won't close."

251

"Then there must be something jamming it."

I pulled the basket all the way out and handed it to Susan while I examined the interior of the autoclave. I quickly realized it was going to be impossible to see through the water in order to find what was keeping the basket from seating all the way.

"Looks like we'll have to empty out the water so we can take a look inside."

Susan visibly slumped. "I really need to get out of here as soon as I can tonight, Dr. Raymond. It's my boyfriend's birthday."

I thought about that and looked over at the second autoclave. "Is the other one working?"

She nodded.

"Do we have enough instruments for tomorrow?"

"Probably not."

I looked through the basket to see what we might be short on and something caught my eye. I fished an explorer out from among the rest of the instruments and saw that the tip had been broken off. I looked again at the pan of water and then had an idea. "Hang on a second. I'll be right back."

Across the hall in my office I took a large magnet off of my file cabinet that was currently holding up my kids' school calendar. Back in the darkroom I pulled on a latex glove, inserted my hand inside the autoclave, and ran the magnet by feel over the bottom of the pan. A minute later I brought my hand back out of the opening and observed that the bottom of the magnet had retained the small tip of the explorer.

"Cool," Susan said, as she slipped the instrument tray into the autoclave. The door closed easily and she started up the machine. "I must have looked in there a hundred times. I never would have seen that."

"Well, once you know what you're looking for it's a lot easier to find it."

"Thanks, Dr. Raymond. I'm all done now. If it's okay I'm going to take off."

"With my blessing."

Susan ran back to the break room to retrieve her coat as I put back the magnet. Eventually I managed to make my way up to the reception desk—my initial destination—where my receptionist, Nona, looked at me over her glasses and nodded toward the waiting room. I looked out of the sliding glass window to see Lieutenant Dan Lasky leafing through a six-month-old copy of Newsweek.

"Major crisis?" Nona asked, and for a second I thought she was talking about Dan. Then I realized what she was referring to.

"Nah, just the autoclave. It's working now, though."

Nona is an attractive brunette in her early forties, and has been my most valuable employee for over a decade. She runs the office for me, leaving me free to devote my full attention to the patients who trust their dental care to Steve Raymond, D.D.S.

"He came in while you were helping Susan. It sounds urgent."

"Dan?" I said, opening the door to the waiting room.

He tossed the magazine on a table and stood to shake hands. There was a time when the sight of his rumpled brown suit would cause me to suppress a grin, but by now I was inured to his disheveled sartorial style. "Hey, Steve. Could I talk to you in private for a second?"

"Sure," I said, and led him back to my office.

Other than a pathologist that I had gone to school with, Dan Lasky was about the best friend I had in Seattle. He was one of my first patients—a walk in, no less—when I began my practice in the professional building where I lease office space, just across the street from the Elliott Bay Medical Center. A lieutenant in the Seattle Police Department's Magnolia

Precinct, Dan has rescued me on more than one occasion when I've run afoul of the law—something odd, I know, for a dentist to say, but, well . . . you had to be there. I was just making for my desk when he closed the door behind him and started in without sitting down.

"I was wondering if you could come with me and take a look at something."

"What?"

"A murder scene."

"Are you serious?"

"Yeah. I'd really appreciate it."

"Well, okay, I guess. When would you want me to do this?"

"Right now."

I looked at my watch. I was going to be late getting home for dinner as it was. Then I looked up at Dan. His dark hair was shot through with gray and looked as if he'd just crawled out of bed. The five o'clock shadow on his face and dark smudges under his eyes reminded me of his dedication to the job. He wasn't exactly pleading—that wasn't his style—but I could tell it was important to him.

"All right. Just let me call Janet and tell her I'm going to be late."

II

Nona walked out with us and I locked up for the night. Stepping out of my air-conditioned office into the humid evening was like slipping into a hot bath. Seattle was having one of its rare heat waves. Normally this time in June it would be raining, but for the last week the thermometer had been in the low nineties at midday. Now, just after six, it was still eighty and sticky with salt air coming off of Puget Sound. I said goodbye to Nona and climbed in the passenger side of Dan's Ford Taurus while he filled me in.

"Three days ago, Monday morning when the woman didn't show up for work, her office called but there was no answer. A co-worker who lives close by stopped in after work and found her car out front. When she couldn't get an answer at the door or on the woman's cell phone she let herself in. She had a key because she waters the plants and stops in occasionally when they were on longer trips. As soon as she saw the body she called the cops. Medical examiner said she'd been dead since Friday night."

"Jesus . . ."

My office is next to the Elliott Bay Medical Center, and Dan pulled into hospital traffic and headed north up Magnolia Boulevard toward Discovery Park. The windows in the car were down and each of us had an arm perched on the door as we drove through the upper-class neighborhood filled with expensive homes and surrounded by manicured lawns and towering evergreens. There was enough noise through the open windows that Dan elected to forgo further conversation until we arrived at the scene. As it turned out he took us all the way up to the park, turned left on Emerson toward the water, and then into a cul-de-sac at the end of the road. There were three homes there, and it was pretty easy to spot which one we were going into: it was the one surrounded by yellow crime-scene tape.

"Are you still processing the scene?" I asked as we climbed out of the Taurus.

"Not exactly," he said, and I had to hustle to keep up with him as he went up the front walk to the door.

The house itself was fairly unremarkable, a brown split-level with a small lawn in front, a woodpile on the side, and landscaped beds with a few rhododendron bushes. There were also three-foot metal stakes in the ground strung with the yellow tape surrounding the house, and not one but two yellow stickers listing the laws being broken with illegal entry into the crime scene. Dan cut the stickers with a pocketknife and stripped them off the door, then took me inside and up the stairs. Two things were immediately noticeable upon entry. The first was the smell.

Had I not known what had happened here I might have chalked it up to poor housekeeping. It wasn't strong, and it may have even been my imagination, but the knowledge that a dead body had been lying here for three days in this heat made my stomach turn. The second thing was the heat itself: it felt as if I had stepped into a sauna. The view, however, was incredible. Huge windows looked out across the water of Puget Sound to Bainbridge Island through a frame of spruce and Douglas fir. The sun was still well above the horizon, having a couple more hours before it would dip behind the island, and had raised the temperature in the house considerably higher that it was outside. I could feel sweat trickle down my sides as I looked over the living room furnishings. Beautiful hardwood floors covered with oriental rugs supported elegant furniture and expensive audio and video equipment.

"Down here," Dan yelled from the hallway, and I realized I had been staring at the room and hadn't seen him leave.

He was standing at the end of the hall outside the master bedroom: more windows looking out at the water, one of them mercifully open, and a king-sized bed, stripped to the mattress, with a large brown stain in the middle. I was about to ask him what the hell I could possibly do that trained investigators hadn't already done with much more skill, when he continued with the facts of the case as he leaned on the door frame.

"Her name was Kami Browning, 36. Husband, Rico Browning, 47, some big-deal public relations guy with a software company in town, Walker, Richer and Quinn. When the officers arrived, the woman who'd called in was waiting for them outside. Found her here." He motioned toward the bed. "Twelve stab wounds to the abdomen. No signs of sexual assault, no signs of struggle, no defensive wounds, nothing except a bite mark that didn't quite break the skin on her shoulder."

"The killer?"

"That's what it's supposed to look like."

I smiled. "Interesting choice of words."

Dan took out a small notebook and began reading. "Browning wasn't a big woman. M.E. says she was most likely pinned down by the weight of the assailant and died fairly quickly from internal bleeding. The guy's clothes, if he was wearing any, would have been covered in blood, but the only blood found was on the bed. Initial tox screen shows nothing that would prevent her from fighting back. The bite mark . . ." He flipped his notebook closed and stuck it back in his coat pocket. "Made *after* he killed her."

"So," I said, "find the guy who bit her and you have the killer?"

"Exactly, and that's where things get a little too strange. Come here."

I followed Dan out to the kitchen and he walked over and opened the door of a well-stocked refrigerator. The cool air spilling out of the fridge felt great. I looked inside and then back up at Dan. "Yeah?"

"Take a good look."

Examining the contents more closely this time I found little out of the ordinary, except for some lunchmeat with a bite taken out of it. There was also a piece of chocolate cake with a corner missing. I pulled out the crisper drawer saw an apple with a big brown spot in the middle. There was also a bag of rolls, one of them with a conspicuous bite out of the middle. Finally I looked back up at Dan. "Everything has a bite taken out of it."

He nodded. "Eight in all." Neither of us made a move to close the refrigerator door and we stood there while he told me what was bothering him.

"The bite marks in the fridge match the one on the victim. The two items with the best impressions we took down to the lab to make models, a brand-new brick of Tillamook cheddar with the corner bitten off and a carrot with the end bitten off. Now, the M.E. says its 50-50 that we could get a conviction on the body bite-mark alone because of having to match dental records with a bruise on the body, but with the additional matches from the cheese and carrot the odds are better."

"So, how do you find out whose teeth they are?"

"Already have."

That surprised me. "Then what am I doing here?"

Dan walked over to sit at the circular kitchen table. He pulled out his notebook again, plopped it on the tabletop and pulled out a chair while I took a seat across from him. We left the refrigerator door open.

He flipped open the book. "Fingerprints everywhere, as you can imagine. So we decide to concentrate in the master bedroom and bathroom, and the kitchen. Bathroom surfaces are good for prints, and maybe above the bed we'll get something from the guy bracing himself. Anyway, four sets come up regular. The first is the wife, second is the husband, and the third is the cleaning woman."

"The fourth are the killers?"

"Supposedly."

"You keep saying that. What's up?"

"Well, we run the fourth set of prints to see what comes up and we get a match. A guy named Don Winslow, late thirties, in the Air Force reserve so he's in the system. We pick him up at his apartment in Bothell and he tells us that he's been having an affair with Mrs. Browning for the last two years, but that she called it off three months ago."

"And you don't believe him?"

Dan frowned, more to himself than to me. "No, the problem is I do believe him. He says they spent about half the time in his apartment and half in the house in Magnolia. That's consistent with the prints we found. And so is the fact that he hadn't been here in a while. There were far fewer of his than the other three."

"I don't understand. Wouldn't that make him a prime suspect if she called it off and he couldn't accept it?"

"Sure, but answer me this. When he was first brought in for questioning he seemed genuinely upset, not about himself but about the Browning woman. During questioning he doesn't ask for a lawyer. We even offer and he says he has nothing to hide. At that point the detectives in charge figure they have nothing to lose and ask him if he'd give them an impression of his teeth—just to rule him out—and he agrees. When the M.E.

tells the detectives it's a perfect match they book him. Suddenly he lawyers up and now they're trying to get the statement thrown out, the impression thrown out, everything they can to make up for the mistakes this guy made during questioning.

"So why did he do it? If the guy's a nut case and wanted to get caught, why all the backtracking? And if he really was trying to get away with it, why did he give us everything we needed to convict him?"

"I would say it looked as if he didn't think he was guilty."

Dan nodded and put away his notebook. "That's what I think, too."

"So who else had a motive? The husband?"

"The husband was in San Jose all weekend."

"I thought you said it happened Friday night?"

"Yeah. It's O.J. all over again. He took a flight out of Sea-Tac at nine."

"So he could have done it."

"Yeah."

"What about the boyfriend's alibi?"

"Home alone watching a baseball game on the tube."

"Hmm."

"Yeah."

We sat in silence for a while, Dan chewing over information he probably knew by heart. After a minute I said, "What exactly was it that you needed me for?"

"I'm not sure. I guess I just wanted to run it by you and see if anything jumped out at you, something I may not have thought of."

"I don't know, Dan. Don't you have trained forensic dentists who do this sort of thing all the time?"

He frowned again. "You know what he said when I asked him about the stuff in the fridge? He said, 'I guess the guy must have been hungry.'"

"So they don't think there's anything left to investigate?"

Eyes rolled. "The detectives in charge were just about pissing in their pants when they got the dental match. They're not looking for anything more."

I stood up and walked over to the fridge to take another look. I picked up the package of lunchmeat and opened it up to look inside. There were several dark crumbs inside that I started to fish out and then stopped myself. "Is it okay if I touch this?"

"Sure. They finished processing the crime scene Monday night."

I turned to face him. "Then why is the house still sealed? Isn't the husband back yet?"

Dan stood and walked back over to the cool of the fridge. "Yeah. That's why I sealed the place. I've been over here every night after work, crawling over this place inch by inch."

"For the knife?"

He nodded. "I don't want the husband back in here until I'm positive there's no evidence he can destroy."

I turned my attention back to the bag of lunchmeat and instantly noticed how much darker it had become in the house since we'd first arrived. The sun had already dipped below the tops of the trees on the property outside and the back light from the fridge made it almost impossible to see. I looked around for a light switch and found one on the wall next to the toaster. But before I could flip it up the overhead lights went on. Dan, from a switch near a second doorway into the kitchen, said, "I think that's the garbage disposal."

I was glad he'd known what I was looking for. The noise probably would have scared the shit out of me. I pulled out one of the crumbs and took a tentative smell. It was obviously the chocolate cake. The slice of cake and the plate it was on yielded nothing and I moved on to the apple. Tiny smears of what looked to be dried cheese were on the skin just above and below the bite mark. Then I examined the rolls, where I found brown specs that felt and smelled like decayed apple pulp.

Dan could obviously see the look on my face and said, "What?"

"Just an idea. You know, there's only one way I can think of that you could have someone's teeth in a place that they weren't."

"Dentures?"

"Oh, well that's another, I guess. But I was thinking about dental models. If you were having some bridgework done and there had been a model made of both your upper and lower teeth, they would be mounted on a hinge that could simulate a bite pretty well. You couldn't do that with dentures."

"That's an idea, but how could you prove it?"

"Well, the one thing you wouldn't have if you were using dental models that you would if someone was using their own mouth is lips."

Dan snapped his fingers. "There should be saliva on the body where she was bitten."

I laughed. "I hadn't thought of that, either. This is what I noticed." I pointed out the bits of food that I'd seen and said, "Normally, if you're biting into something your lips would keep everything in your mouth. But with a dental model it would still be hanging on the teeth and then could be transferred to the next item of food."

"Where would the food go, the stuff that had been bitten off?"

"I would just fall out the back, I suppose."

Both of us looked down at the bottom shelf of the fridge and saw quite few cake crumbs.

Dan squatted down to get a better look. "He probably did the cake first because it was just sitting on the plate, but it made such a mess that he decided to stay with things like the carrot and cheese that wouldn't break apart."

I looked around for a garbage can and finally found it under the sink. "This is empty."

"We already have it," Dan said. "Standard operating procedure."

"Have they looked through it yet?"

"Not a chance, now that they think they know who did it."

"Do you think the husband did it?"

He shook his head. "I don't think that way. As much as possible I try to let the evidence speak for itself. I have pretty good reason to believe that the boyfriend is innocent, but I still don't have anything on the husband. For one thing, why would the husband kill his wife if the affair had already been over for three months?"

I thought back to a rough patch Janet and I had gone through a few years before and how long it had taken to heal. "Maybe it took him that long to realize he wasn't ever going to get over it. Or maybe he found out it wasn't really over. Maybe the boyfriend was lying."

Dan chuckled morosely.

"What?"

"They always lie, Steve. Even when they didn't do it, suspects always lie." Dan took another look at the refrigerator and, as if he hated to do it, shut the door. "Let's get out of here."

III

Dan dropped me off back at work and said he'd be in touch if the dental model theory panned out. We said our good-byes and I climbed into the cab of my Toyota pickup. In the garage at home I have an Acura 3.2 TL that I bought when I traded in my dad's Porsche, but I always seem to gravitate toward the truck when I go to work. Old habits die hard. I was busy sorting through the facts of Dan's case in my mind and wasn't thinking when I turned over the engine. The frenetic sounds of Fats Navarro and Don Lanphere negotiating Lanphere's "Go" came blasting out of my stereo speakers, cranked up from my morning commute. Though I eased back the volume, my heart was still racing as I rooted in my tape case for something a bit more sedate. I exchanged Navarro for Tina Brooks' *True Blue* in the tape deck and the minor melody of "Theme for Doris" leaked out of the speakers as I turned the truck toward the 520 Bridge and home.

As I came over the western rise of the bridge at Montlake the surface of Lake Washington looked as calm as I'd ever seen it, and the cool breezed normally associated with dropping down onto the floating bridge deck was conspicuous by its absence. There was no a/c in the truck—I almost never need it in Seattle—and even with both windows down it was about as cool as a blast furnace in the cab. I took the first exit on the far side of the bridge down 84th to my house in Medina, and parked behind the Acura.

Drenched in sweat, I made my way into the cool, inviting interior of my home. My ten-year-old daughter and seven-year-old son had long ago abandoned greeting me at the door when I returned home from work, and I was still having trouble adjusting. I eventually found my wife in the bedroom upstairs, dinner long over, with paperwork covering the bed.

"What happened to you?" she said with a grin.

I quickly stripped off my shirt in preparation for a shower. "Something you'll never believe."

Her eyebrows raised.

"Dan Lasky called me in to consult on a case."

The eyebrows plummeted. "Why wouldn't he?"

"Am I mistaken or aren't you the one who told me that Dan didn't like me butting in on his cases?"

"Sure, but it's hardly butting in if he *asks* for your help."

There was no winning an argument with a lawyer, so I shifted the topic. "It's a murder investigation over by Discovery Park."

"The one where the woman was stabbed to death?"

"Yeah, that's it."

"So what did Dan want you to do?"

"There was a bite mark on the victim that matched up with the man she was having an affair with. It looks like someone may have been used a dental model of his teeth to implicate him as the murderer."

She nodded and said, "Rico Browning."

"That's the husband. How do you know all this?"

"I actually met him once, at some function over at WRQ. Take my word for it—I'm a defense attorney but I sure wouldn't want to defend him."

I dropped my pants and sat on the bed to remove them. "You think he's capable?"

"Ask Dan about him," she said. "He's short, bald, Cuban, and mean, and not necessarily in that order."

"How does a guy like that get put in charge of public relations?"

"I didn't say he was stupid. He's very good at what he does, and most people get along with him just fine, but there's an undercurrent of menace about the man that gave me the creeps."

"Hmm. And you think he did it?"

"I don't know about that. Just don't give him my phone number." She smiled to let me know it was a joke, and I headed for the shower.

After toweling off and putting on some khaki shorts and a t-shirt, I went down to make dinner for myself. Cathie and Tim came in to the kitchen to say goodnight to me a few minutes later. I put the rest of the Caesar salad Janet had made into a bowl, sliced some sourdough bread to go with it and took it out to the table. Then I popped the top on a Heineken and sat down to eat. But before I could even get the first bite into my mouth, the phone rang.

I inherited a large, three-story house from my father that came with an intercom system to allow communication with the rest of the house. The primary unit was located next to the kitchen phone and because of that, the only time someone answers the phone upstairs is if there is no one downstairs. Since I was closest to the phone I knew I would have to answer. I was surprised to hear Dan Lasky's voice on the other end.

"Steve. I got the name of Winslow's dentist."

"That was fast."

"I'm going to talk to him tomorrow about the models. You want to come?"

"I have patients in the morning."

"How about lunch time?"

"Okay."

"Good. I'll pick you up at noon."

IV

The next morning Nona was able to switch a couple of my afternoon appointments, giving me until 2:30 before I had to be back. When he picked me up, Dan said we were heading north to Mill Creek. A solid blanket of high, white clouds had moved in overnight and dropped the temperature about ten degrees. Unfortunately they had made absolutely no impact on the humidity and now, instead of hot and muggy, it was just overcast and muggy. We drove with the windows up and the a/c on.

"Doc's name is Roy Kaldestad," Dan said once we were heading north on I-5. "Ever heard of him?"

I chuckled and said, "I'm pretty sure I went to dental school with him at the U dub."

Dan took his eyes off the road to look at me. "Well, now I'm glad I waited to take you along."

Dr. Kaldestad's office was located in what looked to be a new professional medical building, next door to a Group Health clinic. We walked inside a cheerfully decorated waiting room done in a sports theme. Most of the framed posters on the wall were of Mariner and Seahawk players. When Dan told the receptionist who he was she said to take a seat, that the doctor was expecting us. And sure enough, he stuck his head out the door before we had a chance to sit down.

"Hey, guys. Come on back to my office."

I recognized him immediately. Kaldestad led the way down a hallway that was liberally decorated with framed photos of Seattle sports figures. All were autographed. In among them I saw quite a few photos of Jacksonville Jaguars and Florida Marlins. "Did you grow up in Florida?" I asked as I walked by him into his office. He gave me a funny look and I said, "I just noticed the photos in the hall."

"Oh, no. I did a year in Jacksonville after dental school, an advanced program in general dentistry." But Kaldestad was still giving me the once over.

"I'm not sure if you remember me, Dr. Kaldestad, but we went to dental school together. My name's—"

"Steve Raymond," he blurted out. "Sure." Then we shook hands. "You were a year ahead of me. You look different with your hair cut."

In college and dental school, and for a few years after, I wore my hair very long and tied back in a ponytail. For the last year and a half, though, I'd been wearing my hair in a buzz cut. I ran my hand over the half-inch of hair on my head. "Yeah, I figured it was time for me to start looking like a respectable dentist."

Kaldestad was only about five-eight, but had a lean face and an engaging smile. I knew that he was only 37 or 38, and yet he looked much younger. He was obviously in great shape, too. He wore a short sleeved lab coat that showed off his well-developed arms. "I forget," I said. "Were you into wrestling or weight lifting?"

"Weights," he said. "Still am."

"Hmm. Do you think that has much of an effect on the fine muscle control in your hands—"

Dan cleared his throat and Kaldestad turned to him.

"I'm sorry. Detective . . . ?"

"Lieutenant Lasky."

"Have a seat, Lieutenant. Both of you. Your office told me that you were interested in looking at some dental records."

"Yes, for a Don Winslow."

"I already pulled his file this morning." Kaldestad picked up a file from his desk. "Do you have the warrant?"

Dan produced a folded piece of paper from his jacket pocket and handed it to the doctor. "Okay, this looks all right. What do you want to know?"

Dan looked over to me.

"I guess I can explain what we need. I'm sort of consulting on a case Lieutenant Lasky is investigating. We need to know if Mr. Winslow ever had any bridge work done, or extensive crown work that would have required a full model of his teeth."

Kaldestad looked at the file and said, "Yeah. I had a bridge made for him a year, no, year and a half ago. I'm sure I would have taken a complete impression for that."

"Did you ever give the models to Mr. Winslow?" Dan asked hopefully.

Kaldestad shook his head.

"Do you think anyone in your office would have kept them, or have given them to Mr. Winslow—or to someone else?"

"Not a chance. I mean, there's only me and a couple of the assistants who do the lab work. You can ask them, but that would have been so weird I'm sure I would have remembered it."

"Do you still have the models?" Dan asked.

Kaldestad actually laughed then, a high sort of giggle that clearly pissed Dan off.

I tried to smooth things over. "Well, we almost never keep the models after we seat the appliance. They just go back to the lab." To Kaldestad I said, "Do you usually send the whole model back to the lab or just knock them off the articulator?"

"The whole thing. We wait until we have a box full and then send them back when they come to pick up new impressions."

"Which lab do you use?"

"Oral Dynamics in Edmonds."

Now it was my turn to laugh. "That's really what it's called?"

"Yeah, but they do good work. Who do you use?"

"Nakanishi in Bellevue."

"Yeah, I've heard they're good, but that's too far south for me."

Another throat clearing from Dan and we stood to thank Dr. Kaldestad for his time. I told him it was good to see him again—even though we didn't really know each other—and he said the same. Dan couldn't wait to get out of there and when we were in the car he turned to me and said, "Asshole." For the briefest of seconds I thought he was talking about me. Then he said, "How the hell am I supposed to know what they do with those things?"

"Do you want to check out the dental lab?"

"Do you have time?"

I still had over an hour-and-half before I had to be back to work. "Sure. But let's grab some lunch first."

We ate wonderfully greasy fish and chips down by the ferry dock in Edmonds, sweating at a picnic table as we watched the Kingston ferries deposit and collect their cargo. Afterward we consulted the phone book to determine where Oral Dynamics was located. The place was a block off of Main Street on Bell, between an automotive repair shop and a self-storage place. The front door opened into a tiny waiting room that contained exactly two orange, plastic molded chairs and didn't look as if anyone had spent time waiting there in a while. Dan flashed his badge, and we milled around while the receptionist retrieved the owner—a Mr. Hamid Sajjadi was the name on the business cards—to come out and talk with us. When Dan had informed him as to the nature of our visit we were ushered into a small office that looked as little used as the waiting room.

Sajjadi was dark complexioned with black hair and piercing

eyes that could have been of anything from North African to Middle Eastern to East Indian descent for all I knew. He asked what our visit was all about and Dan filled him in.

"We're conducting a murder investigation, Mr. Sajjadi, and we need to talk to some of your people."

Wide-eyed, he said, "You think they had something to do with it?"

"No, sir. Not at all. We're simply looking for evidence and want to talk to the people here who make up the models for Dr. Kaldestad."

He seemed even more puzzled now. Dan pushed on. "How long have your people been working here—the ones who make the models?"

"Nancy's been here five years, Glen for two. They work in the model room."

"Great. Would it be possible to talk to them?"

Sajjadi hesitated.

"This is just informal questioning. They don't have to stop working."

That was all it took and he quickly led the way into the lab. We were on the left side of the lab as we entered. The primary work of casting and finishing crowns, bridgework and dentures was going on out in the large space to the right, but off the hall to the left was a good-sized alcove that served as the model room. A counter along the perimeter of the entire area contained a couple of sinks, large dispensers for the powdered modeling compounds that came in white, buff, and blue to determine the strength of the models, a compressed air station for drying the impressions, a large grinder to shape the model bases when they were dry, and four stations with vibrators, pins, and tiny jig saws where the actual casting was done. A couple of bins in the back held four types of articulators, left side, right side, full mouth, and more complex ones for dentures. Dozens of poured impressions we drying in racks above the stations and a boom-box on a corner shelf emitted rap music at a volume that was just a notch above comfortable.

Nancy, as it turned out, was the supervisor of the model room. She was a good-looking brunette with long, curly hair who might have been thirty, barely. Once Sajjadi had left she confessed that she occasionally took some of the compound home for craft projects but had never taken a model home or given one to anybody. At that moment a driver came in with half-a-dozen new impressions and she suggested we talk to Glen.

Glen was no more than twenty-four and wore a red headband and a green hospital scrub suit. "You guys really cops?" he asked. He was just finishing up attaching four models to articulators by using the white compound and a rounded putty knife to temporarily cement them to the hinges. We followed him over to the sink where he rinsed out the large flexible rubber bowl he had been using for the compound.

"I'm Lieutenant Lasky, and this is Dr. Raymond. He's consulting on the case."

"What kind of doctor?"

"I'm a dentist in Seattle."

"Glenn, can you grab a couple of these?" Nancy said, and he walked over to select two impressions from the group of six and take them back to his workstation.

"Sorry guys, but I kind of have to get these done while the impressions are still wet." He grabbed a smaller version of the dark green rubber bowl and mixed up some of the blue powder with warm water.

Dan said, "We're trying to find out if you ever gave away a model of someone's teeth."

"Nah. I have a couple of cool ones at home in my bedroom," then his voice lowered, "only don't tell Mr. Sajjadi, because the articulators are his."

272

I nodded. "Glen, this would have been a full impression, upper and lower."

He was thinking but his head was unconsciously moving back and forth.

"This would have been about a year or year and a half ago."

"Oh." He finally turned to us. That seemed to change everything. "There was a guy. Hey, Nancy, remember that teacher dude—"

"I was on maternity leave."

"Oh, right. Well, anyway, there was this teacher dude who came in and said he wanted to show some models to his class. Sajjadi said it was okay as long as he brought 'em back."

"Did he?" Dan asked.

Glen smiled. "Nope."

"Do you remember whose model you gave him?"

Head shaking, "Not the patient, but I do remember he only wanted to look at one dentist's models."

"Kaldestad?" I offered.

He shrugged. "I don't know. All I remember is that he came back every week for a month. He must have found something, but I don't actually remember what he took." Glen lifted the wet paper towels from around the impressions and took the trays over to the compressed air to remove the water from the mold. When he returned to his station he flipped on the vibrator and began to work. "Sorry, but I gotta finish this."

First he set the rubber bowl on the vibrator and expelled all the air bubbles from the compound, then quickly picked up a small spatula and exchanged the bowl for the impression tray. Carefully, he took a tiny dollop of the blue compound and ran it down the side of the tooth that had been prepped for a crown. He pressed down on the impression tray, increasing the vibration of the machine until all the air bubbles were out of the compound in the prep, then quickly filled the prep with increasingly greater amounts of compound. When it had spilled over and filled the two adjacent teeth, he moved on to the next impression. After that one was finished he took the bowl and set it on the vibrator letting the material flow into the remaining molds for the teeth, just up to the gum lines.

I was impressed. Back when I had done my own lab work I had two or three crowns a week at most. Glen was very good, and very fast. "How many of these do you do in a week?" I asked him.

"I don't know. A hundred, maybe." No wonder he was so quick. Returning to the sink again he rinsed out the bowl and then walked past us. "Hang on," he said. "I just have to set the pins now."

Back at his station he took two brass pins and set them, one each, into the compound just above where the crown preps were. After adjusting the angles and making sure they wouldn't fall over he looked up at us.

"Is there anything else about this teacher you can tell us?" Dan asked. "Where he was teaching, what his name was—"

"Wait a minute." Glen's face brightened. "I did remember his name. It was a gun, I think."

Dan and I looked across the top of the kid's head at each other. I don't think either of us had taken Glen for a World War II buff. I raised my eyebrows to Dan but he shook his head. "Winchester?" he offered to Glen.

"Nah, it was a whole name. The gun I mean."

When it became clear after a few minutes that it wasn't going to come, Dan finally said, "Browning?"

"Browning Automatic Rifle," the kid shouted, beaming. "Yeah, that's it. A B.A.R."

"Oh, shit." It was Nancy. "I think we got another delivery. Glen, I need you to pour up the rest of these so I can start on the new impressions."

"Sorry, guys."

Dan fished a business card from his wallet and handed it to

Glen. "Listen, I don't think this is going to happen, but if Mr. Browning tries to contact you again, or comes in, please give me a call. It's very important."

"Sure thing," he said, holding up the card, then set it on the counter and ran over to help Nancy."

During our conversation I'd noticed that Sajjadi had poked his head into the model room a couple of times and he was waiting for us as we left. "I appreciate your cooperation," Dan told him, and he let us show ourselves out.

While we were driving back to the office Dan was quiet.

"Does this mean you'll let Winslow go, now that you know Browning had the models?"

"Winslow's already out on bail." Dan sighed heavily. "My real problem is that I don't have any physical evidence. Unless we find either the knife or the model, there's nothing solid to link either one of them to the murder."

"What about the bite marks?"

"Unfortunately that only muddies the water. The defense for either suspect would argue that because the bite was made with a model, that it's theoretically possible for anyone to have made the bite. Winslow's attorney has already made a motion to dismiss the case on account of the model."

"Huh. It sounds like I may have made things worse."

He was shaking his head before I'd finished. "No, not possible. As far as I'm concerned any evidence is good evidence. The fact that we know about the models may make it impossible to get a conviction, but it's the truth, it's what actually happened. And for me, anyway, that's the most important thing."

V

Thunderstorms the next day brought nearly everyone in the Elliott Bay Dental Health Center outside to see the lightning. And though they threatened, the dark clouds brought neither rain nor a decrease in the humidity. I had trouble concentrating on work all day, and it had nothing to do with the thunderclaps that rocked the building that morning. I was preoccupied with the facts surrounding Kami Browning's murder, trying to think of something that would help Dan with his case.

He called me that morning to tell me the bad news. A careful inventory of the garbage seized from the kitchen had not turned up the missing bites of food, and Dan predicted that they had already worked their way through San Jose's water treatment system the previous weekend via Rico Browning's gastrointestinal tract. Unfortunately that was probably the most likely scenario. He also informed me that he was going to have to let Browning back into the house the next day. He thanked me for helping him and I had the impression that my services as a consultant were no longer required. Later that day, however, it became more than an impression.

I had just finished assessing the need for Mr. Ogren, a retired teacher, to have a partial denture which, of course, he was resisting—a denture is the last stop before the old folks home—when Laurie poked her head in the door. "Nona says not to come up front. She'll be back in a minute."

"What's going on?"

"Couple of suits waiting in your office," she said, and took off.

I made a few notations in Mr. Ogren's chart and told him again how the extensive restorations he needed were ultimately not going to cure the problems he was experiencing. Nona showed up shortly after to escort Mr. Ogren out.

"Rico Browning's in your office," she said without preamble.

"What?"

She shook her head. "I couldn't stop him. He has his lawyer with him and he doesn't look happy."

She took Mr. Ogren and I followed them down the hall. I hit a wall of cologne just outside my office and only reluctantly shut the door as I went inside. It was Rico Browning all right, just as Janet had described. He looked like a caged animal as he paced behind his lawyer, a distinguished looking gentleman with gray hair and a matching moustache. Both were wearing charcoal-gray, three-piece suits with white shirts and red power ties, as if they'd called each other up in the morning to coordinate wardrobes.

Browning was on me with a fat finger in my chest before I could even make it behind the protective barrier of my desk. "Listen to me, *Doctor*—" as though he hated having to use a term of respect "—I want you to stay away from my house, stay away from my office, and stay away from the cops or I'll have your ass thrown in jail so fast you won't remember how it got there."

I wasn't afraid of jail—I'd been there before. Rico Browning, however, was another matter. He was a full head shorter than me, but no less intimidating for it. His bald head was shiny with perspiration from the humidity. I wanted to be able to dismiss him because of his height, but not only did he reek of cologne, he inexplicably reeked of power. I pointedly turned from him without a word and retreated behind my desk. Since Browning had clearly staked out the other direction for himself, I elected to take the high road. "Would one of you care to tell me what this is all about?"

"As if you didn't know."

"Rico—" the lawyer attempted.

"Shut up. When I need your advice I'll ask for it." Then it was back to me. "I know you're working for the cops and it's going to stop right now. You come within a hundred yards of my house again, buddy, and you're going to jail."

"I happen to be working for Lieutenant Lasky as a consultant on a case."

"Lasky doesn't have the power to hire anyone. If you're really working for the Seattle Police Department then I want to see some documentation to that effect."

Now I could see where this was going. "I'm simply helping Lieutenant Lasky informally."

"Well it stops. Now. Towner?"

Evidentially that was the lawyer's name. He pulled a briefcase to his lap and extracted some papers, which he handed to me after he stood. "This is a restraining order barring you from coming within one hundred yards of Mr. Browning's office or residence, and an injunction barring you from further consultation with the Seattle Police Department without your officially being employed by the city or the county."

I took it, but I wasn't happy about it. And I wasn't about to argue—I had a lawyer, too. "Anything else, gentlemen?"

"That's enough," Browning jumped in. "You just keep away from me and keep away from the cops, or I'm warning you—"

"Rico—"

"Jail is just the beginning. I'll sue your ass for every penny you've got. You won't be able to *brush* anyone's teeth in this town again. Are we clear on that?"

"Perfectly," I said through clenched teeth.

"Good. Let's go, Towner." Then Browning stormed out of the office without waiting.

Towner hesitated at the door and said, "I don't have to tell you that Mr. Browning only recently lost his wife and should not have to be subjected to spurious investigations by . . . amateurs."

I'd had enough. "Yeah, I heard your master the first time."

"I don't threaten, Dr. Raymond, the way my *master* does, but just a friendly word of warning. He means what he says." With that, Towner disappeared too.

I threw down the papers on my desk and picked up the phone. I was punching out Dan's number when Laurie leaned into the office and said, "Ms. Schaben's here."

Shit. "I'll be right there."

I went back to work and it wasn't until I was done with my last patient at 4:30 that I made it back to the phone in my office. The place still stunk of Browning and his mouthpiece. When I finally got Dan on the line I said, "Guess who was here in my office today, threatening me with jail time?"

"I know. Browning."

"What the hell's going on, Dan?"

"Tell me what he said." I outlined the threats that Browning had made and Dan said, "Well, I don't know what else you can do except stay away from the guy."

"I've never even been near him before."

"You know what I mean."

"I feel like going over to his house just to spite him."

"Don't." It was not a request. "Look, there's nothing left for you to do on this thing anyway. Browning's just throwing his weight around because he can."

"So he can get away with murder?"

"We don't know that, Steve. Just let it go."

I collected myself for a moment and said, "All right, but you'll have to do me one favor first."

Tentatively: "What?"

"Nail his ass to the wall."

I could hear Dan laughing in the background as he hung up on me. He was right, of course. I had absolutely no plans to do anything about Browning, and still wouldn't if the asshole hadn't threatened me. I didn't feel much like talking about it, so instead of going up front to confide in Nona, I went back to the lab to make a denture repair I needed to finish before going home. I hit the tape deck before I sat down and Dizzy Gillespie's "Groovin' High" came on half way through Charlie Parker's solo. That was more like it. Now I could work.

The model I'd poured that morning of Mr. Bernard's upper gums had hardened and one of my assistants had ground the base so it would lie flat on the lab bench. I put a grinding wheel on my hand-piece, removed material on both sides of the split where the corner of the denture had come off, and placed the denture back on the model. Then I mixed up the repair compound and began filling in the gap with new material. It only needed to dry for a few minutes, but while I sat there waiting my eye was drawn to a full model of teeth I kept above my lab bench. I smiled. They were Janet's from when I'd had to make a couple of onlays for her a few years ago.

I took the model down from the shelf, opened and closed the buff-colored teeth, then looked around for something they could bite. Digging a wide, flat strip of pink wax from a box in a drawer to my left, I slipped it between her central incisors and pressed down. The teeth bit into the wax and I pulled it apart to examine the bite. Because it was so thin, there would be little to differentiate it from a real bite. Something with more thickness, though, like the brick of cheese, would have revealed imperfections in the model—especially if it was a couple of years old.

Pulling apart the teeth, the wax stuck to the model. I took a waxing instrument and scraped away the excess, stuck it to the small end that had been bitten off, and tossed the whole thing into the big, galvanized garbage can by the back door. My throw was short, however, and the wax clunked into the aluminum sink. A thought began to form in my mind that I couldn't quite grasp, something I was trying to remember, but Nona appeared at the door before it could surface.

"Another crisis?"

"Ah, just your basic threat of legal action and jail time."

"The murder investigation?"

"Yeah. He's the prime suspect now, and I think he's feeling the heat."

"Mr. Bernard just called . . ." She motioned her head toward the denture.

I nodded. "Tell him to come in. It'll be ready."

Nona left and I put a polishing wheel on my hand-piece and began to smooth down the repair. When I'd finished, I put the denture back in the travel case it had been delivered in and cleaned up the lab bench. On my way out I reached for the light switch and that's when the thought that I'd almost had finally came to me. Once I'd delivered the denture out front to Nona, I ran back to my office and put in a call to Dan. I now had a pretty good idea what had happened to the bites of food.

After I told him he said, "I hadn't even thought of that. I'll get a crime scene unit down there right away and let you know if we find anything."

As I hung up the phone the faint whiff of Browning that remained in my office gave me only smug satisfaction. Don't get mad; get even. With any luck, my information would lead to the arrest and conviction of Rico Browning for the murder of his wife. I was going to be like a kid on Christmas Eve that night, waiting for Dan to break the news the next day.

VI

But Dan called later that night. "You were right, Steve. The food was in the garbage disposal. He'd run water in the sink to get rid of the crumbs but hadn't turned on the disposal."

"Is it going to help?"

"Well, there was a beautiful thumb print on the cheese—"

"That's great."

"Unfortunately when the cheese dried it sort of deformed. It's definitely a match but, you know defense lawyers, it's not a hundred percent."

"Well, at least you know who did it. That should help."

"Yeah, it already has."

"What do you mean?"

"We have a witness, too."

"Not to the murder."

"No, but . . . Well, look. Can you come down tomorrow? He's going to make a statement. I'd like you to be there."

That seemed to run contrary to the advice Dan had given me just a few hours before. "What if Browning and his lawyer find out?"

"Oh, I don't think we have to worry about that."

For some reason his reassurance made me even more nervous. "Are you sure about this, Dan?"

"Positive. When can you be here?"

"I have patients all morning. Is noon okay?"

"I'll see you then."

The rains finally came, and with them brisk winds and cooler temperatures. After a week in the grip of oppressive humidity, it was nice to have the moisture in the air where you could see it. Of course traffic was a mess. Because of the slick cement and heavy volume of water on the roadway I got stuck in bridge traffic, which actually caused a rare occurrence for me: being late for work. Saturday morning is a busy time for me anyway, and I had to hustle to catch up before lunch so that I could get over to the Magnolia Precinct in time to see Dan's witness.

At noon the rain had tapered off to a drizzle, typical early summer weather for Seattle, and in two minutes I was standing in front of the desk sergeant asking to see Lieutenant Lasky. Dan was grinning when he came out to meet me.

Suspicious, I asked, "What's going on?"

"You'll see."

He led me down a hallway in the opposite direction from his office, and into a small interrogation room. Seated at the table, I was surprised to see, was Glen from Oral Dynamics, in jeans this time but still sporting the medical scrub top. "Hey, Doc."

"Hi, Glen."

Dan moved me in so that I could stand behind the witness and look over his shoulder, then he leaned over the table next to him. Two detectives stood against the wall on the opposite side of the room, looking bored. "Glen," Dan said. "I appreciate your coming in like this to make a statement."

"No problem."

"Dr. Raymond and I didn't really get a chance to ask you all of the questions we needed to when we were over at the dental lab the other day. What I need to do is show you a group of pictures and ask you to identify the man that you gave the model to."

"Browning? Sure."

I looked over at Dan but he only smiled. He set down a plastic photo album page with eight sleeves for pictures. All of them contained headshots of men in suits, half of them military. Immediately my eyes were drawn to the smiling face of Rico Browning, no doubt taken from the files of the business desk at the *Seattle Times*, or a promo piece for WRQ. I found myself grinning as Glen looked over the photos and said, "There he is."

I was shocked, however, when he pointed to someone else.

"Thank you, Glen. Detectives Benjamin and Elliot will go ahead and take a written statement from you now. Just tell them everything you can remember about him."

Dan clapped me on the shoulder and led me out into the hall.

"Who the hell was that?"

"Think about it," he said.

The Air Force uniform is what finally did it. "The boyfriend?"

"We picked up Winslow last night. This morning the judge revoked his bail. Apparently he figured that the phony bite marks would be too obvious and get him off the hook. He'll have a hard time squirming out of this one, especially with the new evidence."

"Did you know that Glen was going to pick him out?"

He nodded. "I called him up last night and when I asked him to describe Browning I knew he'd really been talking to Winslow."

We were almost to Dan's office before I realized it. "I can't believe it. I was so sure it had to be Browning."

"Well, he may be guilty of being a son of a bitch, but unfortunately that's not against the law."

"Yeah. I suppose the important thing is that you figured out who did it."

"Thanks to you. If we hadn't found that fingerprint, I'm

not sure I would have thought to go back to talk to the kid at the lab."

I held out my hand and we shook. "Anytime."

"Well, thanks again." Then I heard Dan say something that had a vaguely familiar ring to it. "Once you know what you're looking for, it's sure a lot easier to find it."

About the Author

Eric B. Olsen is the author of six works of fiction in three different genres. He has written a medical thriller entitled *Death's Head*, as well as the horror novel *Dark Imaginings*. He is also the author of three mystery novels, *Proximal to Murder* and *Death in the Dentist's Chair* featuring amateur sleuth Steve Raymond, D.D.S., and *The Seattle Changes* featuring private detective Ray Neslowe. In addition, he is the author of *If I Should Wake Before I Die*, a book of short horror fiction.

Today Mr. Olsen writes primarily non-fiction, including *The Death of Education*, an exposé of the public school system in America, *The Films of Jon Garcia: 2009-2013*, an analysis of the work of the acclaimed Portland independent filmmaker, and a book of essays entitled *The Intellectual American*. Mr. Olsen lives in the Pacific Northwest with his wife.

Please visit the author's web site at https://sites.google.com/ericbolsenauthor/home or contact by email at neslowepublishing@gmail.com.

Printed in the United States
By Bookmasters